A FOOL THERE WAS

Recent Titles by Betty Rowlands from Severn House

ALPHA, BETA, GAMMA . . . DEAD
COPYCAT
DEADLY OBSESSION
DEATH AT DEARLY MANOR
DIRTY WORK
A HIVE OF BEES
AN INCONSIDERATE DEATH
PARTY TO MURDER
SMOKESCREEN
TOUCH ME NOT

A FOOL THERE WAS

Betty Rowlands

This first world edition published 2009
in Great Britain and in the USA by
SEVERN HOUSE PUBLISHERS LTD of
9–15 High Street, Sutton, Surrey, England, SM1 1DF.
Trade paperback edition published
in Great Britain and the USA 2009 by
SEVERN HOUSE PUBLISHERS LTD

British Library Cataloguing in Publication Data

Rowlands, Betty.
    A Fool There Was.
    1. Reynolds, Sukey (Fictitious character)–Fiction.
    2. Policewomen–Great Britain–Fiction. 3. Detective and
    mystery stories.
    I. Title
    823.9'14-dc22

ISBN-13: 978-0-7278-6786-5   (cased)
ISBN-13: 978-1-84751-151-5   (trade paper)

All Severn House titles are printed on acid-free paper.

Typeset by Palimpsest Book Production Ltd.,
Grangemouth, Stirlingshire, Scotland.
Printed and bound in Great Britain by
MPG Books Ltd., Bodmin, Cornwall.

ONE

'Time for a change of driver,' said Sukey. 'Why don't you pull in at the Membury service area? It's only a mile further on.'

'Good idea.' Vicky checked her door mirror before switching to the nearside lane. 'It'll do us good to stretch our legs – and I could murder a coffee.'

Darkness was falling as they pulled off the motorway. It was several minutes before Vicky found a space in the car park some distance from the main building. The wind that had made their Channel crossing a less than enjoyable experience had begun to subside, but a sudden flurry of rain made the two friends, on their way home to Bristol after a touring holiday in France, go scurrying for shelter.

Once indoors they made for the coffee shop, where they found a long queue. Beyond the checkout a young man with a shaven head was deftly guiding a trolley between the tables in the seating area, sweeping the debris left by previous customers into a plastic bag and wiping up spilt milk and sugar with a grubby-looking cloth. A depressed-looking, grey-haired woman trailed in his wake, gathering discarded items from the floor with a long-handled dustpan and broom. Amid the chatter of voices and the clink of crockery, advertisements promoting everything from exotic holidays to motor insurance streamed across a video screen in a continuous loop.

It was some time before they were served and managed to find a free table. They sat in silence for several minutes, contentedly drinking their coffee, when they were startled to hear someone call their names. They looked up to see two uniformed members of the Wiltshire Constabulary – PCs Jilly Swinton and Keith Kelly, whom they had met recently on a case involving their combined forces – approaching a neighbouring table. They returned the greeting and invited the two to sit with them.

'So what are you doing on our patch?' asked Keith as he

sat down. 'Do Avon and Somerset Constabulary need our assistance again?'

'Not as far as we know, but I'm sure you're welcome to ours
if you need it,' Vicky retorted.

'We'll bear it in mind.' Keith opened a packet of chocolate
biscuits and offered them round. 'Have some nourishment.'

'Shouldn't really, but thanks.' Vicky reached out and took one.
'We resisted temptation at the counter because we're being fed
as soon as we hit Bristol. My partner's doing the cooking.'

'Lucky old you,' said Jilly with a sigh of envy.

'Thanks,' said Sukey as she too accepted a chocolate biscuit.
'There was food on the ferry, but the sea didn't do much for our
appetites,' she added with a grimace.

'So where have you been?' asked Jilly.

'France,' said Vicky. 'We did a tour round Brittany and ended
up for the last few days in Paris.'

'Helping Maigret with his latest case?' said Keith with a sly
wink.

'Of course,' said Sukey cheerfully, 'when he heard we were
in the country, the head of the Sûreté immediately appealed to
us for help.'

'We managed to track down a couple of killers and a drug
baron for him in between shopping and cultural things like the
Louvre and Notre Dame,' added Vicky.

'I'm sure he was most appreciative.'

'Oh, he was. He's promised to write to the Chief Constable
and recommend us for promotion.' Sukey put down her empty
mug and stood up. 'It's time we were on our way. Nice meeting
you guys – see you around!'

They had just reached their car and Sukey was about to climb
into the driver's seat when Vicky said in a sharp undertone,
'What do you reckon's going on over there?' She nodded in the
direction of a car parked about six spaces along the row. The
driver's window was wound down and a man in a dark coat
with a soft hat pulled down over his eyes and his collar turned
up against the rain was bending down talking him. The two off-
duty detectives could not catch what he was saying, but his
body language suggested agitation. He appeared to be trying to
give what looked like a padded envelope to the driver, who

looked at it without taking it from the man's hand before shaking his head and attempting to close the window. With one gloved hand on the glass in an attempt to prevent it rising, the man tried to push the envelope through the rapidly closing gap. The next moment the car door was flung open so violently that he staggered back and crashed against the adjacent car, setting off the automatic alarm, while the envelope fell from his hand into a puddle. As he bent to retrieve it, the driver slammed the door, started his engine and drove away. With the envelope in his hand, the first man made a futile effort to pursue the car before stopping and looking around in what the two off-duty detectives later described as 'a helpless sort of way'.

'Something fishy going on there,' said Sukey. 'Let's keep an eye on him.'

They got into their car and waited to see what the man would do next. He turned his head from side to side to glance across the lines of parked cars and for the first time they caught a glimpse of his face. Under the yellow sodium lights it was difficult to judge his colouring, but beneath the low brim of his hat they got a glimpse of thin, clean-shaven features with deep furrows running from nose to mouth. He began to walk along the lines of cars, slowly, like a man sleepwalking.

Vicky clutched Sukey's arm. 'Look, over there!' she whispered. While they had been watching, another car had driven into a space a couple of rows away. The driver, a thickset man in an anorak, got out and glanced round as if in search of someone. The first man spotted him, scurried across and appeared to check the registration number of his car before offering him the envelope, which he accepted without hesitation. The two spoke briefly; the newcomer appeared to be putting the envelope in his glove box while the first man made his way, more purposefully this time, to a black Volvo. He got in, started the engine and drove slowly towards the exit.

'Mission accomplished, by the looks of things,' said Vicky. 'Get his number.'

'I already have.' Sukey held up the notebook she kept on the shelf below the steering column. 'That could be a drugs drop. How about alerting Jilly and Keith?'

'I was about to suggest it.' They got out of the car and watched the second man, who had left his car and was walking towards the service building. 'He's making a phone call,' Vicky went on, seeing him pull out a cell phone and put it to his ear. 'Reporting a successful handover, no doubt.'

'He doesn't seem in too much of a hurry, does he?' said Sukey. 'He obviously has no idea we were watching. I think I'll get his number too.'

'Not bothered by the car alarm either,' said Vicky, as the device continued its monotonous wailing. 'Not that anyone else seems to be either,' she added with a shrug. 'It's like burglar alarms, half the time no one takes any notice of them.'

They strolled across the intervening lines of cars as if making a short cut to the service area. Sukey jotted down the number of the man's white Peugeot before they followed him at a discreet distance. By the time they had reached the entrance their quarry was inside and they caught a glimpse of him disappearing round the corner in the direction of the toilets.

'Why don't you wait here to see where he goes next while I have a word with Jilly and Keith?' said Vicky.

'Right.' Sukey stood by a display of cut flowers and pretended to be making a decision about which bunch to select while keeping an eye on the point where the man was likely to emerge. A short while later he reappeared and in the stronger light she got a good look at his face. He was about sixty years old, clean-shaven with regular features, a fresh, healthy colour and thinning grey hair smoothed back from a high brow. She watched as he walked towards the exit; outside the rain was falling more heavily and he pulled up the hood of his anorak before setting off across the car park.

Sukey swung round and almost bumped into Vicky as she returned with Jilly and Keith. 'He's just leaving – he was only going to the loo,' she told them. She pointed to the man, who had just reached his car and was about to get in. 'That's him, over there.'

'Right, we'll have a word.' The two officers set off across the car park at the double but they had gone only a few yards when the Peugeot's headlights came on; the car pulled out and followed the directions to the exit.

'Sod this one-way system!' said Keith. 'If it had led him this way we could have flagged him down. At least we've got his number.' He grabbed his radio, gave his call sign and outlined the situation to the control room. 'We're starting in pursuit. Target seems to have no idea he's been spotted so there shouldn't be a problem.' He sprinted to their car with Jilly at his heels; Sukey and Vicky returned to their car and watched them leave.

'So what are we waiting for?' asked Vicky, as Sukey sat with the engine running but made no move to drive away.

'I've just had a thought,' said Sukey. 'Did you happen to notice the car that first man drove – the one who refused to take the envelope?'

Vicky closed her eyes and thought for a moment. 'I'm pretty sure it was white . . . yes, a white Peugeot.' She opened her eyes and drew a quick breath. 'I see what you're driving at!' she exclaimed. 'The man who accepted the envelope was driving a white Peugeot as well. Now, what was the number of the first one? I can't say I was paying much attention, but—'

'It began with MO,' Sukey said confidently. 'I remember thinking modus operandi . . . but I can't remember what came next I'm afraid.' She pulled out her notebook and switched on the interior light. 'Yes, that explains it. The second white Peugeot – the one the woodies are following – has a number starting with MO as well. It looks as if the bloke in the black Volvo – the one who handed over the envelope – confused the numbers and picked on the wrong car.'

'No wonder white Peugeot Mark One refused to take it,' Vicky chuckled. 'He must have thought the first bloke was trying to sell him crack or something.'

'Maybe that's exactly what he was doing,' said Sukey soberly. 'Well, we should soon find out.' She put the car in gear and drove slowly towards the exit.

Shortly after they turned off the M4 on the final stretch of their journey home, Sukey noticed brake lights ahead and slowed down. Vicky, who had been dozing, woke with a start. 'What's up?' she said.

As Sukey brought the car to a halt behind the queue an ambulance bore down on them, siren wailing and blue light flashing. 'RTA by the looks of it,' she said as it tore past, closely followed by a police car and a fire engine.

They crawled forward. A considerable time elapsed before they saw police officers in fluorescent yellow jackets directing the queue. As Sukey steered slowly past the scene of the accident Vicky peered through the passenger window and gave a sudden gasp.

Without taking her eyes off the road, Sukey said quietly, 'What is it?'

'Tell you in a minute.' Vicky waited until the road ahead was clear and they were able to pick up speed again before saying, 'Three cars involved – a red Mercedes, a silver BMW . . . and a black Volvo. The Volvo's on its roof and I guess it's rolled over more than once – it's badly crushed.'

'I don't suppose you got the number?'

'As it happens I did. Give me your notebook.' Sukey took it from the shelf behind the steering wheel and handed it over. 'Yes, it's our friend's car all right,' said Vicky grimly. 'It looked pretty bad – I doubt if he survived.'

TWO

'I've been thinking about that guy in the black Volvo,' said Sukey. 'I know we joked about how he might be acting as runner for a drugs ring, but on second thoughts it doesn't seem very likely.'

'I've been thinking the same thing,' said Vicky. 'It's not the way the stuff is usually delivered. The pros hand it over so discreetly and unobtrusively that unless you were on the watch you'd never spot it.'

'And this man was anything but a pro,' Sukey continued, 'he was as jumpy as a cat on hot bricks and he didn't even check the car number properly. And he seemed desperate to get away. My guess is he'd never done that sort of thing before.'

'I'd give a lot to know what was in that envelope,' said Vicky. She took out her mobile phone and jabbed buttons. 'I'm just giving Chris a call to let him know we'll be with him in fifteen minutes or so – ten if we're lucky.'

'Help yourselves to Parmesan.' Chris Capaldi indicated a dish of freshly grated cheese while ladling generous helpings of pasta on to warmed plates and passing them to the two hungry women. They accepted gratefully, inhaling the appetizing smell of the food before tucking in with relish.

'Chris, darling, you're a genius!' sighed Vicky. She reached out to grab his hand and give it a squeeze before he sat down.

'Hear hear!' Sukey waved her fork in appreciation before plunging it into her plate for another mouthful. 'Is this a family recipe handed down through generations of Capaldis?'

Chris chuckled. 'Something like that! My nonna insisted I bring it back with me last time I visited her in Rome. She's convinced no one in England knows how to cook half-decent pasta so I do it sometimes for my dad.'

'Chris's mum's English,' Vicky explained in response to Sukey's slightly puzzled expression.

'And she's a wonderful cook,' said Chris. 'She taught me lots of things and she makes a mean steak and kidney pie, but Dad insists no one can do pasta like Nonna – except me, of course. It's the only weakness in an otherwise perfect marriage.'

The three were dining in the flat on the northern outskirts of Bristol that Vicky shared with Chris, who was a chef at a local hotel. It was on the top floor in a small development of four blocks close to the Downs and from the sitting room window they could just glimpse the towers of the Clifton Suspension Bridge. They ate in a contented silence for a few minutes before Chris continued, 'Anyway, tell me about your trip. I gathered from Vicky's texts that you really enjoyed Brittany and Paris.'

'Yes, it was fine,' said Sukey. 'We shared the driving and only fell out once over which was the right direction.' She laid down her fork with a sigh of appreciation. 'Chris, that was divine.'

'How about some tiramisu to follow?'

'Lovely.'

They finished their meal and sat down in the cosy sitting room while Chris served coffee and almond biscuits. Presently Sukey put down her cup, looked at her watch and said, 'I think it's time I went home. The trouble with coming back on a Sunday is having to go to work the next day.'

'At least we aren't on the early shift,' said Vicky. 'I've just had a thought,' she added as Sukey got up to leave. 'Do you think we should report that business with the envelope?'

Sukey considered for a moment. 'It didn't happen on our patch and the local force were on to it before we left, so I wouldn't have thought . . . but I suppose it wouldn't hurt to mention it. Jilly and Keith know us so they may send a report back to our people. It wouldn't look good if we hadn't mentioned it.'

'There's the RTA as well and that did happen on our patch,' said Vicky, 'and it was the driver of the Volvo who handed over the envelope. We should at least tell DS Rathbone.'

'What business was this?' Chris wanted to know. They gave him a brief description of the behaviour of the two men. 'It doesn't sound to me like anything to do with drugs,' he said. 'Ten to one when your friends catch up with the suspect there'll be something quite innocent in the envelope and he'll complain of police harassment.'

'You're probably right,' Vicky agreed, 'but just the same, it looked distinctly fishy.'

'Maybe this guy was acting as some sort of go-between,' Sukey suggested.

'What sort of go-between?' asked Chris.

'I've no idea,' Sukey admitted. 'Goodnight, Vicky, see you tomorrow.' She slipped her arms into the jacket that Chris held out for her. 'Goodnight, Chris, and thanks for a wonderful meal.'

On the short drive to Clifton she stopped at an all night convenience store to pick up bread, milk and eggs before returning to the flat off Whiteladies Road where she had lived since moving from Gloucester to Bristol. It was a converted hayloft that was once part of the stable block on a country estate and boasted a small roof terrace with a panoramic view across the city. Once home, she gathered up a week's accumulation of mail, lugged her bulging suitcase up the two flights of stairs and dumped it on the floor beside her bed. Having taken out her toilet bag she closed the suitcase, kicked it into a corner and began to undress, throwing the discarded garments on the floor beside it. An unexpected wave of tiredness flowed through her limbs; she was still feeling the effect of many hours spent sitting in the car and her immediate need was for a prolonged, hot, soothing shower.

Half an hour later, relaxed and revived in clean nightclothes and dressing gown, she went into the kitchen and heated some milk in the microwave. She drank it slowly, wandering from room to room in her little domain as she did so, absorbing the familiar surroundings with each leisurely mouthful. She glanced through the pile of mail, sorted out the obvious junk, briefly scrutinizing the rest of the items before putting them all to one side. There was nothing that couldn't wait till tomorrow. She checked her voicemail and decided the few messages could keep as well. She rinsed the empty mug at the sink, went to bed and switched out the light. It was good to be home.

When Sukey and Vicky reported for duty at two o'clock the following afternoon they were greeted by colleagues making the usual enquiries about their holiday. DS Greg Rathbone was on the phone when they arrived; when he had finished his conversation he put the phone down and beckoned to them.

'Good to have you back,' he said by way of a greeting. 'We were up to our eyes all last week – the DCI wanted a special operation mounted on a dealer suspected of using kids as runners outside Westfield Comprehensive so we've been pretty stretched. We got a sort of result – at least, we nailed the dealer but of course we can't touch the kids, they're far too young and the parents refused to admit their little darlings would do anything so diabolical as delivering drugs.'

'And meanwhile the customers will go in search of another source of supply I suppose,' said Vicky.

Rathbone shrugged. 'No doubt. Yes, what is it?' he said as Anna, the civilian worker in the CID office whose responsibilities included liaising with police forces in other areas, approached with a sheet of paper in her hand.

'This fax just came in, Sarge,' she said. 'It's about an incident involving two men acting suspiciously in the Membury services area on the M4.'

'That's in Wiltshire. What's it got to do with us?'

'It appears two of our off-duty CID officers reported the incident to two of their PCs who happened to be there at the time.'

Her glance in the direction of Vicky and Sukey was not lost on Rathbone, who swung round and said sharply, 'Do you two know anything about this?'

'Yes, Sarge,' said Vicky, 'we were in the car park at Membury and we observed two men acting suspiciously and thought it advisable to alert PCs Swinton and Kelly. We knew them by sight – we just happened to meet them in the coffee shop a short while beforehand.'

'One other thing, Sarge,' Sukey added, 'the first man drove off in a black Volvo that was subsequently involved in an RTA on the M32.'

'You witnessed the accident?'

'No, Sarge, but we'd already noted the registration number and Vicky checked it as we passed the wreckage. It's definitely the same car.'

'I see. You'd better give me a report.'

'Got mine right here, Sarge.'

'Me too!' said Vicky.

Rathbone allowed himself a glimpse of a smile. 'OK, let's have them.'

They handed them over and waited while he read through them, hoping – since they had written them independently without comparing notes – that they agreed in every essential. He appeared satisfied; when he had finished he thought for a few moments before saying, 'The two Wiltshire officers you met in the coffee shop were uniformed?'

Vicky nodded. 'Yes, Sarge, but as they were setting off in pursuit of the white Peugeot they alerted their HQ, so maybe their CID thought it worth looking into.'

'This could be tricky,' said Rathbone thoughtfully. 'Since the RTA happened on our patch there may be something this end that calls for investigation, but I don't want to tread on anyone's toes. I think I'll have a word with DCI Leach before I take any action.' He picked up his phone and punched out a number. 'Two of my team have become involved in something that concerns the Wiltshire force, sir,' he said. He outlined the details and continued, 'I'd like some guidance from you if you could spare a minute. That's fine, thank you sir.' He put the phone down and said, 'In his office in half an hour. You can use the time to update on last week's incidents.'

'So, you two managed to put in a spot of sleuthing on your way home from leave?' DCI Leach looked at Sukey and Vicky with a characteristic humorous glint in his keen blue eyes. 'I've got the report on the RTA from the Traffic Division. The driver of the Volvo was cut from the wreckage but was pronounced dead at the scene. According to the driving licence found in his pocket he's Tobias Mayhew of 14 Tyndale Gardens, Horfield. Nothing known about him and so far we haven't been able to trace his next of kin.' He picked up the two reports. 'I've read through these and I've got one or two questions. First of all, exactly what was it about this man that roused your suspicions? Vicky, I gather you were the first to spot him.'

'That's right, sir. It was curiosity at first, rather than suspicion. We couldn't understand why, when the man in the white Peugeot wouldn't accept the envelope he was trying to give him, he made such desperate efforts to force it on him. It wasn't until a second man in an identical white Peugeot parked a short distance away and was obviously looking out for this man – the one with the envelope – that it dawned on us that the first guy had probably mistaken the car. The similarity in the numbers confirmed it.'

'Anything to add to that, Sukey?'

'The first man had his collar turned up and his hat pulled down, sir, so we only got a brief glimpse of his face. It might have been simply protection against the weather, but it could have been an attempt at concealment.'

'But the second man, the man who took the envelope, didn't make any attempt to hide his face,' Vicky interpolated.

'And he seemed perfectly relaxed,' Sukey added.

'I see.' Leach thought for a minute or two and then said, 'It didn't occur to either of you that Mayhew was so jumpy because he needed a fix?'

The two women exchanged slightly embarrassed glances and shook their heads. 'We did think the envelope might have contained drugs, sir, which was why we alerted the two Wiltshire PCs,' said Vicky.

'And we thought it must have been the first time he'd carried out that kind of mission, which would account for his nervousness,' said Sukey. 'Sir,' she added hastily as he fixed her with a penetrating – and this time unsmiling – gaze.

'It's the sort of thing you have to bear in mind all the time in this kind of situation,' said Leach, 'although in this case I doubt if anything you did could have prevented the RTA. In fact, if there'd been a pursuit it might have resulted in something even worse and the pursuing officers might have got the blame. As it is, the people in the other cars escaped with minor injuries. Inquiries into the cause of the accident are at an early stage, but first reports are that the Volvo was driving at an excessive speed and switched lanes without warning. The coroner has been informed and one of you should attend the inquest – both if DS Rathbone can spare you. The PM should reveal any alcohol or drugs in the body.'

'Excuse me, sir,' said Sukey, 'has there been any feedback from Wiltshire about the second driver?'

'There certainly has.' Leach picked up another sheet of paper. 'The two officers you alerted at Membury pulled him over as he was about to leave a filling station. He was pretty miffed at being questioned; he gave them a mouthful about harassment of law-abiding citizens and why weren't they doing something useful like catching criminals – the usual stuff – but eventually he allowed them to examine the envelope. It contained –' Leach consulted his notes – 'a woman's handkerchief, a pendant with a carved ornament that looked like ivory or bone, and a locket containing a curl of dark hair.' He threw the notebook down and fixed the two with a steely gaze. 'In other words, items of purely sentimental value.'

'Looks like a lot of police time was wasted, thanks to us, sir,' said Sukey in a subdued voice.

Leach nodded. 'True, but your suspicions were understand-able and this won't count against you. In fact, since the woodies haven't managed to contact anyone who knows Mayhew, it mightn't be a bad idea if we did a little ferreting around. I'll have a word about that and let you know what's agreed, Greg.'

'Right, sir.'

Leach switched his gaze back to the two women. 'Incidentally, has either of you attended a post-mortem?' They shook their heads. 'In that case, it's time you did. Greg, take one of them with you – they can toss for the privilege. That's all for now.'

THREE

'On the assumption that DCI Leach will want us to take over the search for Mayhew's next of kin from uniformed,' said Rathbone when they returned to the CID office, 'I suggest you read over our report on Warren Chesney. He's the dealer we nicked last week and he lives a few streets away from Tyndale Gardens. If, as DCI Leach seems to suspect, Mayhew is a crackhead, there may be a link.' His flat tone gave no indication as to whether or not he had any views on the matter.

Ten minutes later he came over to them and said, 'It's been agreed we check up on Mayhew, so book a car, get yourselves over to Tyndale Gardens and see what you can turn up.'

'Now, or when we've finished reading the Chesney report, Sarge?' asked Vicky.

'You might as well go now and leave the report till later. You can always go back if necessary.'

'I've a feeling DCI Leach is in one of his ornery moods today,' said Sukey as she and Vicky went downstairs.

'What gives you that idea?'

'I'm sure I detected a hint of fiendish glee in his eye when he sentenced one of us to attend the PM on Mayhew, as if he hoped whoever went would disgrace herself by throwing up or passing out.'

'If I get the short straw he may well have his hopes realized,' said Vicky. 'I'm told it's the smell that turns some people's stomachs,' she added with a grimace.

Sukey nodded. 'When I was a SOCO I once had to go to the morgue to take fingerprints from a corpse, and you're right, the smell is a bit stomach churning, but manipulating the cold hands was the worst bit. I felt the chill even through my gloves. And I once had to photograph a headless body that had been immersed in water for several days,' she added after a moment's reflection. 'That wasn't a pretty sight either, but I managed not to throw up.'

Vicky shuddered. 'Sounds gruesome. I'm surprised you've

never attended a PM, though,' she added. 'I thought taking pictures of each stage of the proceedings was part of a SOCO's job.'

'It is, but dear old Sergeant George Barnes who was in charge of the team in Gloucester had some quaint ideas about what was and what wasn't a suitable job for a woman and he always sent one of the men to do it. Taking pictures of murder victims was one thing, but he drew the line about making me watch them being carved up.'

'Well DCI Leach obviously has no such misgivings so one of us will have to face it,' said Vicky, 'although sooner or later I guess we'll both have to.' They picked up the car keys and went out into the yard. 'Will you drive or shall I?'

Tyndale Gardens was a leafy cul-de-sac of semi-detached dwellings backing on to a playing field. Each had a small, neatly tended front garden with its own driveway and at the end were half a dozen parking spaces for visitors, two of which were already occupied. As Vicky backed into one of the free spaces another car pulled in beside her. Three ladies, each clutching a folder, got out and knocked on the door of number fifteen where another woman, who was evidently expecting them, opened the door. One of the visitors said something and glanced back to where the two detectives were still sitting in their car and the woman responded by subjecting them to a close scrutiny for several seconds before closing the door.

'Looks like a meeting of the local Women's Institute,' Vicky commented.

'More likely the Neighbourhood Watch committee,' said Sukey. 'I noticed the sign at the end of the road – maybe she runs the local branch. What's the betting she took our number?'

Vicky nodded. 'In which case, she'll be the ideal one to ask about her next-door neighbour. She probably won't welcome our presence at her meeting, but I think we should make ourselves known and perhaps fix a more convenient time to come back. And she might be happier if she knew we weren't a couple of villains casing the joint,' she added with a grin.

Sukey chuckled. 'You're probably right. And if she doesn't want to talk to us now we can always call at some of the other houses in the meantime.'

They left the car and knocked at number fifteen. There was a short interval before the door was opened and the woman fixed them with an unfriendly stare. 'If you're selling something—' she began and then broke off as the detectives showed their warrant cards. Her hostile expression changed to one of alarm. 'Police? Is something wrong? Has there been a burglary?'

'Not that we know of,' Sukey assured her, 'we're just making some inquiries about one of your neighbours.'

'We realize this may not be a convenient time,' Vicky added. 'If you prefer, we could arrange to come back later when you're free. And perhaps you wouldn't mind telling us your name?'

'Of course. I'm Mrs Unwin . . . Marian Unwin.' She glanced at her watch. 'I have a meeting of the Ladies' Circle at present – we're planning our programme for the next few months but it should be over in an hour or so. Would you like to come back about half past four? By the way, which neighbour are you interested in?'

'Thank you, we'll be back at half past four,' said Sukey politely.

Mrs Unwin nodded. 'I *quite* understand why you don't want to give any confidential information at this stage,' she said with a knowing smile. 'Goodbye, see you later.'

As they closed Mrs Unwin's front gate Sukey said quietly, 'Did you notice how her eyes flicked in the direction of number fourteen when she asked which neighbour we're interested in?'

Vicky nodded. 'She's probably heard about the woodies who've been trying to contact Mayhew's next of kin.'

'It's quite likely they called on her,' Sukey agreed, 'but as she didn't mention it she was probably out.'

'She might have heard about it from the other neighbours,' Vicky pointed out. 'I wonder if they were told the reason for the enquiries.'

'You mean, did the woodies tell anyone Mayhew's dead? I wouldn't have thought so.'

'So let's assume they don't know.' Vicky glanced along the row of houses. 'Where shall we try next?'

'There's a car on the drive at number thirteen so someone's probably at home,' said Sukey. 'Let's begin there.'

As they walked up the path of number thirteen they noticed a movement behind the lace curtain at the front window of number twelve. 'But soft, we are observed!' said Vicky in a stage whisper as she pressed the bell at number thirteen.

A man with white hair and moustache and an upright bearing that suggested a military background opened the door. 'Good morning ladies,' he said jovially, 'what can I do for you? Oh, CID eh?' he went on as they displayed their warrant cards. 'Come to check on the local villains?' He gave a throaty chuckle. 'Come along in!' He closed the door behind them before saying, 'It's about young Toby Mayhew, I suppose? I heard from the woman next door that your people – or at least, the uniformed bunch – were here yesterday, asking about his next of kin. Wouldn't tell her what it was about of course. She was quite cross,' he added mischievously. 'Between you and me, she's a bit of a busybody, likes to know everything that's going on. Good heart, though.'

'Do you happen to know where we can contact Mr Mayhew's next of kin, sir?' asked Sukey.

His expression became serious and he shook his head. 'I'm afraid not, but I might be able to help you find them. Come in and sit down.' He led them into a comfortably furnished front room and pulled up two armchairs. 'My name's Driver – George Driver, Colonel, retired,' he went on. 'Known to the ranks as 'Slave Driver', of course,' he added with a wink. 'Only in a jokey sort of way, mind you. Always had a good relationship with my men. May I offer you ladies some refreshment?'

'No thank you, Colonel Driver,' said Sukey. 'We don't want to take up too much of your time, but—'

'No need to worry about that,' Driver assured them. Having seen them comfortably seated he settled in a high-backed, winged armchair and stretched out his legs, displaying highly polished brown shoes, striped socks and sharply creased fawn trousers above which he wore a checked shirt and plain green tie under a well-cut tweed jacket. 'Time is something I have plenty of these days,' he went on. 'Mustn't grumble though, I've had a good life in the army and my two sons and their wives visit regularly with the grandchildren.'

'That must be a comfort,' said Vicky. 'Now sir, would you mind telling us how well you know Tobias Mayhew?'

'Sad business, that,' said Driver with a solemn shake of the head. 'Happens too often nowadays. Saw it with some of my

own men . . . ruined their lives. Some of them anyway – others
managed to pick up the pieces. Strength of character counts for
a lot y'know.'

'I'm sure it does,' said Vicky politely.

'Some are willing to talk things over and go for what they
call counselling nowadays. In my day it was a case of the old
stiff upper lip, what?'

'So what can you tell us about Toby Mayhew, Colonel Driver?'
asked Sukey, who had been privately wondering whether they
would ever get him to the point.

'Ah yes, young Toby.' Driver stroked his moustache with a
thoughtful expression. You're trying to contact his next of kin.
Can't say I know the fellow all that well,' he went on. 'When
he moved into the place next door – that would be a couple of
years ago now – he hardly showed his face for a week or so.
Then he started wandering down his garden and looking over
the wall across the playing fields. Quite often there'd be kids
out there and now and again I saw him chatting to them. If I
happened to be in my own garden I'd give him a friendly "good
day"; sometimes he'd smile and return the greeting, but other
times he'd stare right through me. It occurred to me he might
be in a state of depression.' Driver broke off as a clock on the
mantelpiece chimed a quarter to four. 'I say, are you sure you
wouldn't like some tea? I usually have a cup about now.'

'Well, if it wouldn't be any trouble . . .' said Vicky and Driver
beamed and leapt to his feet.

'Ready in a jiffy,' he said and hurried from the room. In the
interval that followed they heard the sound of a kettle being
filled and the rattling of cups and saucers.

'D'you reckon he's really got anything to tell us or is he just
glad of a bit of company?' said Sukey in a low voice.

'I'm hoping he's got something interesting to tell us, but we'll
have to wait and see,' Vicky whispered back.

A few minutes later Driver returned wheeling a trolley and
proceeded to pour tea from a silver teapot into bone china cups.
He pulled out two small tables and placed one beside each chair,
got out silver coasters on which he placed their cups of tea, gave
each a matching china plate and offered chocolate biscuits. When
he was satisfied that they had everything they wanted he served

himself with tea and biscuits and went back to his own chair. After two deep swallows from his cup he set it down on its saucer with a sigh of appreciation.

'That's better,' he said contentedly. 'Now ladies, what else do you want to know about young Toby? He went out yesterday and he hasn't come back – at least, his car isn't there. I hope he isn't in any kind of trouble?'

'Have you any reason to think he might be?' asked Sukey. 'You hinted he had some problem that was making him depressed.'

Driver nodded. 'That's right. I could see he needed cheering up so I invited him round for a snifter one evening. The first time he refused – quite rudely, as I remember, but I persevered and the next time he jumped at the invitation. After a couple of scotches he relaxed and then became very emotional and poured his heart out to me. He was in the army, got an unexpected weekend pass and thought he'd give his wife a surprise.' Driver gave a slightly sardonic smile. 'She got a surprise all right, and so did he . . . and his best friend as well. He found them in bed together.'

'That must have been a nasty shock all round,' said Sukey, conscious of the triteness of the comment but recognizing from Driver's expression that he expected some kind of response.

'Very nasty,' agreed Vicky. 'What did he do?'

'Pitched the boyfriend out into the street stark naked and chucked his clothes after him,' said Driver with obvious relish. 'If he'd left it at that, all would have been well,' he went on, becoming serious again, 'but unfortunately he went back and beat up the wife. Wound up with six months in the glasshouse followed by dishonourable discharge.'

'That's a really sad story,' said Sukey. 'You said he's only lived here for a couple of years so presumably all this happened somewhere else.'

'That's right, but I'm afraid I don't know where. All he told me is that when she came out of hospital his wife went and shacked up with her lover.'

'Has he ever mentioned any other relatives?' asked Vicky. 'His parents, brother or sisters, for example?'

'I gather his parents disowned him after he was kicked out of the army. His father was a sergeant and put pressure on young Toby to follow in his footsteps. I don't think his heart was in it but it seems dad was a bit of a bully. And my understanding is that he was an only child.'

'But you don't know where his parents live?'

Driver shook his head. 'No, but army records will show where he was living when he joined up. I suggest you start there.'

'We'll certainly do that, thank you.' Vicky made a note.

'By the way,' said Sukey, 'does he have a job, do you know?'

Driver shook his head. 'I've no idea. He's never mentioned a regular job, but he runs a car so I suppose he has some sort of income.'

Sukey, whose chair faced the window, happened to spot a group of ladies leaving number fifteen and returning to their cars. She glanced at the clock on the mantelpiece; it was a little after four thirty.

'Thank you very much, Colonel Driver,' she said. 'You've been a great help. You'll excuse us if we leave now, but we have some other people to talk to.'

'And thank you for the tea,' added Vicky.

'Delighted to be of assistance,' said the colonel as he escorted them to the door. 'If I think of anything else, who shall I ask for?'

Vicky fished in her pocket for one of her cards and gave it to him. 'The number to call is on this,' she said, 'and I suggest you ask for DS Rathbone.'

'Well, we actually learned something useful,' said Vicky in a low voice after the door closed behind them. 'I was beginning to wonder whether he just invited us in for a chat because he was lonely.'

'I had the same impression at first,' said Sukey. 'I don't suppose everyone we call on will be quite so helpful.'

But in this assumption she was considerably wide of the mark.

FOUR

As they were closing Colonel Driver's gate behind them the door of number twelve opened and a high-pitched female voice said, 'Excuse me!'

They turned to see a small, slight woman of about sixty hurrying down the path to speak to them. 'Ahem, excuse me!' she repeated in a conspiratorial whisper, 'I couldn't help over-hearing you telling my neighbour that you're from the CID. If it's young Mr Mayhew you're interested in, I may be able to help you. I tried to tell the officers who came before,' she went on before they could answer, 'but when I said I didn't know where they could find his next of kin they didn't seem inter-ested.' Her glance switched from Sukey to Vicky and back again. *'You could almost see her nose twitching!'* Vicky told Rathbone later.

'Thank you very much, madam,' said Sukey politely. 'We'd certainly appreciate any help you can give us. We have an appoint-ment with another of your neighbours at half past four, but perhaps we may come back to you later?'

'Ah, that'll be her at number fifteen I suppose,' said the woman. She gave a slightly dismissive sniff. 'I doubt if *she* can tell you much. Keeps herself to herself, she does, not at all neighbourly. See you in a little while, then?' She gave an ingratiating smile and went back indoors.

'By "not at all neighbourly" I imagine she means Mrs Unwin doesn't keep her up to date with all the details of her private life,' Vicky remarked as they walked the few yards to number fifteen. 'I wonder if she had better luck with Mayhew. I don't imagine he'd have been likely to open his heart to her the way he did to Colonel Driver.'

'Probably not, but I'll bet there's not much goes on round here that she doesn't know,' said Sukey. 'We know she was watching when we went to his house and I noticed a little window next to her front door is cracked open. It's probably the downstairs loo – maybe she scuttled in there when we knocked on the Colonel's door and heard us say we were CID.'

'Do come in,' said Mrs Unwin with a smile as she opened the door in response to their knock. She was a plump woman of about fifty who spoke with a soft Welsh accent. 'I'm sorry I had to ask you to come back. Would you like some tea?'

'Actually, we've just had some,' said Vicky, 'but thank you all the same.'

'Come this way, then.' Their hostess betrayed no curiosity as she ushered them into the back room, which overlooked the garden and the playing field beyond. It was furnished as a dining room and had apparently been the scene of the meeting of the Ladies' Circle, since an open Manila folder and some loose papers lay on the table. Mrs Unwin gathered up the papers, put them in the folder and closed it before sitting down and signalling to Sukey and Vicky to do the same. 'We've only just finished our meeting,' she said, placing her hands on the folder as if she felt it necessary to account for its presence. 'I'm the secretary so I have to write the minutes.'

'I promise we won't take up too much of your time,' said Vicky. 'We need to contact Tobias Mayhew's next of kin. Do you happen to know where they live?'

'His next of kin?' Mrs Unwin gave an anxious frown. 'Is he in some kind of trouble? Has he been hurt?'

'If you wouldn't mind just answering the question,' said Sukey.

Mrs Unwin looked embarrassed, as if fearing she had appeared over-inquisitive. 'The simple answer is "no",' she said hastily. 'In fact, I've hardly spoken to the man since he moved in next door. I tried being neighbourly without appearing nosy – unlike some people I could mention – but all I ever got in response to my "Good morning" or "Good day" was a grunt and I've heard from others that he reacts to them in the same way. Colonel Driver at number thirteen might know more than I do,' she went on after a brief pause. 'I've seen them once or twice chatting over the garden fence.'

'We have spoken to the colonel, but our enquiries are still continuing,' said Vicky. 'Are you sure you can't think of anything that might help us? Have you noticed any regular callers to his house, for example?'

Mrs Unwin frowned and shook her head. 'I hope you don't think I'm in the habit of spying on my neighbours,' she said reproachfully.

'No, of course not,' Vicky said hastily, anxious to smooth apparently ruffled feathers. 'We're just wondering if you'd happened to notice anyone – just the odd person, for example.'

'I can't say I have – except the postman or the bin men, of course.'

'You have a very nice garden,' Sukey commented. She glanced out of the window at the immaculate lawn and trim borders, at present bare of colour in the dying light of the February afternoon. 'You must spend quite a lot of time out there in the summer.'

Mrs Unwin's laugh held a hint of sadness. 'Oh dear, no,' she said, 'at least, only to enjoy it from in here or sit outside if the weather's warm enough. My husband was very keen; he spent a lot of time out there, but since he died I've had to employ a gardener. As a matter of fact, I've been thinking of selling this house and moving into a flat. But you don't want to hear about me,' she went on. 'It's Mr Mayhew you're interested in. I'm really sorry I can't be more helpful.'

'So you've never even had occasion to talk to him over the fence?' Sukey persisted.

'I'm afraid not. I suggest you try Mrs Scott at number twelve. She's our Neighbourhood Watch co-ordinator; she knows more about what goes on round here than anyone and what she doesn't know she makes it her business to find out. Not that she isn't a good neighbour,' she hurried on, as if anxious not to be thought uncharitable. 'She was very kind to me when Wilf died . . . but then, so was everyone else, but they didn't swamp me with advice on how to run the rest of my life.'

'I have a feeling,' said Sukey as, having taken their leave of Mrs Unwin, she and Vicky headed back to Mrs Scott's house, 'that we are about to glean some useful additions to what Colonel Driver gave us.'

'Me too,' said Vicky.

Mrs Scott received them with enthusiasm and showed them into a cosy room that ran the length of the house with windows overlooking both the back garden and the road. It was evident that when the house was built the room was divided in two and

Sukey found herself wondering mischievously whether the conversion had been made by the Scotts or whether they had been attracted by that particular feature.

'It's nice to have company now and again,' Mrs Scott began. 'Albert – my husband that is – retired last year, but I seem to see less of him than when he was working. He's either off playing golf or doing some committee work or other. Today it's the Probus Club. I call it his geriatric playgroup,' she added with a slightly girlish laugh, to which Sukey and Vicky responded with polite smiles. 'Now, I believe you want to know about Toby Mayhew?'

'We want to contact his next of kin and we're wondering if you can help us,' said Vicky. 'We understand he's lived next door to you for about two years.'

Mrs Scott nodded. 'Two years on the thirty-first of January,' she said without hesitation. 'I remember the date because it's Albert's birthday. We were going out to dinner in the evening; the removal van came in the morning of course and I remember thinking it was funny there was no woman to tell the men where to put the furniture and things, just this rather grumpy-looking man. I noticed it was all new stuff and I thought he must be making a home for his new wife . . . or then again, maybe they'd lost everything in a fire . . . you never know do you?'

Sukey took advantage of a brief pause in the reminiscences to ask, 'Did you ever find out?'

'Absolutely not. A most *uncommunicative* young man,' she said, with emphasis on every syllable. 'His next of kin?' she went on with a slight start, as if the significance of the question had only just struck her. 'No, I've no idea – but what's happened? Isn't that what the police want to know if someone's been killed?'

'That isn't the only reason,' Vicky said. 'Is there anything you can think of that might help us?'

'I knocked on the door after the removal men had gone to introduce myself. I'm the Neighbourhood Watch co-ordinator and naturally I make a point of introducing myself to newcomers. In fact, I invited him round for a cup of tea,' Mrs Scott went on, 'but he was quite rude, didn't even say "Thank you", practically shut the door in my face. He never even told me his name – I got it from the postman after he'd been here a couple of weeks

– and he showed no sign of being neighbourly. It's almost as if he's got something to hide. I've noticed him chatting to Colonel Driver out in the garden,' she added resentfully, 'and I know the Colonel invites him round once in a while, but I've no idea what they talk about. As I said, I could never get a word out of him and neither could Albert . . . but I have seen him talk to the children now and again.'

'You mean the neighbours' children?'

'No, the children who play in the park. He spends a lot of time leaning over the wall at the end of his garden and now and again one of the boys – it's usually boys – will run up and speak to him. Sometimes I've had the impression he gave the child something . . . sweets, I suppose, for the small ones and maybe cigarettes to the bigger ones. I thought it was rather suspicious and I told Frank Barker at number twenty-one – he's a local councillor.'

'You suspect Mr Mayhew of being a paedophile?' asked Vicky.

Mrs Scott shuddered slightly at the word. 'Well, not *exactly* that,' she said hastily, 'but you hear so many dreadful stories don't you? You can't be too careful.'

'I notice you call him Toby,' said Vicky, 'so he must at least have told you his first name?'

'Not at all!' Mrs Scott snapped. 'I just happened to overhear a man call him that – a man who called a day or two after he moved in. The same man still calls from time to time and gets invited in so I suppose he's a friend or something to do with his job.'

Little by little, under patient questioning, the two detectives managed to elicit a considerable amount of information about Toby Mayhew's visitor. They thanked her politely, declined her offer of refreshment and took their leave. By now it was getting on for six o'clock; after a quick word with DS Rathbone they drove back to the station to report their findings so far.

'It seems you've come back with as many questions as answers,' Rathbone commented. 'Assuming Mayhew is his real name and the story about beating up the wife and being chucked out of the army is true, we shouldn't have any difficulty in checking where his parents live – or used to live. At the same time, especially in

the light of what the SIO said, I'm thinking we should be looking
into a possible drugs link. This man who used to call on him –
I see Mrs Scott gave you a description of sorts and it just could
be Warren Chesney, so you'd better go back tomorrow and show
her a mug shot. If she can't identify him I suggest you go round
to a few more neighbours and show it to them. Maybe someone
got a good enough look at him to do an E-FIT. We'll do a check
on the car details Mrs Scott gave you, of course. If there's a link
with Chesney it would be a bonus, but I'm not holding my breath.
I'm interested in the contact with the kids, though. They might
have been runners for Chesney, delivering supplies to the
customers.

'You don't think there's anything in the paedophile suggestion, Sarge?' said Sukey.

Rathbone shrugged. 'The head of the local comprehensive was
very helpful with our enquiries about Chesney, but there was
never any suggestion as far as I know of that sort of problem. I
suppose that's another box we'll have to tick. OK, I'll see what
help the Ministry can give us and in the meantime you'd better
pay another visit to Tyndale Gardens. By the way, don't forget
you're back on early shift as from tomorrow.'

When Sukey and Vicky returned to Tyndale Gardens the following
day and showed the photo of Warren Chesney to Mrs Scott she
was very positive that he was indeed the man she had seen calling
on Toby Mayhew. 'But I don't recall seeing him lately,' she said,
both her tone and her expression indicating an eagerness for
further information. They thanked her for her help, knocked at
Colonel Driver's door and showed him the photo. While not
having taken so much interest in the comings and goings of
Mayhew's visitors as his neighbour, he recalled having on one
occasion seen someone looking very like Chesney leaving his
house at the same time as he himself was returning home. 'Can't
say exactly when it was,' he apologized, 'but I reckon that could
be him.'

They returned to headquarters in some triumph to report to
DS Rathbone, but they had barely begun when he received an
urgent call from DCI Leach. When he returned he said,
'Something new has come up. Sukey, put your coat on, we're

going to Clevedon. Vicky, write out your report and I'll see it later.'

'What is it, Sarge?' asked Sukey as she followed Rathbone downstairs.

'Something nasty on the beach,' he said tersely as he collected the keys of a pool car and tossed them to Sukey. 'I'm taking you instead of Vicky because I've a feeling you've got a stronger stomach.' As she started the engine he added, 'A woman's head has been washed up by the tide. No body, just the head.'

FIVE

The seafront at Clevedon, normally quiet at this time of year apart from a few locals exercising their dogs, was already a scene of intense police activity by the time Sukey and Rathbone arrived. A uniformed officer directed them to a parking space close to the pier alongside a number of police vehicles and two white vans belonging to crime scene investigators. Word of the gruesome discovery had evidently got around, for a small crowd had gathered as close to the scene of action as the police allowed and were craning over the wrought-iron handrail that ran the length of the high wall overlooking the beach in an effort to see what was going on below them. About halfway along the pier, a handful of anglers appeared more interested in the police activity than their fishing lines.

A wide area of the foreshore was also cordoned off and a team of uniformed officers stood by while the CSIs examined and recorded the scene. A steep, narrow iron stairway led down to the beach. At the bottom, sitting on the edge of a concrete slipway where members of the local sailing club launched their boats at high tide, was a young woman. She had her hands over her eyes and was evidently in a state of shock, for she was shaking violently and uttering little whimpering noises. A uniformed woman police officer, crouched down beside her, looked up as the two detectives approached.

'Is she the one who found it?' asked Rathbone. 'DS Rathbone and DC Reynolds,' he added, as the officer seemed about to question their right to be there.

She hastily got to her feet. 'Oh – er, PC Annie Darby, Sarge,' she said. 'Yes, that's right. I'm trying to get her to move,' she added in a low voice. 'She was in hysterics when we got here, staring at it like she was hypnotized. I've managed to get her this far and quieten her down but if she sees it again . . . it is pretty gruesome,' she added with a grimace.

He gave a sympathetic chuckle. 'From the colour of your face I guess you've had a glimpse yourself,' he said and she managed a shaky smile. 'But you can tell her she needn't worry, she won't be asked if she can identify the lady. Just the same she's an important witness and we'll need to question her.' He jerked his head towards the staircase. 'There's a café over the road that looks as if it's open. She could probably use a hot drink – see what you can do.'

'I'll do my best, Sarge.'

'Good girl.' He strode on with Sukey at his heels. One of the officers came to meet them.

'Inspector Reg Hutchins,' he announced. 'I take it you're DS Rathbone?'

'That's right, sir, and this is DC Sukey Reynolds.'

'You'd better have a look at exhibit A as soon as the CSIs have done their stuff,' said Hutchins. 'I hope you've got strong stomachs,' he added with some feeling. Sukey had the impression that he too had found 'exhibit A' a trifle unnerving and hoped she would manage to hold on to her breakfast.

They watched the masked figures in their white overalls as they went methodically about their work, one with a camera and the other taking and recording measurements. It crossed Sukey's mind that at a cursory glance from that distance the thing lying on the wet brown mud might have been mistaken for just another of the large, round boulders covered in seaweed that lay strewn around below the high-water line.

It was several minutes before the CSIs carefully picked their way back to the place where Hutchins and the detectives were waiting. 'Finished?' the inspector said brusquely.

The one with the camera nodded and said 'Yes, Guv.'

The second, evidently more affected than his colleague, hastily tore off his mask, clapped a hand over his mouth and took several deep, shuddering breaths. 'Not a pretty sight,' he said apologetically.

Hutchins turned to Rathbone. 'OK, she's all yours,' he said. 'I suppose we don't need to send for a doctor to pronounce the victim dead?' he added with a twitch at one side of his mouth that might have been mistaken for a smile.

'I think we can safely make that assumption for ourselves, sir,' Rathbone replied dryly and there was a general lessening of tension at the hint of grim humour in the exchange. 'The coroner will want a time when death was certified, but I guess the nearest we can give is the time when the first of your men arrived.'

'What about the pathologist?' asked Hutchins.

'He'll have to be informed, of course,' said Rathbone. 'There doesn't seem much point in bringing him here, but I'd better check with my SIO.' He moved away and switched on his mobile. After a few moments he returned and said, 'DCI Leach agrees, sir. He says we're to contain the scene as best we can while it's still exposed and have a good look round for possible evidence. In the meantime he'll organize some kind of sterile container to pack the thing in for transfer to the morgue.' He turned to Sukey. 'Right, let's get this over.' It was clear from his tone that, like herself, he was not looking forward to their next immediate task.

As they drew near, the brownish mass with the appearance of seaweed growing on a rock suddenly metamorphosed into long dark hair clinging damply to the disembodied head of a woman. It was lying half on its side; as they moved carefully round it they could see her profile, with one wide-open eye staring blankly at the sky.

Sukey took a deep breath and swallowed hard. 'Oh, dear God!' she said softly.

'I've seen some pretty grisly sights in my time, but this beats all,' muttered Rathbone. He too breathed deeply and put a handkerchief over his mouth; for a moment she thought he was going to gag but he managed to steady himself before saying shakily, 'You OK?'

Sukey nodded. 'Just about, Sarge.'

'Looks like it's suffered some damage,' he said gruffly, indicating an area at the corner of the mouth where the flesh appeared to have been torn. ' Maybe it's been dashed by the tide against some submerged object.' He glanced round him, a little helplessly. 'How in the world do we set about establishing exactly where it entered the water? It could have been miles along the coast – or from a boat some distance out to sea.'

'Or from the end of the pier?' Sukey suggested.

He nodded gloomily. 'That too, I suppose. We'll need some expert advice on tides. And let's hope Doc Hanley will be able to give us some idea after he's done the PM of how long it's been in the water. It would help if he could say if death occurred before or after decapitation, but maybe that's too much to ask. The CSIs will have recorded any prints in the sand – we'll have to compare them with the girl's footwear once we have their report.' He took a final look round in all directions before saying, 'Not much point in hanging round here is there, Sukey?'

'Not really, Sarge.' They went back to Inspector Hutchins. 'Who found it, sir?' asked Rathbone.

'The young woman you spoke to when you arrived.' He indicated with a jerk of his head the spot where the girl had been sitting. 'It appears she was walking along the wet sand at the water's edge and suddenly came across it. All she could do was scream and point, which is what she was still doing when we got here. She seemed hypnotized – we had the devil of a job to get her to move.'

'So she isn't the one who reported it?'

'No. A man walking his dog heard the screaming and hurried down to investigate. He called us on his mobile and waited with the girl till we got here. By that time a few more people had been drawn to the spot by the noise and we had to shoo them away so that we could contain the scene.'

'Is that witness still here?'

Hutchins shook his head. 'He was pretty shaken himself; he gave us his name and address and we told him he could go home and someone would get in touch later. I think he said something about having a drink in the pub over the road – you might catch him there,' he added. 'He's a Mr Giles Russell.'

'Thank you, sir, that's a great help. Do you happen to know the state of the tide, by the way?'

Hutchins glanced at his watch. 'It's almost on the turn. It'll be back where the thing's lying in a couple of hours or so.'

'Right, there's no time to lose.' Rathbone made a further call on his mobile. When he had finished he said, 'I've put the DCI in the picture and he's going to get the container to us as quickly as possible.' He turned to Sukey. 'Right, I think we'll try the pub first – with luck Russell may still be there. I'll check; you go and find out if that woman's going to be fit to talk to us – say in fifteen minutes or so – and then come and join me.'

*   *   *

Sukey found the girl sitting beside PC Annie Darby at a corner
table in the café, where the only customers apart from Annie
and her protégée were two middle-aged ladies who were tucking
into toasted teacakes and showing no interest in anything or
anyone else. She appeared to be in her late teens or early twen-
ties, with untidy blonde hair round a face that Sukey guessed
would normally be pretty but was presently pinched and white
with shock. Her hands were tightly clasped round a mug, but
her teeth were chattering so much that she was having difficulty
in drinking the contents. On seeing Sukey she appeared to make
an effort to pull herself together.

'Sorry to be such a wimp,' she said weakly.

'She's beginning to feel better,' said Annie. 'Try and drink
your tea, Kelly,' she said persuasively and the girl obediently
took a few swallows.

Sukey sat down at the table and introduced herself. 'My
sergeant and I would like to ask you some questions in a few
minutes' time,' she began, 'but if you don't feel well enough to
talk now we'll arrange for you to be taken home and we can see
you tomorrow. Do you mind telling me your full name?'

'Kelly Steele.'

'And how old are you?'

'Twenty-one.'

'That means we can ask you some questions now if you feel
up to it. Or we could take you back to our headquarters and
arrange for a family liaison officer to be with you while we talk.'

Kelly looked down at the remains of her tea and pulled a face.
'It's gone cold,' she said apologetically as she handed the half-
empty mug to Annie. Already, the colour had started to return to
her face. 'Yes, that'd be OK,' she said. 'I'd like to get it over with.'

'Good girl,' said Sukey. 'Why don't you have some fresh tea
– and maybe a little something to eat? I'll be back shortly.'

Giles Russell was a man of about sixty with thinning grey hair and
a matching moustache. When Sukey entered the crowded saloon
bar of the Moon and Sixpence she found him ensconced in a corner
with a black and white Welsh collie at his feet and Rathbone facing
him across a table on which stood a pint tankard of ale, a glass of
orange juice and an opened packet of crisps.

'Can I get you anything?' said Rathbone as she sat down.

'Not just now, thank you, Sarge,' she said.

'Right.' Rathbone took a mouthful of orange juice before saying, 'Mr Russell has promised to do what he can to help us.'

'That's great,' she said. She took out her notebook, opened it and waited. The man nodded, smiled and raised the tankard in salute before taking several copious swallows.

'Now, Mr Russell,' Rathbone continued, 'I understand you've lived in Clevedon all your life?'

The man nodded. 'Pretty well,' he said in a voice that had a strong West Country burr. 'I've been walking along the front here for a good many years now and I've never seen anything like *that* before.' He glanced towards the window, which commanded a view of the sea and the pier. On the foreshore the police were gathered in a protective ring around the gruesome evidence as they waited for the promised container. 'It quite shook me up for the moment, especially with that woman screeching her head off. It upset Bessie, too.' He reached down to caress the dog's head and it wagged its tail and licked his hand.

'Yes, it must have been a bit unnerving.' Rathbone said while Sukey made sympathetic noises. She suspected that Russell was rather enjoying the attention and meant to make the most of it. 'So,' Rathbone continued, 'you walk this way with Bessie most days, is that right?'

'Pretty well. I walk along the front as far as the kids' playground and usually pop in here for a noggin on the way back.' Russell drained his tankard and glanced hopefully at Rathbone, who picked it up and went to the bar.

Russell turned to Sukey and treated her to a smile that showed an immaculate set of teeth while his eyes, of a bright greyish blue, sparkled with undisguised admiration. 'I must say,' he said, 'I find it very strange to meet a young lady in such unpleasant circumstances. Strange, but most agreeable nonetheless,' he added gallantly.

Sukey smiled politely in return and murmured something noncommittal while mentally hoping that Rathbone would not be long delayed at the bar. To her relief, he returned before Russell had time to pursue the conversation. He set down another foaming tankard, from which Russell drank deeply before waiting expectantly for the next question.

'Right, Mr Russell,' said Rathbone. 'I imagine you often meet the same people on your daily walks?'

He nodded. 'Oh yes, indeed. There's Charlie Hastings from the bowls club, and Mickey Graham – he's captain of the local cricket team – and then there's old Mrs Higgins with her Poppy, we always stop for a chat don't we Bessie? And—'

'Perhaps after we've had our talk you wouldn't mind jotting down their names so that we can have a word with them?' Rathbone said hastily when Russell paused for breath. 'Just for now, we'd like to know if you've noticed anyone strange, or acting strangely, say during the past week or so? Particularly if the person was carrying a bag with something that looked like it had something heavy in it?'

Russell's thought processes called for several deep draughts of beer. Eventually, he shook his head. 'I can't say as I have,' he said, with evident regret.

'Can you recall any of your friends mentioning anything of the sort?' suggested Sukey.

Russell still appeared to be cogitating while the level in his tankard dropped at a significant rate. Rathbone and Sukey were exchanging resigned glances when a hearty masculine voice behind them said, 'Hello, Giles!' A plump, rosy-cheeked man of about the same age as Russell reached across the table to shake him by the hand. 'What's all the excitement? Boys in blue everywhere – what's going on? Oh, sorry if I'm intruding,' he went on, giving the detectives an apologetic nod. 'I'm Ken Lowe from the angling club. Giles and I have long chats while we're waiting for the fish to bite.'

'Perhaps you'll allow me to explain, Mr Lowe.' Having introduced himself and Sukey, Rathbone outlined the situation while Russell, looking distinctly embarrassed, sat fiddling with his tankard.

Lowe gave a soft whistle. 'Bless my soul!' he said. 'I wonder if . . . I thought at the time that it must have been a rock, although in that particular spot it seemed unlikely.' A look of horror spread across his genial features. 'To think it might have been *that*!' He hastily got to his feet. 'I need a drink.'

SIX

The others waited in silence while Lowe went to the bar, returning a minute or two later with a large scotch. He sat down and took several hasty gulps before saying shakily, 'That's better. Sorry about that. It was just the realization . . . came as a bit of a shock . . . I told you, didn't I Giles . . . no, on second thoughts you were with me that day when my line got caught, don't you remember? One day last week – Thursday, was it, or maybe Friday? We both thought at the time, it must have been on a rock only it seemed strange because there aren't that many that far out, not on the port side of the pier anyway.'

Russell, evidently feeling rather foolish at not having recalled this incident and its possible relevance to this morning's discovery, nodded, drained his glass and said lamely, 'I confess it didn't occur to me that—'

To save him further embarrassment and, Sukey secretly guessed, to avoid the necessity of buying him yet another pint, Rathbone said, 'It's obvious that you have some information that could be highly significant to our inquiries, gentlemen, but I'd prefer not to continue this discussion in public.' He broke off and glanced round the crowded lounge before adding, 'Especially as most of the people here seem to have only one thing on their minds. Would you mind coming to the station with us?'

'Fine by me.' Lowe downed the rest of his scotch and stood up. 'How about you, Giles?'

'Yes, of course.' Russell got to his feet and tugged gently at Bessie's leash. 'Come on, lass, we're going to the cop shop.' He staggered slightly as he followed Lowe to the door, hesitated and changed direction. 'Got to pay a call,' he explained. 'Hold Bessie for me, Ken.' He thrust the dog's leash at Lowe and headed for the toilet.

'Hardly surprising after all that beer,' Rathbone muttered out of the corner of his mouth. 'By the way, Sukey, you'd better run

back to the café and tell Annie to take Kelly home. We'll get
her statement later.'

'Right, Sarge.'

'And while you're at it, tell her we'll need Kelly's footwear
for checking by forensics.'

'Will do.'

Kelly's face fell on being told of the new arrangement as,
having recovered from the initial shock of her gruesome
discovery, she had evidently been looking forward to being interviewed at police headquarters. Her disappointment turned to
alarm when she was asked to hand over her trainers. It took
several minutes for her to grasp the reason for the request, but
eventually she accepted that she was not under suspicion. By
the time Sukey got back to the car Rathbone was sitting in the
front passenger seat while Lowe and Russell were in the back
with Bessie between them. Rathbone accepted her apology for
the delay without comment.

'Change of plan,' he announced. 'Mr Lowe has had a word
with his wife and she has very kindly invited us to their house.
She recalls the incident very well so she may be able to help
us. And Mr Lowe assures us she is a very sensible lady and quite
understands the situation,' he added as an afterthought.

Ken Lowe's house was a semi-detached bungalow a short
distance from the town centre. His wife Margaret was a softly
spoken woman with bobbed pepper and salt hair and a fresh,
ruddy complexion that spoke of many years of exposure to sun
and sea air.

'What a dreadful thing to happen,' she said as she ushered
them into a comfortable sitting room with French windows overlooking a pleasant garden. 'And what a horrible shock for that
poor young woman! Whatever kind of person would cut off a
lady's head and throw it into the sea just like that? And what do
you suppose has happened to the rest of the poor creature?'

'That's what we have to find out,' said Rathbone. 'At the
moment we are as much in the dark as you are, so we'll be most
grateful for any help you can give us.'

'I'll do what I can. Would you like some coffee?' Her
husband and Russell declined, but the two detectives gratefully
accepted.

When they were all settled and Bessie had been given a drink of water, Rathbone said, 'Mr Lowe, I understand that on a recent occasion, when you and Mr Russell were fishing on the pier, your line became entangled in something in the water?'

'That's right.'

'Did you manage to free it?'

'I did, but it took me quite a time. I reeled in to make sure the hook and sinker were still there and not damaged, and they were all right. The bait had gone of course . . . but there was no fish,' he added ruefully.'

'Did you get the impression that whatever your line was caught in was actually on the seabed?'

'I think it must have been. We thought it was a rock, didn't we, Giles?'

Russell nodded. 'We couldn't think of anything else it might be. You kept saying it was too heavy to reel in without damaging your tackle.'

'Whereabouts on the pier were you?' asked Rathbone.

'Fairly near the end, as far as I remember,' said Lowe.

'I'm pretty sure you said it was near the end,' said his wife. 'And as to the day, it was Saturday of last week. I went to the matinée in Bristol that afternoon and I remember you told me about it when I got home.'

'Is that where you normally fish?' asked Sukey.

The two anglers glanced at one another. 'Mostly we cast our lines about halfway along,' said Lowe after a pause. 'Now why did we . . .?'

'It was neap tide last Saturday,' said Russell, suddenly regaining confidence on being able to contribute some positive information. 'And the tide was just about on the turn,' he added.

'So you moved further along the pier because the water would have been too shallow from your usual spot?' The two men nodded. 'So between last Saturday and this morning, the object that wasn't a rock but in fact was the severed head of a woman somehow shifted from the place where your line caught it to the point where it was found?'

'Well, there's no mystery about that,' said Mrs Lowe briskly. 'It can't have been embedded in the sand or it wouldn't have moved. Anything lying loose on the bottom would have rolled to and fro with the movement of the waves – especially something round, like a human head,' she added, pulling a face.

'I'm sure you know, Sergeant, that the rise and fall of the tide on this part of the coast is the highest in the country,' Russell put in. 'The water comes sweeping in very fast up the Bristol Channel . . . and of course, every so often we have the Severn Bore,' he added with a touch of pride.

'Yes, indeed,' said Sukey, who had acquired this information very early in her career with the Avon and Somerset CID. 'I've seen it and it's very impressive. We don't know yet, of course, how long the head has been in the water, but supposing it was dropped in, say, four or five days ago, could you make some sort of estimate as to where along the estuary it might have started its journey?'

'It wouldn't have been anywhere near the coast or it would probably have come ashore sooner,' said Lowe after a short silence while the three considered the question. 'And if it was only a short distance down from Clevedon it would have been carried further upstream and come ashore nearer Portishead. My guess is that it was dropped from a boat out in the middle of the estuary, say somewhere between Sand Point and Cardiff – but that's only a guess, mind you.'

'I wonder if the rest of the body was dumped at the same time,' Mrs Lowe speculated.

'Good question,' said Rathbone approvingly. 'If so, then it will presumably appear within the next day or two.'

'I wonder if the murderer has cut it into any more bits?' From the grin on his flushed face it appeared that Giles Russell was taking a ghoulish pleasure at this turn in the discussion. It crossed Sukey's mind that the number of pints he had consumed in the Moon and Sixpence were having a delayed effect.

Before anyone could respond, Rathbone's mobile rang. With a murmured excuse he left the room, returning shortly with a more than usually serious expression.

'I'm afraid we'll have to curtail this discussion,' he said. 'Something has come up that means we have to go back to headquarters. Thank you all for your help – and especially for the coffee, Mrs Lowe.'

Once back in the car he said, 'You can probably guess what's happened?'

'More bits of body washed up?' said Sukey.
'Got it in one.'

Two days later all the missing parts of the murdered woman had been found at intervals along the eastern banks of the River Severn, the naked torso upstream of Portishead and the limbs washed up at various points beyond Avonmouth. On Thursday afternoon, DCI Leach summoned his team to his office and told them that the investigation now covered two separate areas – Avon and Somerset and South Gloucestershire – and that a major investigation team was being set up.

'There's no need for me to tell you we're dealing with a pretty nasty type of crime,' he began. 'Our first priority of course is to establish the identity of the victim – until we know who she is and who her associates are we have no idea where to start the hunt for her killer. The face is recognizable to anyone who knew her well, but it's suffered some damage so rather than publish a photograph the Super has ordered an artist's impression after she's been tidied up. He's holding a press conference this afternoon and he'll promise a further statement after the PM. We hope Doc Hanley will be able to give us some idea of how long the parts have been in the water. And of course we'll be checking in case there's a possible tie up with any recent reports of a woman going missing.'

'Do we know what caused the damage to the face, sir?' asked Sukey. 'Could it have been done when Mr Lowe's hook got caught?'

Leach shook his head. 'Hanley doesn't think so. He thinks it's more likely that it was caused by hungry fish nibbling at it.' He grimaced; it was rare for him to show signs of being affected by the most grisly details, but Sukey noticed that even he appeared to find this possibility hard to stomach. She felt a contraction in her own anatomy and was aware that Vicky, sitting at her side, was having a similar problem. 'Early reports suggest there was similar damage to the other bits,' Leach went on. 'When Hanley's completed his examination he'll be able to give us some idea of the woman's age, how long she's been in the water and so on, but he's warned us that there's bound to be a certain amount of guesswork.'

'I imagine our tidal experts will be asked to comment on Lowe's suggestion as to where the bits might have been dropped in the water, sir?' suggested Rathbone.

'Naturally. Of course, they can't begin to make a serious estimate until we have an idea how long ago it happened. Any more questions?'

'I take it the victim's clothes haven't been found?' said Vicky.

Leach glanced at Rathbone, who said, 'No reports of any findings so far. It's possible some garments may have been washed up but not so far discovered.'

Leach made a note. 'I'll mention it to the Super and no doubt he'll make sure the MIT will keep their eyes open. Anything else?'

'What should we do while we're waiting for Doc Hanley's report, sir?' asked Rathbone.

'What were you doing when this lot broke?'

'Trying to track down Toby Mayhew's next of kin – the man Sukey and Vicky observed acting suspiciously in the motorway services who was subsequently killed in an RTA.'

'Ah yes, I remember. There's some suggestion he may be involved in drugs, I believe. Well, you might as well go back to that for the time being.'

SEVEN

When they returned to the CID office there was a message in Rathbone's in-tray. He scanned it briefly and gave a grunt of satisfaction.

'It's a reply to our enquiry about Mayhew, giving us the address where he was living when he enlisted in the army, which was about seven years ago,' he said. 'Your Colonel Driver seemed to think he was living at home at the time, so you'd better start by checking whether anyone of that name is still there. If there is, it'll most likely be his parents; if not, then they've either moved or died, in which case the neighbours might be able to help.' He tossed the message on his desk. 'With luck, you'll be able to tick one box – informing the next of kin.'

Sukey picked up the note, read the contents, and handed it to Vicky. 'And then what, Sarge?' she asked.

'Don't expect me to do all your thinking for you,' he said curtly. 'Try giving me some ideas of your own.'

'We'd like to know what Mayhew's been living on since he moved to Tyndale Gardens,' said Vicky. 'From what Colonel Driver told us, he didn't appear to have a regular job but he could have been drawing some kind of benefit. Social Services might be able to help us there.'

'If he was a junkie he'd have needed money – quite a lot of it, and certainly more than the average job seeker's allowance,' Sukey pointed out. 'It would be interesting to find out what he was giving those kids. Mrs Scott suggested sweets or cigarettes, but it could have been drugs. We're pretty sure Warren Chesney called at his house more than once and we suspect that was where he was getting his own supply, but he might have been part of Chesney's distribution set-up. Maybe he was supplying the kids and other local crackheads as well. D'you think we should get a warrant to search his house, Sarge?'

Rathbone nodded. 'Good thinking, Sukey,' he said. His moment-ary irritation seemed to have passed. 'It might be an idea to have

another talk to the residents of Tyndale Gardens in case there
have been any other suspicious callers at the house since you made
your enquiries. If so we'll consider putting the place under
surveillance. As to the search warrant, let's put that on hold until
you've tracked down the next of kin. If it's the parents they may
be entitled to be present while any search is carried out. And be
tactful . . . make sure you've got the right people before you go
blundering in.' Rathbone stood up. 'Right, you two get on with
that and I'll see what's been going on in the rest of the depart-
ment.'

As they went down to collect a car, Vicky hissed in Sukey's
ear, 'He's a fine one to talk about tact – as if we were a pair of
rookies. He's not always the soul of diplomacy himself, anyway.'

Sukey grinned. 'I reckon it does his ego a bit of good to talk
down to us now and again,' she whispered back.

A check in the phone book showed that a Joseph W. Mayhew
was living at the address Toby Mayhew had given when he
enlisted in the army. 'Looks promising,' said Sukey. 'Let's get
over there right away.'

The house was on the northern side of Bristol, in a street of
semi-detached houses close to the parish church. They were all
built in a style suggesting they were originally part of a local
authority housing development, but from the various improvements
in the way of porches, replacement windows and individual front
doors, and a general air of modest pride in their appearance, it was
evident that many of them had passed into private ownership. The
Mayhews' house had a neat front garden, part of which had been
converted into hardstanding for a fairly new, dark-blue Toyota.

A slight, grey-haired woman opened the door in response to
their knock.

'Mrs Mayhew?' said Vicky.

The woman nodded. 'Yes, what do you want?'

'We're from Avon and Somerset CID,' said Vicky. The two
Detective Constables introduced themselves by name and held
up their ID cards.

Mrs Mayhew gave a welcoming smile and held the door wide
open. 'Please come in,' she said cordially. 'We've been hoping
to hear from you. Have you recovered our property?' Without

waiting for a reply she half turned and called, 'Joe! It's the police again. I think they've got some news for us.'

A man of about sixty, with a slightly florid, clean-shaven complexion and a square chin, appeared from a room at the back of the house. 'About time too. Let's hear it then,' he said.

'Mr Mayhew?' said Vicky.

'Who else?' His tone was far from affable as he added, a trifle suspiciously, 'You aren't the officers who came last time.'

'No,' said Sukey, aware that this was going to be even trickier than they had anticipated. 'We aren't here to talk about missing property, I'm afraid. We're here on a different matter.'

'Which is?'

'It concerns a man called Tobias Mayhew. We have reason to believe you have a son of that name.'

'Oh, that young wastrel!' said Mayhew shortly. 'I'm afraid he's been a great disappointment to us. Haven't seen hide nor hair of him lately. What mischief has he been up to now?'

Sukey cleared her throat. 'I'm afraid it's rather more serious than mischief,' she said. 'I wonder –' she glanced at his wife, who was beginning to show signs of agitation – 'could we possibly sit down?'

Mayhew shrugged and showed them into a cosy sitting room with French windows overlooking a small garden. Beyond the back fence, a green open space ran downhill to the little River Trym, shortly before it flowed into the Avon. A woman was throwing a ball for a dog, while a child ran excitedly up and down in pursuit of both. In response to a gesture from her husband, Mrs Mayhew sat on a settee facing the window, while he remained standing. The two detectives sat either side of her, knowing that the news they brought would be a parent's worst nightmare.

Mrs Mayhew turned from one to the other, her eyes full of fear. 'Please tell us what's happened to Toby,' she pleaded. 'Is he in trouble? Is he ill?'

Sukey took her hand and said gently, 'I'm very sorry to have to tell you –' she glanced from one parent to the other before continuing – 'that a man we believe to be your son was killed in a recent road accident.'

Mrs Mayhew gave a gasp of horror and put a hand to her

mouth, then said eagerly, 'You only believe it's him . . . you mean there may be some mistake—?'

'According to the items found on the body – a driving licence and a bank card – we are almost certain the dead man was your son, but we're afraid that in order to put the matter beyond all doubt we have to ask one of you to identify him.'

'Oh, no!' The mother burst into uncontrollable weeping. Sukey put an arm round her shoulders. Vicky spotted a box of tissues on a low table and hastily pulled out a handful to mop up the tears while both women did their best to comfort her. It was several minutes before she was able to speak; in the meantime, her husband strode up and down the small room, his head down and his hands clenched at his sides.

At last he said, 'A car accident, was it? Thought so. When did this happen?'

'Last Sunday,' said Vicky.

'Took your time letting us know,' he said gruffly.

'We're sorry about that, but it took us a while to trace you,' said Vicky.

Mayhew shrugged. 'He was full of bloody drugs I suppose. Knew he'd come to a bad end once he got hooked on that filthy stuff. I warned him . . . I did warn him, didn't I Millie . . . we both did, but he wouldn't listen.'

'It was that wicked woman who was his undoing!' Mrs Mayhew wailed.

'Now Millie, don't let's wash our dirty linen in front of these ladies,' said her husband. 'What's done is done . . . we did our best to help him after that bit of trouble but once he got in with that fellow Chesney—'

'Chesney, did you say?' said Vicky.

'Warren Chesney. I heard a rumour he'd been arrested recently – is that true? No, I can't expect you to answer that,' he added before either detective had time to comment. 'If I had my way he'd be shot, along with others like him. Parasites they are, ruining young lives.' For a moment his voice faltered; he turned to face the window and furtively brushed a hand over his eyes.

'Mr Mayhew . . . Mrs Mayhew,' Sukey began. She felt her excitement rising as a new idea came into her mind and it was with difficulty that she kept her voice even as she went on, 'We do have reason to believe that your son knew Warren Chesney and it's possible that you may be able to help us with our enquiries into another case. Perhaps, when you've had time to get over the initial shock –' she was about to say 'of your son's death' but changed it to 'of our visit' – 'we could arrange to come and see you again. In the meantime, would you like us to take you –' again she hesitated, reluctant to mention the morgue – 'to see him?'

'I suppose we have to,' said Mrs Mayhew sadly. Her eyes were red with weeping but she had managed to regain her composure.

'The answer to your other question, by the way, is yes,' said Mayhew. 'Anything we can do to smash any of that lot, we'll do.'

Standing beside the parents of Toby Mayhew while the sheet covering his body was gently drawn back to reveal his face, Sukey offered a prayer of thankfulness that apart from a bruise on the right temple, the damage to the features was minimal. It must be devastating, she thought, to have to look on the mutilated face of a loved one, or to have to identify a hideously injured body by operation scars or birthmarks. As it was, the father said huskily, 'Yes, that's our son,' while the mother, tears once more streaming unchecked from her eyes, laid a hand on the lifeless head for a moment before walking away clinging to her husband's arm.

'Thank you, that must have been an ordeal for you,' said Sukey.

'Had to be done,' said Joseph Mayhew. 'Never easy though. I once had to identify one of my comrades killed in action. He was just a lad – younger than ours.'

'The inquest is fixed for tomorrow,' said Sukey, 'and of course you are free to attend, but it will almost certainly be adjourned until after the post-mortem.'

'The post-mortem? You mean, he's going to be cut open?' Mrs Mayhew burst into a fresh bout of weeping and buried her face in her husband's shoulder.

'I'm afraid so,' said Vicky, who was visibly moved by the mother's distress.

'It's to check for drugs I suppose?' said Mayhew.

'It's principally to determine the cause of death,' Sukey explained. 'We're assuming for the moment that in your son's case it was a direct result of the accident, but it happens sometimes that a person has a stroke or a heart attack that causes them to lose control of the car. Naturally, we'll keep you informed.'

'Thank you. And in the meantime, please let us know what help we can give in tracking any members of Chesney's mob. Not that I hold out any great hopes – these bastards are pretty good at covering their tracks.'

'They are indeed,' said Sukey. 'We'll be in touch.'

'So,' said Vicky as, after driving the Mayhews home, they headed back to headquarters, 'it seems Toby's dad isn't quite the monster he led Colonel Driver to believe.'

'That's right,' Sukey agreed. 'I wonder what other porkies he told?'

'It'll be interesting to find out. No doubt Sergeant Rathbone will want us to follow it up, although I doubt if we'll uncover anything useful.'

'You're probably right,' Sukey sighed.

As it later turned out, their pessimism was not entirely justified.

EIGHT

By the time Sukey and Vicky had driven Toby Mayhew's parents back home it was after four o'clock. As Vicky turned the car round she said, 'D'you fancy a cup of tea? I spotted a café as we came through the village.'

'Good idea,' Sukey agreed.

'And while we're having our cuppa,' Vicky added, 'we can work out a plan of action.'

There were only a few customers in the café and they had no difficulty in finding a table tucked away in a corner where they were unlikely to be overheard. When they were served with tea and toasted teacakes – the latter at Vicky's insistence – Sukey said, 'My feeling is that it'd be better to leave Toby's parents alone until next week. The inquest will be adjourned straight away; they'll probably want to attend and they may find it a bit upsetting – particularly Mrs M.'

'I doubt if the SIO will wear that,' said Vicky. 'He'll want the house searched without delay for drugs and any clues to Toby's other associates.'

Sukey nodded. 'Yes, of course, and Toby's father did say he'd do anything he could to help. In any case he's probably entitled to be present when we enter the house. Do you think we should go back to Tyndale Gardens when we've had our tea?' she went on. 'We only spoke to three of the neighbours, but maybe some of the others noticed something.'

'Could be,' said Vicky in between bites from her teacake, 'but I wonder if it might be an idea to start with Mrs Scott. I'll bet she's been doing her neighbourhood watch thing ever since our visit. She or one of the others might have spotted some unusual activity at number fourteen.'

'She knows how to contact us,' Sukey pointed out. 'She'd have been on to us like a shot if she'd seen anything worth reporting. Or what she considers worth reporting,' she added with a hint of scepticism. 'Now she's got the bit between her teeth she'll probably mount a round the clock surveillance with the rest of her team and make a note to tell us every time a dog barks.'

'Don't knock the person who gave us the strongest lead we have so far,' said Vicky. At that moment her cell phone rang. She put down her half-eaten teacake and hurried outside. When she came back she said, 'Guess who?'

'Mrs Scott?'

Vicky nodded. 'She rang the office – very excited. She thinks there's been "something fishy" going on at Toby's and wants us to go and see her.'

'What sort of fishy?'

'She wouldn't go into details. I said we were thinking of going back to Tyndale Gardens anyway and they could tell her we're on our way.'

'So what are we waiting for?'

'For me to finish my tea.' Vicky hastily swallowed the last mouthful.

'After your first visit the other day,' said Mrs Scott as she ushered the two detectives into the sitting room at number twelve Tyndale Gardens, 'Monday afternoon wasn't it? Yes, that's right, Monday afternoon because Albert –' she indicated the dough-faced man who had momentarily lifted a plump posterior a few inches from his chair to greet them and immediately sat down again – 'Albert was at his Probus Club and when he came home I told him all about it and I said to him, I said, "I reckon they suspect young Toby of being mixed up in drugs". Didn't I say that, Albert?'

'Yes, dear, you did say that,' said Albert with a grave nod.

'And lo and behold, when you ladies came again on Tuesday morning and showed me that photograph you'll remember I said at once, "Yes, that's definitely the man who used to call on young Toby". You'd gone to the shops, hadn't you, Albert, and when you got home I said, "You'll never guess what, those two lady detectives I told you about came again and showed me a photograph and I recognized the man straight away as the man we'd seen calling on young Toby". You remember me saying that, don't you, Albert?'

'Yes, dear, I remember,' said Albert obediently.

'And it's my belief the man in the photograph is suspected of dealing in drugs,' his wife continued, 'so you see, don't you, Albert, I was right all the time wasn't I?'

In response to this final question, delivered with a smile of triumph, Albert cautiously responded, 'Yes, dear, you were probably right.'

'Mrs Scott,' said Sukey hastily before Mrs Scott had a chance to launch on a further review of past history, 'the fact that you were able to identify the man in that photograph as the man who regularly visited Tobias Mayhew was of considerable help to us. We understand that you may now have some further information.'

'That's right,' said Mrs Scott eagerly.

'How about a cup of tea, Carrie?' said Albert.

Mrs Scott tut-tutted. 'Of course, of course, how rude of me. I'm sure you ladies would like—'

'Not for us, thank you,' said Vicky firmly. 'If you could just tell us what you rang about . . . ?'

'Yes, of course. Your time is precious isn't it . . . well, after you came on Tuesday and we knew we were right about young Toby being mixed up with drugs I said to Albert, I said, "They've arrested one man but from what we read in the papers there'll be others and we ought to keep a lookout, didn't we?" I said that right away, didn't I, Albert? And then –' for once she hurried on without waiting for confirmation – 'I put a note through every door in Tyndale Gardens right away asking the residents to keep a lookout for any suspicious-looking callers at his house.'

'You were going to put, "any callers at all", Carrie,' said Albert, for the first time showing some initiative. 'I suggested you put "suspicious-looking" so as not to waste police time reporting people like the Jehovah's Witnesses who knock at everyone's door.'

'That's right, Albert, so you did.' She gave him the kind of smile a proud mother gives a child who has successfully answered a question.

'And you've had a result?' said Vicky.

'Young Mr Dobbie at number twenty-five opposite – he's a musician, if you can call what he plays music but that's how he describes himself – he plays at some nightclub in the city and never gets home until the small hours. Last night he happened to look out of his window just before getting into bed and he thought he saw something move in young Toby's front garden. He waited for a couple of minutes but nothing happened and he thought he must have been mistaken. When he got up this afternoon – he sleeps until very late, of course, being up half the night – he remembered my note and rang me to tell me about it. I said I'd report it right away. I rang him back to say you were coming and invited him to join us, but he said to tell you he'll be in until six o'clock if you'd like to speak to him yourself.' Her recital ended on a slightly petulant note; evidently she considered her status as Neighbourhood Watch co-ordinator entitled her to be present at the interview with Mr Dobbie and resented being excluded.

After a swift exchange of glances, Sukey and Vicky got to their feet. 'We'll go and see him straight away,' said Vicky, 'and thank you both very much, you've been very helpful.'

'And please keep up the good work,' said Sukey.

'By the way,' said Mrs Scott as she let them out, 'did you manage to find Toby's next of kin?'

'Oh yes, thank you very much,' they said in chorus, and made their escape before she had a chance to ask any more questions.

Jason Dobbie had a shaven head and a quantity of metalwork attached to various parts of his face. He wore ragged jeans and a sleeveless khaki top that revealed a dragon tattooed on his right shoulder. He greeted them in a surprisingly cultured voice and his friendly smile revealed perfect teeth. As he held the door open for them, Sukey noticed him giving a sharp glance over her shoulder in the direction of the Scotts' house.

'You managed to shed Scotty the Sleuth then?' he said with a mischievous wink. 'She's a good soul but she loves to know everything that's going on and there are times when you feel like throwing her off the scent just for the hell of it.'

'She did seem a bit miffed at being left out of this meeting,' said Vicky.

'I can imagine. She tried every trick in the book to persuade me to meet you at her house.' He led them along the hall and opened a door at the far end. 'This is my den.' He showed them into what in most similar houses would be a sitting room; this one contained little furniture other than a table, a computer station and some expensive-looking audio equipment. The floor was covered with a shabby carpet on which were scattered, apparently at random, a few cushions and a large number of discs.

Glancing down at the labels, Sukey recognized some recent best-selling albums by various British and American groups. 'Mrs Scott told us you were a musician,' she remarked, 'but I guess disc jockey would be nearer the mark?'

'Got it in one!' Jason grinned. 'She was on her rounds a few weeks ago with her newsletter as she calls it while I was playing some new numbers. She banged on my door – so's she could deliver the thing personally she said, but I reckoned it was just an excuse to get her nose inside the house. I took the newsletter, thanked her politely and shut the door.' He chuckled at the recollection. 'Poor old duck, foiled again! Now, you're here because I told her I might have seen a movement outside number fourteen, right?'

'That's right,' said Sukey. 'Can you tell us exactly what it was you saw?'

'To be honest, the more I think about it, the less certain I am that it wasn't my imagination. It was about four o'clock in the morning and I went into my bedroom to draw the curtains before getting undressed for bed. I work in a nightclub in the city centre – but no doubt Scotty told you that already.'

'She did,' said Vicky. 'So what did you see?'

'Like I said, there seemed to be a movement near the front door. I waited for several minutes keeping watch, but didn't see anything else. The front garden's pretty neglected with one or two shrubs that need cutting back, and there was a bit of a wind that night, so after a few minutes I decided I must have imagined it.'

'So why did you bother to tell Mrs Scott then?' asked Sukey.

'I wasn't going to until I remembered that just as I was dropping off to sleep I heard a car start up and I wondered if there was a connection.'

'She didn't say anything about the car,' said Vicky sharply.

Jason grinned again. 'That's because I didn't tell her,' he said.

'Did you happen to notice a car when you looked out?'

'No – at least there were one or two, but I recognized them as belonging to neighbours. Every house has a drive but some families have more than one car so they leave them in the road. In any case, what I heard didn't sound that close.'

'Well, thank you very much anyway,' said Sukey. 'Perhaps you'd continue to keep your eyes open and –' she gave him one of her cards – 'if you do see anything, please let us know right away.'

'It'll probably be in the middle of the night,' he said as he took the card.

'In that case, call 999.'

'What d'you reckon?' said Sukey as, having thanked Jason once again, they left the house and stood for a moment outside the gate. 'Did he see anything or anyone?'

Vicky shrugged. 'Hard to tell. It might be an idea to have a look at Toby's house to see if there are any signs of intruders.'

They crossed the road and pushed open the gate. 'Well, Jason was right about the state of the garden,' Sukey remarked, eyeing the unkempt shrubs and the profusion of weeds springing up through the gravelled drive. 'It would be easy enough to hide behind that,' she went on, indicating an overgrown clump of laurel that reached out towards the front downstairs window of the house.

'It looks like someone's been here,' said Vicky suddenly. She took a step forward and bent down to examine the ground beneath the window sill.

'What is it?' Sukey peered over her shoulder.

Vicky pointed. 'One dog-end, only half smoked. Perhaps someone dropped it while peering through the window.' She stepped back and examined the window sill. 'No sign of any attempt to break in.'

'Any disturbance on the ground?' asked Sukey.

'Can't see any, but the CSIs might spot something. Maybe the Sarge will think it's worth sending them to have a look.'

'Shall we look round the back while we're at it?' Sukey suggested.

Access to the rear of the property was via a path between Toby's house and that of Colonel Driver. It was divided down the middle by a privet hedge, neatly trimmed on the Colonel's side but hanging down over the path on the other. The rear garden was in an equally overgrown state, although a flagged path down one side, probably laid by a previous owner of the house, was reasonably clear of weeds. The garden was separated from the school playing field beyond by a stone wall.

'I suppose that's where he used to stand when Colonel Driver started chatting to him,' said Vicky.

'And where Mrs Scott saw him giving things to the kids,' Sukey reminded her. She craned over the wall and peered at the ground on the other side. 'There are a few dog-ends down there. Maybe Toby dropped them – in which case they'll have his DNA on them. And if there's a different DNA on the one under the laurel bush it'll prove someone has been lurking there.'

'Good thinking,' said Vicky. 'You're the athletic one. Why don't you climb over and pick them up?'

'It's a bit higher than other walls I've climbed, but I'll have a go.' Sukey groped with one foot in search of a toehold and after a few false starts managed to straddle the wall and jump down on the other side. She pulled a sterile envelope from her pocket and scooped up several of the dog-ends lying half hidden in the grass, carefully sealed the envelope and scrambled back over the wall.

'We'd better collect the one from the front as well,' said Vicky.

They checked the back of the house but saw no sign of any attempt at forced entry. 'If anyone was snooping around at the time Jason thought he saw a movement, presumably it was with the intention of breaking in,' said Vicky. 'So why didn't they? It isn't as if he challenged them or did anything else to suggest they'd been spotted.'

'That's true,' Sukey agreed. 'Unless,' she added, 'they don't know Toby's dead, were expecting him home last night and were lying in wait for him.'

'In which case,' said Vicky, 'what made them decide to give up?'

Sukey shook her head. 'You tell me.'

NINE

Returning to the front of the house they retrieved the cigarette end from under the laurel bush and were just about to leave when the door of number thirteen opened and Colonel Driver called out to them.

'Back again, ladies? Found a clue, have you?'

'Possibly,' said Sukey cautiously.

'Any luck with finding young Toby's parents?'

'Yes, we found them, and thank you very much for your help.' said Vicky.

'Anything else I can do?'

'Well, as a matter of fact . . .' Sukey began and he immediately beckoned. 'Come in.' His glance flicked briefly towards the Scotts' house, as if hinting that he would prefer to keep their conversation private. They accepted his invitation to enter but this time politely but firmly declined his offer of tea. 'We have to get back to the station and report to our DS,' Vicky explained. 'I expect you've heard from Mrs Scott . . .'

'. . . asking us to keep a lookout for suspicious characters lurking in the neighbourhood,' the Colonel interposed with a wink. 'Oh yes. I said I'd keep a lookout.' His tone suggested that he had not taken Mrs Scott's injunction very seriously.

'So you haven't seen or heard anything unusual?' said Sukey.

The Colonel shook his head. 'Not really. Now and again someone goes round stuffing leaflets through doors, that sort of thing, but I don't recall seeing anyone lately. As to the night, that's another matter. I sleep like a log – most people of my age can't say that but I'm one of the lucky ones, slept through a thunderstorm a couple of weeks ago. So you managed to track down the Mayhews? Glad I was able to help.' He paused for a moment before saying, 'I suppose there's no point in asking why you were so anxious to find them?'

'Not at the moment, sir,' said Sukey. 'Our search was part of an ongoing police enquiry, and that's why we're here this afternoon.

We have reason to believe that someone has been coming here looking for Toby, possibly during the hours of darkness.'

'Good Lord!' the colonel exclaimed. 'I suppose that's what prompted Mrs Scott's note?'

'Not exactly – rather the other way around.' Sukey told him about the call from Jason Dobbie to Mrs Scott that had brought them back to Tyndale Gardens. He rubbed his hands together in glee on hearing how Jason had insisted on speaking to the detectives alone, but grew more serious as the possible implication dawned on him.

'D'you really think he saw something?'

'We think he may have done.'

The colonel frowned. 'I don't like the sound of this,' he muttered.

'You told us Toby used to lean on the wall at the bottom of his garden,' said Vicky. 'We've noticed some cigarette ends in the grass on the other side; do you think he might have dropped them?'

'So that's what you were after when you climbed over the wall,' Driver chuckled. 'I stood there admiring your athleticism,' he added with an approving nod in Sukey's direction. 'Toby certainly enjoyed a cigarette,' he went on. 'I wouldn't say he was a heavy smoker, mind you, but yes, he might well have dropped his fag-ends into the field.'

'I suppose you don't happen to know what brand he smoked?' said Vicky.

'I do, as it happens. I don't smoke myself but the first time he came here he asked if I minded if he did and I noticed he smoked Chesterfields.'

'Thank you, that might be very useful,' said Vicky.

'Mrs Scott mentioned that she saw Toby talking to the children in the playing field,' said Sukey. 'She seemed to think he gave them something from time to time – possibly sweets or cigarettes, she said. Have you ever noticed anything like that?'

Driver shook his head. 'Can't say I have. She mentioned it to me of course – and to everyone else in the Gardens. Made a great to-do about it – reported it to the Council I believe but we never heard any more. It was a few weeks ago – can't recall exactly when. Do you think there might be something in it? Toby never struck me as being that sort of chap.'

'We have to keep an open mind,' said Sukey.

'Yes, of course,' said Driver. 'Well, I'll certainly keep my eyes open although I can't promise to hear any night-time prowlers.'

Declining his renewed offer of tea – 'or maybe something a little stronger as the time's getting on' – they said goodbye and returned to the station to report to DS Rathbone. He immediately called DCI Leach and within a few minutes the three were summoned to his office.

'There's no doubt we have to take this seriously,' he began when he had listened to Sukey and Vicky giving their account of the visit to Tyndale Gardens. 'If someone has been snooping round Mayhew's house we have to know why, so get a surveillance team set up, Greg.'

'Will do, sir,' said Rathbone.

'And do your best to get the DNA test on the dog-ends fast-tracked,' he went on. He referred to the file on his desk. 'Now, the inquest on the dismembered lady is scheduled for tomorrow morning. It'll be adjourned as a matter of course until after the PM. The inquest on Mayhew will be held a couple of hours later and the same thing will happen; I'll have a word with the coroner and suggest he ask the press not to release his name for the time being. They're usually pretty good in cases where there's an ongoing enquiry but in any case they'll be too exercised over the gruesome details of the morning's proceedings to spare many column inches over a mere RTA. One thing you should know,' he went on, 'a check of Mayhew's mobile revealed that no calls were made or received between the time of the incident in the car park and the time of the accident so we can rule that out as a contributory factor. In fact, the only numbers he ever called were a Chinese takeaway and a dial-a-pizza. A real loner by the sound of it.'

'There's the question of Mayhew's house, sir,' Rathbone pointed out. 'We believe there may be drugs there and possibly information about his contacts other than Warren Chesney. His father is more than willing to help us in any way he can so there shouldn't be a problem about needing a warrant to enter it.'

'Arrange that with him as soon as possible,' said Leach.

He closed the file and slipped it into a drawer. 'That'll be all for now.'

'Excuse me, sir,' said Sukey as they got up to leave, 'do you think there might be a connection between what we've learned today and the incident Vicky and I witnessed in the service area car park last Sunday?'

Leach pursed his lips and frowned as he considered the question. Eventually he shook his head. 'I think it's highly unlikely,' he said. 'It's already been established that the envelope Mayhew handed over contained nothing suspicious and we suspect he was a drug addict in need of a fix, which would account for his erratic behaviour. I've already spoken to Doc Hanley and he's going to take samples for testing at the PM. No doubt there'll be a long wait before the results come back, but you've got plenty of other stuff to go on with.'

'Like the dismembered corpse,' Rathbone remarked as they went back to the CID office. 'We're still waiting for the artist's impression. So far, none of the reports of missing persons has yielded anything promising and there's still no sign of the clothing.'

'Do we know the cause of death yet, Sarge?' asked Sukey.

'No, and Doc Hanley isn't hopeful of establishing it.' He heaved a sigh of resignation. 'Blind alleys all round,' he said despondently.

As expected, Tobias Mayhew's father and mother attended the inquest on their son. Sukey and Vicky met them at the appointed time the following day and had a quiet word with them before the proceedings opened.

'We have reason to believe that certain people who don't know Toby is dead are trying to contact him,' said Sukey. 'The press will be asked not to publish his name for the time being, but we realize you may have already told your friends or other members of your family about his death.'

'We haven't said a word to anyone,' said Joe Mayhew.

'That's good. We'll talk again later.'

As predicted, the inquest was opened, identification was confirmed and the hearing adjourned until a date to be announced. Only a handful of people attended; glancing round the hall Sukey noticed one man, whom she recognized as a reporter from the local paper, taking notes. She hoped the request to withhold Toby's name had reached him.

When the proceedings were over Joe Mayhew said, 'Is there somewhere we can talk?'

'I'll have a word with the caretaker,' said Vicky. She went and spoke to a man who was standing at the door with a bunch of keys in his hand, evidently waiting to lock up when everyone had left. She showed her ID and he invited them to use his office for a few minutes while he attended to some other tasks.

'These people you say are trying to contact Toby,' said Mrs Mayhew uneasily. 'Who do you suppose they are?'

'That's what we're trying to find out,' said Sukey. 'There's a suggestion that someone was prowling around outside his house last night and . . .'

'Just a minute,' said Mayhew. 'Where is this house? We're his next of kin – surely we're entitled to . . .' He broke off and appeared embarrassed, possibly, Sukey suspected, because it had occurred to him that, as Toby's next of kin, the house might well now be his under the laws of inheritance.

'We were coming to that,' said Vicky. 'I'm afraid we have to consider the possibility that Toby made a will leaving his property to someone other than yourselves. We shall be applying for a warrant to search the house and as his next of kin you're entitled to be present if you wish.'

'What do you expect to find?' said Mrs Mayhew.

'Anything that might lead us to the people he was associating with up to the time of his death. Unfortunately his mobile phone hasn't been of much help; is there anything you can think of that might give us a lead?'

The Mayhews looked at each other and then at Sukey. 'We haven't seen or heard from Toby for over two years,' said the mother sadly.

'But you told us you already knew he was on drugs,' said Sukey. 'Can you remember when you first found out?'

'He had some personal troubles,' Joe Mayhew began. 'He split up from his wife and . . .'

'Mr Mayhew,' said Sukey gently, 'We already know the background to his problems because he confided in one of his neighbours.' Mayhew bit his lip and his wife gave a little sob and put a handkerchief to her eyes. 'We don't want to cause you further pain,' Sukey went on, 'but it's possible that the accident in which your son died was partly due to his drug dependency. We know he was acquainted with Warren Chesney, but there are others – part of a ring – who are still out there, supplying drugs and even using children as runners. We need all the help we can get to bring them to justice.'

There was a long pause before Mayhew muttered, 'We need time to think. Give us until after the weekend.'

Sukey and Vicky exchanged glances and nodded. 'All right,' said Vicky, 'we'll call on you first thing on Monday morning. Unless,' she added to Sukey as, having seen the Mayhews to their car, they returned to their own, 'our sergeant decrees otherwise.'

'It strikes me,' said Rathbone when they were back at headquarters, 'that young Toby was a bit of a no-hoper. He led Colonel Driver to believe that his father was a bully and kicked him out when he was dishonourably discharged from the army, yet from what you say both his parents gave him every support they could.'

'So he got mixed up with Chesney's mob and started taking drugs, which were probably the cause of his fatal accident,' said Vicky.

Rathbone frowned. 'Probably,' he agreed, 'and this phantom prowler that Dobbie may or may not have seen is our only link with Warren Chesney's mob. And a pretty tenuous one at that,' he added morosely.

'So once Chesney was put away his supply would have been cut off,' said Sukey. 'Unless, of course, one of the takeaway numbers was a cover-up.'

'They're both genuine fast food outlets and the drugs squad know nothing against them,' said Rathbone. 'I've had a word about a surveillance team,' he went on. 'They're a bit pushed at the moment because of sickness but it should be in place within a day or two. In the meantime . . . well, let's hope if young Jason does spot anyone lurking in the bushes we can get there in time to nick them. Meanwhile,' he referred to a note on his desk pad, 'Doc Hanley phoned to say he's starting the PM on Mayhew this afternoon. One of you will be coming with me and—' He broke off to answer his phone and they saw his expression change. 'Good Lord!' he exclaimed. 'Where did they take him? Right, tell them to keep him alive until we get there.'

'What's up, Sarge?' asked Vicky.

'The postman found a man lying semi-conscious behind the bushes outside Mayhew's house. He's been taken to A and E. Sukey, get a car and wait for me downstairs.' He picked up the phone again.

'What about me, Sarge?' said Vicky.

Rathbone grinned. 'You've drawn the short straw. I'm about to arrange for DS Douglas to attend the PM in my place and you can go along and hold his hand.'

TEN

'Do we know who the casualty is, Sarge?' said Sukey as she settled into the driver's seat and clipped on her safety belt.

'We'll find out when we get there,' Rathbone replied tersely. 'The person who called the emergency services heard a faint moan and found this chap semi-conscious and bleeding from a head wound. He stayed until the ambulance arrived and then left. The sound of the siren alerted a neighbour who got in touch with us straight away.'

'So where do we go first – the hospital or Tyndale Gardens?'

'Hospital,' said Rathbone without hesitation. 'We don't know how badly the victim is hurt or how long he'll survive. If he's even partly conscious he may be able to give us valuable information – provided the medics let us get near him, of course. Uniformed will be on the spot to secure the scene and they'll no doubt be taking statements from the neighbours while the CSIs do their stuff, so we can deal with them later.'

'All I hope is it isn't Jason Dobbie,' said Sukey. 'I told him to dial 999 if he saw anything. It didn't occur to me that he might have a go himself.'

'I hope you and Vicky made it clear that he shouldn't do anything of the kind,' said Rathbone sharply.

'Not in so many words, I'm afraid,' she said lamely. She had already noticed that he was not in the best of moods and he seemed to seize on the omission as an excuse to vent his irritation on her.

Nothing more was said for the rest of the journey, but she was conscious of his silent disapproval. When they reached the hospital an unsmiling receptionist, after making a phone call to announce their arrival, informed them that the man's injuries were still being assessed and that a doctor would see them as soon as possible. She directed them to a room on the second floor, asked them to wait and returned to the magazine she was reading.

'Any chance of a coffee?' asked Rathbone.

'There's a machine on each floor,' she said without looking up.

'Thank you so much.' His pointedly over-polite tone earned him a frosty glare. They found the room and Rathbone pulled out a handful of change, which he held out to Sukey. 'No idea how much they charge for coffee here but it's sure to be a rip-off,' he grumbled. She took the money and went in search of the machine, returning a few minutes later with one mug of coffee and a plastic cup of water. She gave him his change and sat down; he raised an eyebrow on seeing the water, but made no comment.

They waited for what seemed an interminable time, aimlessly turning the pages of out-of-date magazines and frequently glancing at their watches. Every time they heard footsteps in the corridor they sat up and looked expectantly towards the door, but sank back in their chairs as the footsteps died away. It was over an hour before the door finally opened and a man in a white jacket entered.

'Detective Sergeant Rathbone?' he said. Rathbone nodded. 'I'm Francis Lovell, neurological surgeon. You're interested in the condition of Jason Dobbie, I understand? Well, I'm pleased to be able to tell you that, due to an exceptional feature of his cranium, his injury is not life threatening. He has an unusually thick skull,' Lovell explained in response to Rathbone's questioning eyebrows. 'In my opinion, the blow he sustained might well have caused severe brain damage in a person with a skull of average thickness. He's a very fortunate young man.'

Sukey felt a tide of relief wash over her. 'That's excellent news,' she said fervently.

Lovell glanced at her as if he had only just noticed her presence. 'Yes, indeed.' He turned back to Rathbone. 'I take it you'd like to know when it will be possible for you to interview him, Sergeant?'

'It would be helpful, sir.' Rathbone used the same tone in which he had thanked the receptionist, but the innuendo appeared to be lost on Lovell.

'I'm afraid you can't see him today,' he said. 'He's suffering from severe concussion and we've put him under sedation as he was in considerable pain. Give me a number to call and someone will let you know when it's convenient.'

'Thank you, sir.' Rathbone handed over his card. 'It's possible that Dobbie disturbed a dangerous criminal who may, if he finds out that he survived the attack, make a further attempt on his life. We shall therefore need to put him under armed guard for the time being. If it's convenient,' he added.

Lovell's sharp look made it clear that this time the dart had gone home. 'Are you sure you consider that necessary?' he said stiffly.

'We do, sir.'

'Oh, very well.' Without another word, the consultant left the room.

'What a toffee-nosed git!' Rathbone fumed as he and Sukey returned to the car. 'Who the hell does he think he is? Talking down to us as if we were a pair of student nurses . . .' In his indignation he seemed to have forgotten his irritation with Sukey. 'Right, I'll organize an armed round-the-clock guard for Dobbie and then we'll head for Mayhew's house.' He punched a number into his cell phone and gave the necessary instruction before making a second call, this time to DCI Leach's secretary to give a brief report on the visit to the hospital. 'When he comes back, please tell him DC Reynolds and I are on our way to the crime scene in Tyndale Gardens. Thanks, Judy.' He snapped off the phone, settled into his seat and closed his eyes, then opened them for a moment. 'What's the betting Mrs Scott will be the first to pounce on us when we arrive?'

The entire population of Tyndale Gardens appeared to have gathered as close to number fourteen as the police would allow. They stood around in groups, nudging one another, pointing and exchanging whispered comments. Several uniformed officers moved amongst them, asking questions, making notes. An interviewer from a TV station was attracting a considerable amount of interest as he went round with a camera mounted on his shoulder and a microphone in his hand asking a few of the onlookers, apparently at random, for their comments and reactions.

All the familiar trappings of an incident were evident: the blue and white tape, the protective tent over the front garden, the crime scene investigators in their protective overalls bustling to and fro with items of equipment. Sukey pulled up to allow

Rathbone to get out before driving to the place where she and Vicky had parked on their first visit. When she returned she found him talking to the sergeant in charge of the operation; as he had predicted, Mrs Scott was standing a few feet away, impatiently brushing aside a young constable who had approached her, notebook in hand, indicating with words and gestures that she would give her statement to no one but Sergeant Rathbone.

The moment he was free she rushed over and grabbed his arm. 'Is he badly hurt?' she said breathlessly, excitement driving her normally high-pitched voice up a few tones. 'I heard the ambulance . . . I looked out and there was Dick the postman crouching down . . . and then the paramedics came and put him on a stretcher . . . Jason, of course, not the postman . . . and there was a lot of blood . . . he . . . Jason . . . he looked so white and . . . is he going to be all right? What was he doing over here anyway? He must have seen someone . . . why didn't he call 999 like you told us to do if we saw anything?' She broke off – chiefly, Sukey suspected, from shortage of breath rather than for want of anything else to say.

Rathbone took advantage of the break in the torrent of words and said, 'So you heard nothing untoward before the sound of the ambulance siren?'

'Well, no,' she admitted. 'I mean, whoever attacked him must have been very quiet . . . I mean, we sleep in the front bedroom and . . .'

Sukey glanced at her husband, who was standing silently at his wife's side. 'Are we to take it you didn't hear anything either, Mr Scott?'

'Oh . . . Albert!' Mrs Scott jerked her head and gave a slightly disdainful sniff. 'He'd sleep through an earthquake.'

'And how soundly do you sleep, Mrs Scott?'

'I generally sleep very well . . . although if there's anything unusual like a car door slamming or a dog barking, I'm awake immediately,' she added hastily.

Something about her manner suggested to Sukey that she was not entirely comfortable with this line of questioning. 'You said "generally". Was there anything different about last night?'

'Not that I remember.'

There was a hoarse chuckle from her husband. 'I'm not

surprised you don't remember,' he said. 'I warned you about that second glass . . . you never could hold your drink. Not that she was ill . . . nothing like that,' he hastened to add in response to his wife's furious glance. 'The fact is, last night we had a few friends in for a meal and of course we had a few drinks and . . . you might as well admit it, Carrie, you passed out the minute you hit the hay and slept like a log all night.'

'So would it be right to say that you didn't actually hear anything until you were awakened by the sound of the ambulance?' said Sukey.

'I suppose so,' Mrs Scott said sulkily. 'But I was awake and out of bed the minute the ambulance arrived,' she rushed on eagerly. 'I've already told you, I saw them put Jason . . .'

'Yes, and we understand it was you who alerted us,' Rathbone interposed. Sukey sensed his impatience as he said, 'Thank you very much, Mr and Mrs Scott, you've been very helpful. I suggest you go home now and I'll send an officer round to take your formal statement.' It could have been Sukey's imagination, but she was almost sure she caught a surreptitious wink from Mr Scott before he obediently turned to go indoors.

By the time they got back to the station it was almost two o'clock. Rathbone said, 'My stomach thinks my throat's been cut,' got out of the car, slammed the passenger door and strode into the building.

'You think you're the only one?' Sukey muttered at his retreating back. She parked the car and handed in the keys before following him at a slower pace. She went to the cloakroom to freshen up before making her way to the canteen; by the time she got there Rathbone was already sitting in a corner with his back to the door, hunched over a plate of sandwiches. Several tables away she spotted Vicky and DS Douglas. She bought a filled roll and a mug of coffee, put them on a tray and wandered over. 'OK if I join you?'

'Sure,' said Vicky. She was noticeably paler than usual and the sandwich on her plate was only half eaten.

'So how was it – the PM I mean?'

Vicky pulled a face and clasped her stomach. 'Gruesome,' she admitted. 'I didn't disgrace myself though, did I, Sarge?'

'You were a trouper,' Douglas assured her.

'Just the same, I hope the Sarge won't send me to the next one.'

'Which one's that?'

'The dismembered corpse. Now they've found all the bits, Doc Hanley's planning to start later on today. What news of Jason, by the way?'

'He'll be fine by the sound of things,' said Sukey. She described the interview with the consultant and then went on to give a lively account of the conversation with the Scotts.

By the time Vicky had finished laughing colour had begun to return to her cheeks. 'So now we have to wait till Mister High and Mighty Lovell allows us to approach Jason's bedside, I suppose?' she said, dabbing away the tears.

'I've a feeling DCI Leach will want us to be a bit more pro-active than that,' said Sukey. She finished her roll and wiped her fingers. 'It's obvious Jason's injury isn't life threatening and the sooner we can interview him the better. By the way,' she went on, reaching for her mug of coffee, 'any idea what's bitten our sergeant? He's been like a bear with a sore head this morning.'

Vicky shook her head. 'Don't know, unless it's something to do with contact with his kid. I overheard him say something on the phone earlier in the week about a shopping trip at the weekend to buy new sports gear. I think it was the kid he was talking to. Maybe the mother has other ideas. I've heard she can be difficult.'

At that moment Rathbone bore down on them and said, 'The SIO's office in ten minutes,' before making for the door.

'So the one person we might have relied on to give us something useful was in a drunken stupor,' DCI Leach commented. 'Just our luck. Did anyone else hear anything?'

'One or two people reported hearing a car start up,' said Rathbone, 'but nobody could say with any certainty what time it was.'

'That's a fat lot of use.'

'It could be a lot worse, sir,' Rathbone pointed out. 'At least the victim survived and present indications are that we should be able to talk to him soon. Apparently he was trying to say something, but no one could make out what. Maybe when he comes round he'll have more to tell us.'

'So you've no idea what he was trying to say?'

Rathbone shook his head. 'According to the chap who found him it was a series of "Ch . . . ch . . . ch . . ." sounds. Whatever it was, he couldn't make any sense out of it.'

'Let's hope you learn a bit more when you talk to him.'

Back in the CID office, Sukey said, 'Sarge, didn't DCI Leach say one of the numbers on Toby's mobile was a Chinese take-away?'

'Yes. What of it?'

'Maybe Jason was trying to say "Chinese"?'

Rathbone gave her a withering look. 'Or chop suey? Chicken chow mein?' he mocked. 'I doubt if he was thinking about food.' He pulled a message from his in tray, scanned it and gave a low whistle. 'At least there's been possible progress on another front. Some clothing from a recycling centre went with a lot of other stuff to a charity. The woman sorting it noticed bloodstains on some women's underwear and rang her local nick.'

ELEVEN

'A lot of the stuff people put in the clothing banks aren't fit to sell in our shops,' said Mrs Grove, the woman at the sorting centre for 'Help for the Homeless'. It was a cramped room behind a drop-in centre in a slightly run-down part of the city where down-and-outs were offered soup, bread and cheese between ten and four every weekday. 'I'd say that applies to these things. They're pretty fancy, I must say – in more ways than one. Quite disgusting, in fact,' she added. 'I'm sure I wouldn't like to think any daughter of mine would wear anything like *this*.' Wearing an expression of exaggerated disgust, she picked up a plastic bag bearing the logo of a local supermarket, cleared a space on the table and tipped out the contents, which consisted of a bra and a pair of knickers, both made of pink satin, lavishly trimmed with lace and heavily bloodstained.

'Yes, I see what you mean,' Sukey agreed. She put on a pair of plastic gloves before picking up the garments and turning them over, taking care to hide her amusement at the sight of Mrs Grove pointedly averting her gaze. 'They are rather gorgeous though, apart from the blood – and the unusual design features of course,' she added hastily in response to a sniff of disapproval. 'Expensive too, I'll bet. I wonder where they came from? Ah, here's a label. "Naughty Ladies" – well, that figures, doesn't it?'

It was evident that Mrs Grove did not appreciate the humour of the implication. 'I take it you'll want to keep them as evidence of some kind?' she said stiffly.

'Yes, indeed, they may give us an important lead in a murder enquiry,' Sukey assured her. 'We really appreciate your help. By the way, you said they came from a recycling centre – do you happen to know which one?'

Mrs Grove shook her head. 'I've no idea, I'm afraid.'

'And did you find them in this?' Sukey held up the plastic bag.

'Yes, that's right. It gave me quite a shock when I took them out, in fact I felt quite ill for a moment.' Mrs Grove made vague gestures indicative of nausea. 'It wasn't just the blood, it was . . . anyway I pushed them back in the bag and went to wash my hands right away. I felt quite unclean after touching the horrid things,' she added with feeling.

'Yes, I quite understand.' Sukey thanked her, returned to her car and carefully slid the underwear into a sterile bag and the supermarket carrier into another. Back in the CID office she sought out DS Rathbone, who was hunched over his desk with his head in his hands, studying – or pretending to study – an open file.

He looked up as she approached, closed the file and passed a hand over his eyes. 'What've you got there?' he asked. His tone displayed no particular interest.

'A possible lead in the dismembered corpse case,' she said. 'Unless, of course, a complete body with chest wounds turns up in the meantime.' She gave him a brief account of her visit to 'Help for the Homeless' and his expression lightened a little when she mimicked Mrs Grove's facial contortions as she described her feelings on finding the underwear. He even gave a world-weary smile when, by manipulating the items in the first bag, he inspected their unusual features.

The smile faded as he said slowly, 'Whoever wore these almost certainly sustained at least one serious wound in the chest or stomach, and since someone took the trouble to dispose of them I'd say it's safe to assume that the victim died. So we're looking for a body – presumably a woman's but we can't rule out the possibility of a cross-dresser – with either knife or gunshot wounds. When did Doc Hanley say he'd be doing the PM on the dismembered corpse?'

'Vicky said something about later on this afternoon, I think,' said Sukey. 'I think she's hoping you won't ask her to attend that one as well.'

Rathbone grunted. 'Shaken up, was she?'

'A bit, but she's OK.'

'Well, she needn't worry,' he said. 'You and I will do this one. If there's a wound in the torso, and if the DNA in the blood on the undies matches the DNA Doc Hanley extracts from the corpse, we could be a step towards identifying the victim.'

'And if we can track down "Naughty Ladies" they may be able to give us a lead on who they sold those items to,' Sukey said eagerly.

'That might be another step in the right direction,' he agreed.

'And,' she went on, 'if forensics get a different DNA from the bag the things were wrapped in, it might lead us to the murderer.'

'Let's not get too carried away,' he admonished her. 'I'll call the morgue and check what's on the programme for this afternoon.' His mood of lethargy had lifted; he picked up his phone and punched out a number. After exchanging a few words with the person who answered he put down the phone and shook his head. 'Hanley's assistant says he won't be starting on the dismembered lady until Monday. Meanwhile, you'd better get busy tracking down the "Naughty Ladies".'

Sukey's task was surprisingly easy. 'Naughty Ladies' had a remarkably informative website and it was not long, after a brief exchange of emails in which she expressed an interest in their products without revealing her motive in making the enquiry, before she found herself speaking to a lady with a North Country accent who introduced herself as Kay.

'When are you thinking of having your party, luv?' she asked. 'We're fully booked next week, but I could fit you in on Friday the following week if that's any good.' she rattled on, evidently anxious not to lose a potential customer. 'Any idea how many you're planning to invite, luv?'

'Party?' Sukey was momentarily nonplussed. 'Is that how you sell your, er, products?'

'Of course, luv, what did you think? You invite your friends round and our rep brings a range of things for you to try on and maybe play with a little.' Kay gave an arch giggle. 'I'm assuming that's what you had in mind?'

'Not exactly,' said Sukey cautiously. She had a feeling Kay might be frightened off if she had the idea she was being investigated by the police and decided to try diplomacy. 'The fact is,' she said, 'I'd really prefer to come and see you.'

'You're thinking of some special arrangement?' A note of suspicion crept into Kay's voice. 'Look here, luv, this is a legit business and everything we do for our clients is just a bit of harmless fun. If you're looking for some serious hanky-panky you'd better look elsewhere.' Without giving Sukey a chance to protest, Kay slammed down the phone.

Conscious that she had badly mishandled the enquiry and anxious to repair the damage before Rathbone came to check on her progress, Sukey hastily sent another email explaining the situation without going into details and a few minutes later Kay called again. It was evident that she found the misunderstanding not only natural but also highly amusing.

'Why didn't you say you were a copper, luv?' she chuckled. 'We did a party only the other week for a group of coppers' wives. It was a really fun afternoon,' she went on. 'Now, you want me to see if I can identify where one of our products went? Right luv, I'll call round on my way home and have a look at it. In about an hour, say?'

'Our luck's in,' Sukey informed Rathbone after Kay's visit.

'That's good to hear. Luck is something we've been short of lately.'

'Too right,' she agreed. 'It so happens these things are a new line and a bit pricey so Kay placed a trial order to start with. They were offered for the first time at a party in Bradley Stoke about a month ago. Only one person bought them. Kay's given me the hostess's name and phone number so that I can ask permission to check her guest list.'

'So what are you waiting for?'

Sukey glanced pointedly at her watch. 'It's gone six o'clock, it's Friday evening and I haven't had much in the way of food all day,' she said, 'and before you say anything about clock-watching, do you really think it's a good idea to interview ladies about naughty parties at the weekend when their husbands are likely to be around?'

He gave a resigned shrug. 'I suppose you've got a point,' he admitted. 'OK, see you on Monday. Have a good weekend.'

'Thanks.' She put on her jacket and slung her bag over her shoulder. 'You too,' she said over her shoulder.

'Some hopes.'

He sounded so dejected that she turned back. 'Something wrong, Sarge?'

He stood up. 'Have you got time for a quick drink?' He spoke in a low tone, reaching for his jacket in what looked like a deliberate attempt to avoid eye contact. It was the first time he had issued anything remotely like a social invitation. She recalled Vicky's speculation that his uncertain temper might have something to do with marital problems, and recognized that he badly needed company.

'Why not?' she said.

'Where would you like to go?' he asked her on the way to the car park.

'How about one of the pubs down by the marina?'

'Fine by me. You lead the way.'

They found seats in the corner of a recently opened bar whose owner appeared to have expressed a wish for some local colour in the decor. This the interior designer had attempted to achieve by hanging on the walls a series of old sepia photographs of elver and salmon fishermen on the River Severn, interspersed with some of the curiously shaped nets and other traditional implements used in the practice of their trade.

Rathbone brought a pint of beer for himself, a spritzer for Sukey and two bags of crisps to the table, sat down and raised his glass. 'Cheers!' he said.

'You don't look very cheerful,' said Sukey. 'Has the SIO been giving you a hard time?'

He shook his head. 'No more than usual. He's as frustrated as we all are about the lack of progress in both the Mayhew and the dismembered lady cases. Let's hope one of your naughty ladies will give us a lead in that one.' He took another draught of beer and began fumbling with one of the bags of crisps.

'Let's hope so,' she agreed. 'And don't forget Jason Dobbie. Unless there have been complications, he should be fit for interview by Monday. Look, I'm not trying to pry,' she added hesitantly, 'but you've got something else on your mind, haven't you?'

'You could say that.' He gave a heavy sigh and continued to toy with his bag of crisps but without eating any. Sukey, who was feeling hungry, began devouring hers and waited. 'The fact is,' he began at last, 'I was supposed to have Tommy for the weekend, but his mother's taking him to visit her father in Newcastle instead. He's a widower . . . he's got Alzheimer's and she's talking of going to live with him so that she can take care of him.'

'Taking Tommy with her?'

'She'd have to, wouldn't she? I can't look after him . . . not while I'm doing this job and it's the only one I know. It's tricky enough as it is to keep regular contact with him . . . if he's living in Newcastle it'd be impossible.'

'You could always get a transfer.'

He managed a wry grin. 'You trying to get rid of me?'

'No, of course not.' She was on the point of putting a re-assuring hand on his arm, but thought better of it. 'Come to think of it,' she went on, 'leaving his friends, moving to a new environment and settling into a new school while living in a house with a grandfather with dementia . . . it isn't an ideal prospect for a twelve-year-old, is it? To say nothing of seeing less of his dad,' she added hastily.

'That's what's worrying me.'

'Have you talked to her about it?'

'Not really. This was sprung on me last night. There's been a sudden deterioration in her father's condition and his social worker says he's not safe on his own. She was too upset and I was too tired to argue.'

'When does she plan to leave?'

'First thing tomorrow. She couldn't get off work today because so many of the staff are sick.'

Sukey thought for a moment and then, somewhat hesitantly, said, 'She's had this dumped on her at short notice. You said she was upset last night but she's had today to calm down and think more rationally. Why don't you have a word with her when you get home? It doesn't sound very sensible to have Tommy with her when she's got to have discussions with social workers and so on. And if the old chap is behaving oddly it might be distressing for him.'

He finished his beer and put the untouched bag of crisps in his pocket. 'You're right,' he said. 'I'll go home and call her right away. Thanks for that, Sukey, you're a mate.'

'Think nothing of it.' She screwed up her own empty crisp bag and stood up. 'Thanks for the drink. See you Monday.'

TWELVE

On Monday DS Rathbone summoned Sukey and Vicky, together with DC Penny Osborne, another member of DCI Leach's team, and told them that Francis Lovell's secretary had left a message to say that Jason Dobbie had recovered sufficiently to be allowed home.

'I rang the hospital immediately and told the ward sister he was in no circumstances to be allowed to leave the hospital until we could arrange round-the-clock protection for him,' said Rathbone. 'She didn't take too kindly to that – said they needed the bed for another of Mister Lovell's patients. I said we wouldn't keep the great man waiting longer than necessary.' His tone suggested that the conversation had been an acrimonious one. 'Sukey, you and I will go to the hospital and have a chat with Dobbie this morning. Once we've made the necessary arrangements for his protection, we'll let him go home – if that's what he wants of course. That shouldn't take too long; once we've done that we can trot along to the morgue. Doc Hanley said he'd be starting the PM on "Anne Onymous" around ten o'clock. The dismembered lady,' he explained; he allowed himself a faint smile as if pleased with himself at having coined the soubriquet.

'What do you want Vicky and me to do, Sarge?' asked Penny.

'I'm coming to that. Sukey, give Vicky the name of your contact with "Naughty Ladies" and she and Penny can ask her about the people who went to her party.'

'What about the evidence, Sarge?' asked Vicky. 'The undies I mean,' she explained, as he looked blank for a moment.

'Gone to forensics. You did get photographs?' he asked, suddenly rounding on Sukey.

'Of course, Sarge – in glorious Technicolor.' Sukey took an envelope from her in-tray and handed it to Vicky. 'Just for the record, that particular set is listed in the catalogue as "Rambling Rose".'

'Well, if it was Anne Onymous who wore them, she obviously rambled a bit too far,' Rathbone remarked dryly.

'He's cheered up since Friday,' Vicky murmured in Sukey's ear as they separated on their missions. 'Any idea what it was about?'

'Tell you later,' she whispered back. In the car on the way to the hospital she said casually, 'How was your weekend, Sarge?'

'Fine,' he replied with unexpected warmth. 'Lyn agreed with what you said – in fact she'd come to the same conclusion herself so she went to Newcastle on her own. I took Tommy to Berkeley Castle and he really enjoyed it. He's developed an interest in history – especially the gruesome bits,' he added with a chuckle.

'That's great.' Sukey wondered if he would volunteer further information about the family situation, but none was forthcoming; instead he brought her up to date with the report Hanley had sent after the post-mortem on Mayhew.

'Death was due to multiple injuries sustained in the crash,' he said. 'The car was badly crushed and so was Toby. As to the possibility of drugs and/or alcohol in his system, samples have been sent to a local lab but there hasn't been a request for fast tracking. These tests are expensive enough as it is, so it may be weeks before we hear the results. Not that there's any real urgency – we know he associated with Warren Chesney so there's very little doubt he was a junkie. I understand the coroner has released the body for burial. Meanwhile,' he added as Sukey backed into a parking space outside the hospital and switched off the engine, 'there's plenty more for us to do; when we get back to the station you can contact his parents, tell them we're going to check the house for drugs and say they're welcome to be there. I'll set up a team and a sniffer dog. Right, now let's see what young Jason can tell us.'

'Why the joker with the hardware?' Jason Dobbie nodded in the direction of the armed officer sitting in the far corner of the small private room where, clad only in a pair of hospital pyjama trousers, he sat in a chair beside the bed. Apart from the dressing that concealed the wound on his shaven head he looked very much as he had done when Sukey and Vicky first interviewed him.

'Just a precaution,' said Rathbone, his tone deliberately casual. 'We think it's unlikely your assailant knows who you are or where to find you, but we suspect he was working for some very dangerous characters who may see you as a threat to their operations. It's a pity you decided to . . .'

'I know, I should have called 999,' Dobbie interrupted. 'I admit "having a go" was a daft thing to do . . . I'd had a few drinks and I suppose I was feeling lucky.'

'Well, what's done is done,' said Rathbone. 'Now let's see if you can help us track down the villain – or villains; there may have been more than one, of course. Take your time.'

Dobbie shook his head. 'Truth is, I don't remember much about what happened. I've been doing my best, but . . .'

Rathbone put out a hand to check the apology. 'Don't worry, it's not unusual in cases of concussion for the memory to take a while to return.'

'That's what they tell me, but it's so frustrating.'

'Of course it is. Now,' Rathbone continued, speaking in a slow, unhurried manner, 'do you remember the day when DC Reynolds here –' he gestured in Sukey's direction – 'came to see you with her colleague DC Armstrong? You told Mrs Scott you thought you might have seen some movement outside Toby Mayhew's house, which is Number 14, opposite yours.'

'I remember you,' Dobbie nodded at Sukey, 'and yes, you had a friend with you. Mrs Scott . . . ?' He shook his head, looking puzzled.

'Scotty the Sleuth?' Sukey prompted gently and he relaxed and gave a shaky laugh.

'Oh yes, I know her all right, the old busybody. She . . . she gave me a letter . . . now what was it about . . . ?' He frowned and chewed a fingernail.

'She wrote to you and all the neighbours, asking you to look out for suspicious characters lurking around, and a day or two later you told her . . .'

'Yes, of course!' Some of the vagueness lifted from Dobbie's expression. 'I remember now, I did tell her I'd . . . and she called the police . . . and they . . . you came to see me.'

'Well done!' said Rathbone. 'Let's see what else you can remember.'

Little by little, under patient questioning, more fragments of memory began trickling back, but when it came to the moment, in the small hours of Friday morning, when Dobbie – certain this time that there was someone lurking outside Toby Mayhew's house – unwisely went to challenge them instead of calling the police, his mind once more became a blank.

'I'm really sorry,' he said ruefully, putting a hand to the dressing on his head, 'the last thing I remember is leaving the house and crossing the road. After that . . . zilch!' He held up both hands in a gesture of failure.

'Don't worry, you've done brilliantly so far,' Sukey assured him. 'Just for the record, when you were found you were semi-conscious for a short period and you seemed to be trying to say something beginning with "Ch . . . ch . . .". Does that ring a bell at all?'

He shook his head. 'Sorry,' he said after a moment.

Rathbone stood up and signalled to Sukey to do the same. 'I think we'll leave it at that for the time being; we don't want to tire you,' he said.

'So, can I go home?'

'Yes, if that's what you want. PC Riley will take you and stay with you. I'll arrange for someone to relieve him so that you have round-the-clock protection for a while.'

Dobbie shrugged. 'If you say so.' He stood up, opened the bedside cabinet and took out a small holdall. 'I suppose I'd better make myself decent. One of my neighbours called in and left me these' – he held up a sweatshirt and pair of jogging pants – 'because when the paramedics put me in the ambulance she noticed that what I was wearing was bloodstained.'

'That was a Mrs Unwin, Sarge,' PC Riley volunteered. 'A nice lady – she came several times to enquire after Jason and asked me if there was anything she could do.'

'That was kind of her,' said Sukey.

'Yes, wasn't it?' Jason agreed. 'Now, if you'll excuse me . . .' He gestured with the garments, indicating that he wanted them to leave while he changed. As he did so he half turned and Sukey spotted the tattoo on his shoulder. 'I remember seeing that when we called on you,' she remarked. 'It looks Chinese,' she added casually.

He twisted his head to look at it. 'It's supposed to,' he said. 'I had it done for a joke some time ago when I was working in a pub called the Green Dragon. It wasn't Chinese, though – the pub, I mean. It was in a tiny country village somewhere in the Cotswolds.' He gave a sudden exclamation that was almost a gasp, sat down again and put his hands to his eyes. When he spoke the words came out in a series of jerky phrases. 'It was . . . I remember now . . . the man who attacked me . . . I caught a glimpse of him . . . he was coming at me with his arm raised . . . he was holding something . . . I knew he was going to hit me . . . I couldn't get out of the way.' He was shaking and showing signs of distress. Somewhat alarmed, Sukey put her head round the door and beckoned to a nurse who happened to be passing. She hurried to his side and reached for his wrist to check his pulse, but he pulled his arm impatiently away. 'I'm OK, honestly,' he insisted in a slightly shaky but confident voice.

'He was Chinese?' asked Sukey.

'I don't know . . . I didn't see his face . . . he was wearing a mask.'

'Then what?'

'His arm . . . there was a tattoo . . .'

'A dragon like yours?'

He shook his head almost vehemently. 'No . . . it was . . . some sort of writing . . . I couldn't read it of course, but it looked like something in Chinese.'

'It seems you were right about the Chinese connection in what he was trying to say when they found him,' Rathbone admitted as they made their way to the morgue. 'Not that it gets us very far.'

'Maybe he can remember the tattoo accurately enough to draw it for us? Wouldn't that be a help?'

He shrugged. 'It has been known for villains to be identified by tattoos,' he admitted, 'but even if it was a Chinese character I doubt if he'd be able to reproduce it accurately.'

'There might be a connection with the Chinese takeaway – the one with the number on Mayhew's cell phone.'

He shook his head dismissively. 'The "Oriental Garden", you mean? I told you, it's been checked out and it's clean.'

'The restaurant may be, but one of the workers might have dodgy connections,' Sukey persisted.

'OK, we'll bear it in mind,' he said. His slightly patronizing tone suggested that he was only saying it to humour her. 'Right, let's go and watch Doc Hanley at work.'

Hanley drew back the sheet to reveal the body parts, laid out – as Sukey later described it to Vicky – like a macabre jigsaw puzzle. 'There she is in all her glory,' he announced.

'She's quite small,' Rathbone commented. 'An adolescent, would you say?

Hanley shook his head. 'I don't think so. We'll talk about that in a minute. Now, before we go any further I want to draw your attention to a few things.' His gloved fingers moved delicately over the dismembered corpse. 'First, the cut ends of the neck and limbs. Clean as a whistle, possibly done with something like a butcher's cleaver, certainly not with a saw. Cause of death probably this –' the index finger paused over a wound in the stomach – 'although whether it was a fatal blow or death was due to loss of blood remains to be seen. And of course it wasn't inflicted with the tool used to cut her up, most probably a sharp knife or dagger.'

'We've found some bloodstained undergarments,' said Rathbone. 'There may not be a connection, but we could be on the track of the woman who was wearing them. If that's her –' he pointed to the steel slab on which the body parts were lying – 'then we could be a significant step forward in our enquiries.'

'The face is more recognizable now it's cleaned up,' said Sukey. 'She's rather pretty,' she added sadly. Something about the features struck her as unusual and she bent over to take a closer look; what she saw made her catch her breath.

'What is it?' said Rathbone.

'Anything particular about her strike you, Sarge?'

He looked over her shoulder. 'Yes . . . something about the shape of the eyes . . . and the high cheekbones,' he said. 'Yes, I see what you mean . . . she looks slightly oriental.'

Hanley nodded in agreement. 'That's what I was going to say.'

THIRTEEN

'**M**rs Norton?'
'Who's calling?'
'This is DC Armstrong of Avon and Somerset CID. I believe Kay of "Naughty Ladies" has spoken to you on our behalf and that you have very kindly agreed to help us with our enquiries.'

'Yes, I did hear from Kay.' There was a pause. 'I'm not sure . . . what exactly is it you want?'

Vicky put a hand briefly over the transmitter and mouthed 'nervous' at DC Penny Osborne, who was standing beside her, before continuing. 'There is nothing for you to worry about, Mrs Norton, we just want a few minutes of your time.'

'Kay said something about a party I held recently. I assure you, it was all above board and the ladies who attended are all friends . . . neighbours . . . I wouldn't want to get them into trouble . . .'

'There's absolutely no question of trouble for anyone,' Vicky assured her.

'If you could just give me some idea of what it's about?'

'We are trying to trace a lady who ordered some items from the "Naughty Ladies" catalogue. We believe she ordered them at your party.'

'Several ladies ordered items. I couldn't possibly give you their addresses without their permission.'

'We wouldn't ask you to do that.'

'Then what . . . ?'

'Mrs Norton,' said Vicky who was beginning to feel herself losing patience, 'we are investigating a very serious case and we are particularly concerned for the safety of a lady who . . .'

'Safety?' It was evident from the sharp change of tone that the word had set alarm bells ringing. 'It's not Connie is it? I haven't seen her lately and I've been wondering . . . yes, of course, if you're looking for her I'll help in any way I can.'

'Thank you very much,' said Vicky warmly. 'Would it be convenient if we came round to see you now?'

'Yes, of course,' Mrs Norton repeated, and gave the address.

Ash Place was a pleasant cul-de-sac in a recently completed stage of an extensive housing estate on the northern outskirts of Bristol, comprising a sizeable development of detached and semi-detached houses together with amenities such as a library, medical centre, shops and schools. The wide pavements were planted with young trees, the houses gleamed with new paint and the trim front gardens with their miniature lawns and tasteful plant-ings of rose bushes, small shrubs and miniature conifers – many of them still bearing their garden-centre labels – wore a slightly self-conscious air of 'keeping up with the Joneses'.

Vicky parked outside number twenty-two and rang the bell. While she and Penny waited, two young mothers pushing prams eyed them curiously as they passed and stopped a few yards further on to look back. 'Someone's going to get quizzed later on,' Penny remarked with a chuckle.

Vicky nodded. 'I'll bet not much goes on round here without someone making notes,' she agreed. 'They've probably got a Mrs Scott. The self-appointed sleuth of Tyndale Gardens, where Toby Mayhew used to live, is called Mrs Scott,' she explained, in response to Penny's questioning look.

Mrs Norton was a petite, attractive brunette of about thirty. She showed them into a sitting room smelling of new carpets and lavender room-freshener, furnished with a three-piece suite that looked as if it had been delivered that morning. She invited them to sit down and brought coffee in matching mugs and biscuits on matching plates.

'Please, call me Bobbie,' she said after the introductions. 'It's short for Roberta,' she added unnecessarily. 'I'm really worried about Connie,' she went on while dispensing coffee and handing round biscuits, 'and when you said you were concerned about her safety I began to wonder . . . while I was waiting for you to arrive I tried to remember what I knew about her. I'm afraid it isn't very much, but I wrote it down for you.'

'That's very thoughtful of you,' said Vicky warmly.

Bobbie gave a shy smile of pleasure. She reached for a note-book that lay beside the tray on the coffee table and opened it.

'I first met her about six months ago – on the twenty-eighth of September to be precise,' she began. 'We were sitting in the doctor's waiting room and we exchanged a few words. I thought she seemed worried and a bit, well, nervous. I didn't like to ask questions, but I did wonder whether she was afraid she had something seriously wrong with her.'

'When was the next time you saw her?' asked Penny, as Bobby broke off to sip her coffee and nibble a biscuit.

'It was an hour or so later on the same day, in the supermarket. We almost bumped trolleys at the corner of one of the aisles; I made some joke about it, but she didn't laugh and I had the impression she'd been crying. I invited her back here for a cup of tea but she said no and practically ran to the till, paid her bill and disappeared. And I'm sure she hadn't finished her shopping,' Bobbie added as an afterthought.

'You think she was trying to avoid you?'

Bobbie nodded. 'I'm sure of it. I was seriously concerned about her and when Ron – my husband – came home I told him, but he said it was none of my business and not to bother about it.'

'So then what happened?' asked Vicky.

Bobby consulted her notebook. 'The next time I saw her was about two weeks later. We were both on the bus to the Mall and sat next to each other and this time she was more relaxed although she didn't have much to say – not about herself, I mean. We came home together on the bus in the afternoon. After that we bumped into one another quite a few times – in the shops, now and again in the library, and so on.'

'Did you ever go to her house?'

Bobbie shook her head. 'No, never. I invited her once or twice for coffee, but she never invited me back. Once she came when I'd invited a few other friends as well. It was then that one of us, who'd heard about the "Naughty Ladies" parties, suggested we hold one of our own. We thought it was a great idea; we had to be a bit discreet about invitations because there are one or two old sourpusses round here who wouldn't approve and might have told everyone we were "lowering the tone of the neighbourhood".' Bobby gave a gleeful giggle and made quotations marks with her fingers.

'And Connie was one of the guests?'

'That's right. I was quite surprised when she accepted because she seemed so reserved, but anyway she seemed to enjoy it and surprised us all by ordering a *very* naughty bra and knickers. "Rambling Rose", they were called. They had some . . . rather unusual features. We were rather surprised that Kay would offer anything quite so . . . well, shocking, some of us thought. We could see they'd turn on a certain type of man, but . . .' Bobbie made a little *moue* of disgust.

'Did any of the other guests order anything?'

'Oh yes, several of us, but nothing like that. More fun things really but quite innocent, the sort to get our husbands going . . . if you know what I mean.'

Vicky and Penny chuckled and said they knew exactly what she meant. 'So how did the guests get their things? Did they order them through you?'

'That's right. They gave me the money and I sent off a cheque with the order. The parcel came to me; I rang everyone and they came and collected their stuff.'

'So you have Connie's phone number?'

'She never gave it to me. I said the stuff usually came by return and she called round to pick it up a day or two later.' Bobbie handed Vicky a slip of paper. 'Is there anything else I can tell you?'

'Do you happen to know her surname?'

'I'm afraid not. She just said her name was Connie.'

'Can you describe her?'

Bobbie closed her eyes for a moment. 'She's quite small-boned . . . slender, with very dark eyes, almost almond-shaped, and fairly long black hair. High cheekbones . . . I suppose you might say she has a slightly oriental look, although she doesn't have a foreign accent or wear funny clothes.'

'One other thing – may we have the name of your doctor?'

'I see Doctor McCarthy, but I have a feeling she saw one of the other doctors. They'll know at the surgery.'

'Well, thank you Bobbie, you've really been very helpful,' said Vicky.

'Do you think she's all right?' asked Bobbie anxiously as she showed them to the door.

'We don't know. We hope so.'

*   *   *

'What next?' asked Penny as she and Vicky returned to their car.

'We must try and have a word with Connie's doctor,' said Vicky. 'It's significant that when Bobbie met her in the surgery she appeared worried and nervous, and when she saw her a short while later she looked as if she'd been crying. What does that suggest to you?'

'She was afraid she had something seriously wrong . . . and the doctor's diagnosis confirmed it.'

Vicky nodded. 'That thought occurred to me as well.'

The receptionist at the medical centre checked the appointments for the twenty-eighth of September. 'Mrs Connie Gilbert was seen that morning by Doctor Anderson,' she said. 'If you'd like to wait I'll have a word with her between patients and ask if she can spare you a few minutes.'

Doctor Anderson was a woman of about fifty with a pleasant manner that belied her somewhat severe features. 'Yes, Mrs Gilbert is my patient,' she said in answer to Vicky's question. 'What is it you want to know?' Vicky explained and she shook her head doubtfully. 'I am always very reluctant to reveal information about a patient without their consent,' she said slowly. 'You say you are "concerned for her safety" – what are your reasons for this?'

'We are investigating a very nasty, brutal murder, and we think it's possible – although we have no definite proof at the moment – that Mrs Gilbert may be the victim,' said Vicky.

'Oh dear.' Doctor Anderson was visibly shaken. It was several moments before she replied. 'Well, in that case perhaps I should tell you that I had some serious news for her. Not unexpected, but it was a shock to her just the same. She had tested positive for a serious, sexually transmitted disease.'

'Did she give you any idea of how she became infected?'

'She admitted that on more than one occasion she had un-protected sex.'

Doctor Anderson glanced at her watch. 'That's all I can tell you I'm afraid, and I have other patients waiting, so if there's nothing else . . . ?'

'Thank you, Doctor, you've been very helpful,' said Vicky. 'If you do think of anything else, or if Mrs Gilbert should come to see you again, will you please let us know?'

'Certainly.'

When she and Penny were back in the car, Vicky called DS Rathbone's number on her cell phone. It rang several times before he answered.

'I'm at the morgue attending the PM on Anne Onymous,' he said impatiently. 'Can't it wait?'

'We've got a description of "Rambling Rose", Sarge, and thought you might be interested.'

'Well?'

'Does "faintly oriental" ring a bell?'

'So,' said DCI Leach when the team assembled in his office the following morning. 'We seem to be getting closer to an ID for the dismembered lady. This Mrs Gilbert – what have you managed to find out about her?'

'We got her address from the doctor, sir,' said Penny. 'It's a flat over a hairdresser's, number 18A Stoke Parade. We rang the bell, but there was no answer. We enquired at the salon but no one could recall seeing her or anyone else going in or out.'

'But when we went to the fish and chip shop next door we got a very different story,' said Vicky. 'It seems that on numerous occasions men were seen either entering or leaving Connie's flat, mostly in the evening.'

'What sort of men?'

'Various ages . . . mostly well dressed.'

'Well, there doesn't seem to be much doubt about her lifestyle so it's no wonder she picked up an infection,' Leach observed. 'Presumably she was wearing her "Rambling Rose" outfit when she was killed, quite possibly by one of her customers. What about the dismembered corpse, Greg? What news there?' After Rathbone had given his report Leach asked, 'Has she been checked for HIV and so on as well as DNA?'

'Doc Hanley's sent samples and asked for a detailed report, sir.'

'Good. Get a warrant and search her flat and at the same time set up house-to-house and next of kin enquiries. The tenant in the flat adjoining hers might have noticed unusual comings and goings – or noises,' Leach added with a humourless grin.

'Will do, sir. About the Mayhew case, I've arranged with

Sergeant Stafford to bring his team and do a sweep of fourteen Tyndale Gardens tomorrow.'

Leach nodded. 'Keep me posted.'

By the time Sukey and Vicky arrived at Connie Gilbert's flat with the search warrant it was almost midday. Beside the street door, which bore the numbers 18A and 18B, were two corresponding bell pushes. Having first tried 18A – more in hope than expectation – and receiving no response, they tried 18B; after a long interval Vicky tried again, this time keeping her finger on the button for several seconds. They were about to give up and consider their next move when a somnolent voice from a concealed loudspeaker demanded to know who the hell was calling at this ungodly hour.

After Vicky had apologized for the disturbance and stated their business, the voice said grumpily, 'You might as well go up, but if you have to break the door down for God's sake do it quietly.'

The two exchanged amused glances. 'Hung over or hung over?' said Sukey as a buzzer sounded and the street door opened.

'Definitely hung over,' said Vicky.

They climbed the stairs. Facing each other on opposite sides of the landing were two identical front doors. Vicky gave the one marked 18A a tentative push and to their surprise it swung open. 'Whoever used it last didn't bother to close it,' she remarked.

The first thing that struck them as they entered the small entrance hall was the heavy, sensuous perfume. It pervaded the entire flat, which consisted of two rooms, a kitchen and a bathroom. The first room they entered was plainly, almost sparsely furnished with a single bed, a chair, a bedside table on which stood a reading lamp, and a small chest of drawers. Along one wall was a fitted cupboard with a hanging rail and a shelf. 'Not much here to turn the boyfriends on,' commented Vicky.

'She didn't have a very sexy wardrobe either,' said Sukey as they riffled quickly through the small selection of trousers, jackets, sweaters, T-shirts and underwear. 'No sign of anything from the "Naughty Ladies" catalogue either,' she added. 'Let's try the other room.'

The second room told a very different story. Originally intended as a living room with a door to the kitchen, it was furnished and

decorated in what struck the two detectives as a somewhat
amateurish attempt to convey the atmosphere of an oriental
harem. A huge divan was covered with a heavy, richly coloured
throw into which were woven designs that, as Vicky remarked,
'might have come out of the Kama Sutra'. Imitation Persian and
tiger skin rugs were scattered on the floor and the walls were
covered with prints of women in various stages of dress and
undress, many of them in highly suggestive poses.

'And here –' Vicky opened a carved chest, which contained
a tumbled heap of highly provocative outfits and accessories –
'is where she kept her props.'

'Not much doubt about where she entertained the customers,'
Sukey observed. 'It's hardly surprising she never returned
Bobbie's invitations.'

'Not quite the setting for a group of suburban housewives
swapping confidences over the coffee cups,' Vicky agreed. 'We're
talking about her as if we know she's dead, aren't we?' she added
soberly.

'There doesn't seem to be much doubt, does there?' said Sukey.
'Everything looks undisturbed here,' she added thoughtfully, 'and
yet . . . if, as seems probable, she was wearing "Rambling Rose"
when she was stabbed, it's unlikely to have happened anywhere
else so you'd think there'd be . . . I wonder . . .' With a sudden
movement, she grasped one corner of the throw covering the divan
and pulled it back. Both women gasped in horror at the sight of
what had lain hidden beneath it.

FOURTEEN

They stood transfixed for several seconds, staring in shocked silence at the bloodstained bed that spoke mutely of the crime committed on it. 'So this is where she died,' Sukey muttered.

'So it would seem,' Vicky agreed soberly.

'And the next question is,' Sukey continued, almost to herself, 'if Connie Gilbert and Anne Onymous, as our witty sergeant has dubbed the dismembered lady, are the same person, where was she chopped up?'

'We haven't checked the rest of the flat yet, have we?' Vicky reminded her. 'I suppose the kitchen's through that door in the corner.' She crossed the room and pushed it open.

The kitchen was fitted on two sides with cupboards, a cooker and a refrigerator, with a sink and draining board at one end. 'It's not very wide,' Sukey commented as they stood in the doorway, 'but I suppose there'd be room for him to put her on the floor and get to work with his chopper.'

'It'd be sure to make a noise,' Vicky objected. 'Wouldn't someone hear the banging?'

'Not necessarily, not if it happened after the salon closed,' said Sukey, 'but even if they did, they'd probably put it down to someone doing a bit of DIY. That imitation tiling looks like plastic floor covering.' She squatted down in an attempt to examine the surface more closely. 'I can see one or two marks that might have been made by something sharp, but I can't get a close enough look without treading on the floor and we'll be in trouble if we contaminate the scene more than we have done already. I guess we'd better leave that for the CSIs to check.'

Vicky got out her cell phone. 'It's time to report our findings.'

'At last we're getting somewhere,' said Rathbone after learning of the gruesome discovery in flat 18A Stoke Parade. 'Stay there until I arrive; I'll alert the CSIs and get them to attend, meanwhile make sure no one enters or leaves the building without your say-so.'

'The entire building, Sarge?' said Vicky dubiously.

'The entire building.'

'What about Stella's clients?'

'Who the hell is Stella?'

'She runs the hairdressing salon under Connie Gilbert's flat. We can hardly shut her down, can we? We've already spoken to her and neither she nor any of her stylists ever saw any strange men coming or going.'

'OK, but make a note to get a list of all her clients and check with them. And rouse that dozy bugger in number 18B and try and get some sense out of him – all this after uniformed have contained the scene, that is,' he added as an afterthought.

'Will do, Sarge.' Vicky switched off her phone. 'He sounded positively excited – like a bloodhound on the scent,' she reported with a chuckle.

'We know he's been finding the lack of progress frustrating,' said Sukey. 'What with that and his personal problems . . .'

'Oh yes, you can fill me in about that while we're mounting guard at the front door.'

They went downstairs and stood in the doorway awaiting the arrival of reinforcements while Sukey told her about his anxiety over his wife's plan to move to Newcastle to care for her father. 'I hope she finds a better solution than that,' Vicky commented when she had finished.

Sukey nodded. 'Me too. He thinks the world of that kid. And let's hope his optimism over this case is justified. You know,' she went on, 'I still have a hunch there's a connection between Toby Mayhew and this crime.'

'Oh you and your hunches!' Vicky teased. 'Still, they have been known to lead somewhere,' she conceded.

'Supposing,' Sukey went on as if thinking aloud, 'Toby was one of Connie's "clients"?'

'Or suppose the two of them were running rival drug rings,' Vicky suggested. 'Just kidding,' she added in response to Sukey's raised eyebrows. 'Seriously, though,' she went on, 'from what we saw of Toby's jumpiness, can you see him having the nerve to carry out this sort of crime?'

'He might have been a very different character when he was high on drugs,' Sukey countered, 'and he'd done a spell in the army so he'd have gone through some pretty tough training even if he never saw action.'

The arrival of a couple of uniformed officers, who proceeded to erect a barrier across the entrance to the flats, put an end to speculation. Shortly afterwards DS Rathbone arrived. 'Where is it?' he demanded. 'I'd like to have a quick look round before the CSIs get here.'

'Up the stairs and first room on the right – the front door's open,' said Sukey and he went charging up without waiting for them. After a quick word with the two uniformed officers they closed the door and followed him into Connie's bedroom. He studied the bloodstained divan for several seconds before saying, 'Whoever did it must have got blood on his clothes, and yet –' he cast a quick glance round the room – 'he managed to get the body out of the flat without leaving any visible traces apart from what's on the bed. Now, I wonder . . .'

'We think he may have carried it into the kitchen and put it on the floor to chop it up, Sarge, so perhaps he wrapped it in something first,' said Vicky. 'The fact that he covered the blood-stains with the throw suggests he wanted to make sure no one raised the alarm too soon – not until he'd disposed of all the bits anyway.'

'We'll be in a better position to judge the sequence of events after the CSIs have done their stuff,' said Rathbone. 'I've had a word with Doc Hanley and he's promised to come and have a look at the scene. That's probably him now,' he added at the sound of footsteps mounting the stairs.

The pathologist stood looking down at the divan for a while without speaking, absent-mindedly scratching his thin, beaky nose with a tapering forefinger. 'Would I be right in assuming, Greg,' he said at last, 'that you suspect that the person who was attacked in this bed is the woman whose dismembered body was recovered from the sea recently – the one on whom I carried out an autopsy yesterday?'

'We do have reason to believe that's the case,' Rathbone responded cautiously. 'There hasn't been time yet for a detailed examination of the crime scene, but my two DCs have spotted what may be evidence that something – possibly a body – was dismembered in the kitchen of this flat. We hope to build up a clearer picture after the CSIs have made their report.'

Hanley nodded. 'You'll no doubt recall my saying that in my opinion your Anne Onymous died as the result of damage to vital organs caused by several deep stab wounds. None of the wounds cut an artery so there wouldn't have been any spurting of blood. From the way this blood is distributed,' he went on, 'I'd say this victim received fatal injuries – most likely stab wounds – while she was lying on her back.'

'How d'you figure that out?'

'See that area in the middle which is less heavily stained?' said Hanley. 'That suggests to me that she lay there for an interval before death – maybe a few seconds or several minutes, there's no way of telling – while blood welled from the wounds and flowed down on either side of the abdomen. It's not possible to assess what quantity of blood she lost as much of it will have soaked into the mattress.'

'So you can't say how long she lay there bleeding?' Hanley shook his head. 'Or from the state of the blood, how long ago the crime was committed?'

Hanley shook his head again. 'It's almost impossible to tell. It would depend on various factors – the room temperature, how long it was exposed to air before the throw was put over it. Sorry I can't be more precise.'

'Never mind, all this has been of some help,' said Rathbone. 'Just one other thing; how much blood would there be during the butchering process?'

'Not a lot. Blood doesn't flow after death, it just oozes. If it was carried out on a washable surface it wouldn't have taken long to clean up afterwards – although detectable traces would almost certainly be left behind. Samples from the remains have gone for DNA tests, of course, and if this blood yields a matching sample you'll at least have an ID.'

'That would be a great help,' said Rathbone, 'and thanks again, Doc.'

'Oh, one other point,' said Hanley. 'She was probably having sex when – or just before – she was attacked. You'll find references in my report to traces of semen found in the vagina.'

'That could come in useful – if we ever find a suspect, that is,' Rathbone said dryly. 'I'd like to see the rest of the flat before the CSIs get here,' he continued after Hanley had left. 'Somehow or other our murderer must have moved the body to the kitchen – if that is where he chopped it up – yet there's no visible trace of blood anywhere but on the bed.'

'Perhaps he wrapped it in something,' Sukey suggested, 'and if so, whatever he used must be bloodstained.'

'Let's look around,' said Rathbone. 'Where haven't you searched?'

'Only the bathroom.'

'Right, let's look there.'

The small, somewhat cramped bathroom contained a wash-basin, a toilet and a shower compartment. 'No towels,' Sukey remarked, pointing to the empty rail.

Vicky took the lid off a wicker laundry basket. 'Look no further,' she said, indicating the bloodstained heap.

'So,' said Rathbone, 'it looks as if he wrapped her body in the towels – probably so as not to get blood on his clothing – carried her into the kitchen, laid her on the floor and got busy with his chopper. I wonder –' he frowned and thought for a moment – 'whether he brought the chopper with him or used something from Connie's kitchen.'

'Not many people have anything in their kitchen heavy enough to chop up a body, Sarge,' Vicky pointed out. 'Although, now I come to think of it, Chris has a small cleaver in his. My partner – he's a professional chef,' she explained as the sergeant raised an eyebrow.

'Well, we can't do a proper search until the CSIs have checked everything for prints and so on,' he said. 'Let's assume for the moment that when he'd finished his butchery he put the towels in the basket and washed or at least wiped the floor before leaving. His next job was to get the bits out of the flat without arousing suspicion.'

'Plastic bag?' suggested Sukey. 'Or most likely two, one for the torso and another for the head, arms and legs. They'd have to be fairly large, strong bags, the sort people use to put garden rubbish in.'

'Then he'd have to get them to his car,' said Vicky. 'That

would have been a risky business, wouldn't it? Suppose he was spotted?'

Rathbone shrugged. 'If we're right in our assumptions, it's a risk he'd have to take. It's unlikely anyone would have challenged him, but with luck someone might have seen a man carrying apparently heavy plastic bags late at night. We must get on to the press office and tell them to put out an appeal for witnesses.' He checked the time on his watch. 'I'm going back to the station now to get things moving. You two go and see if you can get any sense out of number 18B.'

'I suppose we can forget about lunch until we've done his bidding,' Vicky grumbled as the downstairs door banged behind him. They crossed the landing and knocked at the flat opposite. After a few moments a barefooted young man in black jeans with a towel draped round his naked shoulders opened the door. His head was closely cropped apart from a broad stripe of black hair in the middle, gelled into the shape of a cockscomb, one side of his face was freshly shaven and the other was covered in white foam. He gestured to the two to enter with a wave of the safety razor he was holding.

'I take it you're the two ladies from CID who disturbed my slumbers a while back,' he said with a disarming grin. 'Sorry I was rude – I'm afraid actors don't do mornings.'

'You're an actor?' said Sukey.

'That's right.' He pointed to his head with his left hand while continuing to ply the razor with the other, using a small mirror on the wall beside the door. 'This isn't my normal appearance – I've got a part in a play about a rock band. The name's Don Wyatt by the way, and no, you haven't heard of me and probably never will – not unless I'm up for a serious misdemeanour. Excuse me while I finish this – with you in a moment.' He disappeared into what, from the sound of running water and vigorous splashing that ensued, they assumed was the bathroom. He reappeared moments later, pulling on a black T-shirt. 'Care for some coffee while I help you with your enquiries?'

He led them into the living room, invited them with a theatrical gesture to sit on a large, shabby but comfortable-looking sofa and went into the kitchen. 'Wonder if he's got any biscuits,' Vicky whispered as they waited, 'I'm starving. Oh, joy!' she exclaimed as Don emerged with a tray on which stood a cafetière, three mugs, a carton of milk, a packet of sugar and half a dozen scones on a chipped plate.

'My mother came on Sunday and brought these,' he explained. 'She's convinced I don't eat enough and she always brings far too much stuff, so please tuck in.' He sat down, picked up a mug of coffee, took a deep swig and said, 'Do I take it you're interested in the goings on in 18A?'

FIFTEEN

'What sort of goings on are we talking about?' asked Vicky.

Don Wyatt cocked his head on one side and adopted a quizzical expression that Sukey guessed he had learned at drama school. 'You haven't had any complaints, then? I thought that was why you're here.'

'What sort of complaints do you have in mind?'

He indicated surprise with eyes and hands. 'About Connie in the flat opposite running a one-woman knocking shop of course. She probably calls it a private massage parlour or some other fancy name, but everyone knows what's really on offer.'

'How do you know this?' asked Sukey.

He gave a slightly self-conscious laugh and the two detectives exchanged glances. 'I'm not one of her clients, if that's what you're thinking,' he assured them, 'but if that's not the reason, what's your interest in her? She's not suspected of terrorist activities, is she? I've only set eyes on her a few times . . . but now I come to think about it there is something vaguely foreign-looking about her.'

'We're here because she hasn't been seen lately and her friends are concerned for her safety,' Vicky explained, 'so it would be very helpful if you could tell us exactly what you know about her.'

'Let's begin with the last time you saw her,' prompted Sukey as he appeared at a loss.

He furrowed his brow and closed his eyes. 'That would be about a week ago – or maybe a bit longer, I don't remember exactly,' he said after a few moments. 'She was coming in with a bag of shopping just as I was going out. I only moved in here about three weeks ago,' he hurried on. 'This isn't my flat, by the way, it belongs to a friend who's in America for three months. He's lent it to me while I'm working in Bristol. He told me about Connie and we had a bit of a laugh about it.

He said she entertains most of her clients in the evenings and leads an apparently normal life during the daytime. On the whole she's pretty discreet, I will say that for her. I see comings and goings now and again and sometimes I hear noises – I won't go into details, I'm sure you can imagine the sort of thing.' Despite his air of sophistication, the subject appeared to cause him some embarrassment.

It occurred to Sukey that despite his denial he might know Connie more intimately than he cared to admit. 'Have you ever been inside her flat?' she asked, looking him straight in the eye.

He met her gaze without flinching. 'No, never,' he said emphatically. 'I'm gay,' he added as if to drive the point home.

'Tell us about these noises you've heard from time to time.'

His colour rose and he shifted in his seat. 'You know,' he mumbled. 'Sort of yelps . . . and sometimes groans . . . and giggles and so on. Most of the time it was fairly quiet but now and again the decibels went up.'

'In other words, the sounds you'd associate with sexual activity?'

He nodded. 'Yes, I suppose so. Except once.'

'Yes?' Sukey prompted as he hesitated.

'I remember one night – a week ago last Friday I think it was. I got back a bit late after a heavy night drinking with the rest of the cast. I'd missed the last bus so I got a cab home. She had someone there that night . . . in fact, he was ringing her bell just as I paid off the driver and he went in ahead of me – but the miserable bugger didn't hold the door for me. Being a bit under the weather I had the devil of a job to find my key,' he added petulantly.

'And it was that night you heard something unusual?' said Sukey.

'Well, yes. I've no idea how long after I got home . . . I passed out on the bed but after a while I woke up to go to the bathroom and it was then that I heard it . . . a sort of thump, thump, thump. It went right through my head, like a sledgehammer. I remember pulling the pillow over my head to try and blot it out.'

'How long did it go on?'

Don shook his head. 'I've no idea, I'm afraid. I must have crashed out again. I know I didn't wake up until hours later . . .

with a prince of a hangover.' He put both hands to his head as if reliving the pain. 'It was just as well there was no performance on Saturday afternoon or we'd all have been useless. As it was, *The Queen's English* closed after the evening performance on the Friday, hence the party. You didn't happen to see it, I suppose?' he added. The two detectives shook their heads and he smiled and shrugged. 'Just as well, it's not a very good play.'

'Can we get back to the night you heard this thumping?' said Vicky. 'You say it was definitely the Friday before last? Can you be absolutely sure about this?'

He gave an emphatic nod. 'Quite definitely,' he said.

'About the man you saw that night, the one who was ringing Connie's bell as you were paying off your cab driver,' said Sukey, 'did you get a good look at him?'

He shook his head. 'Not really. He had on dark clothing with something on his head . . . a woollen hat possibly, or a beret, something close fitting anyway.'

'Did you get a glimpse of his face? There's a street lamp a short distance away so maybe—'

'If I did, I don't remember,' he said apologetically. 'He had one hand on the bell and his head slightly bent forward as if he was listening . . . of course, he would be, wouldn't he, he'd be waiting for Connie to answer and then he'd ask her to let him in.'

'And when she unlocked the door he'd have pushed it open and gone in,' said Sukey. With a sudden flash of inspiration, she went on, 'He probably pushed it with one hand. Did you happen to notice which one?'

Don looked slightly bemused at the question. 'The right one, I think. Is it important?'

'Please think very carefully and try to see him in your mind's eye. First of all, was he wearing gloves?'

He shut his eyes for a moment. 'No, I don't think so.'

'So you might have seen his bare wrist?'

'I suppose so. Yes, I did . . . and I remember, I noticed something else. There were some black marks on his wrist.'

Sukey did her best to keep her voice level as she said, 'Could it have been a tattoo?'

He shook his head. 'No, nothing like that, just a few squiggly lines.'

'Some kind of writing, perhaps . . . something in Chinese, for example?'

'I've no idea . . . I suppose it could have been,' he said doubtfully.

'I don't suppose you could draw it for us?'

'You must be kidding! Like I told you, I was pretty well pissed. For all I know it could be something he'd written to remind him of something – Connie's address, for example.' He glanced at his watch. 'Look, if that's all, I've got a rehearsal at three o'clock. I'm afraid I haven't been much help.'

'On the contrary, you've been a great help,' said Vicky. 'And by the way, there's a police guard outside the building, so make sure you've got an ID with you or you might not be allowed back in.'

'Police guard?' His eyes widened. 'Whatever for?'

'Because we have reason to believe that a violent crime – possibly murder – was committed in Connie's flat.'

'After studying all three of your reports, plus Doc Hanley's report on the autopsy, there doesn't seem to be much doubt about it,' said DCI Leach. 'The dismembered body is almost certainly that of Connie Gilbert – if that's her real name, of course – and it seems more than likely that what young Wyatt heard was her killer chopping her up on her own kitchen floor. We have to wait for the results of the samples sent to forensics, of course, and hope they help to fill in some of the gaps. Meanwhile –' he scanned the open file on his desk – 'I see from your report, Greg, that you found a considerable sum of money, mostly in used notes, tucked away in various places in the flat, and you also established from the landlord's agent that the rent was always paid monthly in advance, in cash.'

'That's right, sir – and judging from the amount we picked up business seems to have been pretty brisk,' commented Rathbone dryly.

'Quite so. You didn't find a passport?'

'No sir, but we're making the usual enquiries from the FO. She was, of course, registered at the doctor's surgery, but their records seem to be incomplete. She only consulted them once; they say she asked for an urgent appointment because she had some symptoms that were worrying her.'

'Yes, and we know what lies behind that, don't we?' Leach observed. 'All of this seems to suggest she took particular care to remain anonymous as far as possible.'

'It certainly looks that way,' Rathbone agreed. 'She didn't even have a telephone – at least, there's no landline in the flat and we didn't find a mobile.'

'You found a diary with times and initials so it's obvious she had some kind of appointments system. So –' he glanced at the three detectives seated in front of him – 'how do you suppose the punters got in touch with her? It would have been inconvenient, to say the least, if several of them came knocking at her door at the same time.'

'The same thought occurred to us, sir,' said Sukey. 'Perhaps she used a public pay phone – or had an arrangement with someone who took messages for her.'

'Or maybe she had a mobile but the killer took it away with him, sir,' Vicky suggested. 'He'd guess we'd be searching her flat sooner or later so if his number was on it he'd want to make sure he didn't leave any traces.'

'Good point.' Leach gave a nod of approval. He sat back and thought for a few moments, tapping his front teeth with a ballpoint pen. 'So what's your next step, Greg?'

'We've put out an appeal for witnesses who may have noticed any unusual activity outside or visitors to Connie's flat, of course, and uniformed are conducting house to house enquiries among neighbours and the local businesses. We're going to try and estab-lish if any of the mobile service providers have an account in her name at that address.' He heaved a sigh. 'It's going to be a pretty time-consuming business but it's got to be done.'

'Good.' Leach closed the file on Connie Gilbert and reached for another. 'Now, what about the Tobias Mayhew case? Any movement on that?'

'We're sweeping his house for drugs tomorrow, sir.'

'Ah yes, you did tell me. Well, keep me posted.'

Taking the final words as a sign of dismissal, Rathbone and his two DCs returned to the CID office. 'Any questions arising from that?' he asked.

'There may be nothing in this, Sarge,' Sukey began, 'but if you remember, when Jason Dobbie went to investigate the movement outside Toby Mayhew's house he got a glimpse of a tattoo on the assailant's arm.'

Rathbone nodded. 'I remember. What of it?'

'Jason said it looked like something in Chinese.'

'So?'

'Don Wyatt noticed a similar mark on the arm of a man he saw entering Connie Gilbert's flat. That was three days before Connie's head was washed up on Clevedon beach. Could the man Wyatt saw be the killer? Is it possible that the man who attacked Jason is the same man who killed Connie Gilbert?'

'Stretching it a bit, aren't you?' said Rathbone. 'All Wyatt could swear to – if he could swear to anything, the state he was in at the time – is that he saw, or thought he saw some marks on the man's wrist. I get the impression from your report that you did your best to get him to admit it could have been a tattoo in the form of a Chinese character.'

'He didn't deny it, Sarge, he just said he couldn't be sure,' Sukey pleaded. 'Don't you think it's worth looking into?'

Rathbone shook his head emphatically. 'Like I said, it's stretching coincidence a bit too far.' He reached for his jacket. 'Right, I'm going home. See you tomorrow.'

'You never give up, do you?' said Vicky as she and Sukey cleared their desks. 'You and your hunches!'

SIXTEEN

When Sukey reached home she found a message from her son Fergus, who was currently studying at the University of Gloucester with a view to a career as a forensic psychologist. It was characteristically brief.

'Hi, Mum, sorry I haven't been in touch. Can you call me?'

'Why not?' Sukey said aloud as she switched off the machine and went into the kitchen. Before leaving for work that morning she had taken a pasta dish from the freezer and put it into the refrigerator; having checked that it was fully defrosted she prepared some fresh vegetables and put them ready to cook. She then poured a glass of wine, settled down in an easy chair in the sitting room, picked up the phone and keyed in her son's number. At this hour he was probably having a meal in a café somewhere with his friends, but when he answered the only background noise she heard was a Schubert piano sonata.

'I thought you'd be out with your mates,' she said. 'You're not ill, are you?' she added before he had time to reply.

'Don't worry, Mum, I'm fine. I'm eating in this evening while I do a bit of studying, so it's Indian takeaway and a learned article on criminal behaviour patterns.'

'That sounds interesting. Tell me more.'

'It was the subject of one of last week's lectures about clues left behind by serial offenders, especially killers.'

'There's nothing new about that. It's common knowledge that regular offenders tend to have their own individual methods of working.'

'Yeah, the "this one's got Joe Bloggs's fingerprints all over it" syndrome,' he said with a touch of condescension. 'You're talking about linkage analysis.'

'I am?' Sukey took a deep draught of wine and mentally counted to five. 'All right, I'll buy it.'

'It's a bit difficult to explain,' said Fergus.

'I thought it might be.'

'Of course, if you're not going to take me seriously . . .' he began, evidently sensing a hint of levity in her tone.

'Sorry, didn't mean to sound facetious. It's been a very stressful day and I've just settled down to unwind. You know I'm always interested in what you're doing on your course so do tell me about this new linkage analysis system.'

'There's nothing new about linkage analysis,' he began, 'it's just the latest way of describing what's been done for ages, like you said.'

'You mean modus operandi? Like "personnel" have become "human resources" or "bin men" are now "waste disposal operatives"?'

'If you insist,' he said patiently, 'but what we're looking at now is completely different. It's called "signature analysis" and it's more to do with the way the offender's mind works and the way it affects his behaviour than the way he gains entry to a property or how he disposes of his loot. Some of the cases our tutor quoted are really bizarre . . . and rather disturbing in the way violent attackers – killers and rapists in particular – treat their victims. Some university boffin has developed a computer programme that categorizes various types of behaviour.'

'It sounds fascinating. I'll check with the Chief Constable tomorrow and see if he knows about it.'

'It's still very new so it may not have reached him yet.' This time he appeared to miss the hint of flippancy in the remark. 'Anyway, that's why I phoned – one of the cases we studied has certain features in common with your dismembered lady.'

'Really?' From being mildly amused by his characteristic enthusiasm for a new discovery she became seriously interested. 'Go on.'

'The victim in this case was a man and so far they haven't found all the bits. The head hasn't turned up yet so they can't identify him.'

'How long ago and where were the body parts found?'

'We weren't given all the background details but we do know that the parts were found washed up in various places along a five-mile stretch of coast and appeared to have been in the water for some time. The police questioned a man who worked in a Chinese takeaway not far from where they were found.

He'd once been seen threatening a fellow employee with a cleaver during an argument, but in the end they had to let him go for lack of evidence. He was sacked from his job of course.'

'So what happened to him?'

'It seems the police lost track of him.'

'What happened to the man who was threatened?'

'He gave in his notice – said he was scared the other man would come looking for him. The police haven't been able to trace him either and they think he may be the victim, but on the other hand he might simply have left the district without telling anyone.'

'There should be some employment record,' Sukey pointed out, 'unless he's an illegal, of course.' She finished the last of her wine and checked the time. She was beginning to feel hungry. 'Look, Gus,' she said, 'this is fascinating stuff but I can't see at the moment any connection with our investigation – unless of course you're saying this new computer programme you've been banging on about could help us with our case.'

'It might, but that isn't why I called you. About this other body . . .'

'Gus, we know there have been other cases of bodies being dismembered,' said Sukey, 'including one where the fingers were chopped off. The obvious reason is to delay identification or even make it impossible. The one you've described seems to have been particularly successful from that point of view because the head hasn't been found.'

'Ah, but there is one little titbit I haven't told you yet.'

'All right, let's have it.'

'It says in the evening edition of the *Gloucester Gazette* that the police have been searching a flat in your area.'

'I know, I was there,' said Sukey incautiously.

'You were?' His voice rose to an excited squeak. 'The story goes that a Chinese tom called Connie who lived there has been murdered.'

'Is that what the paparazzi are saying?'

'Something on those lines. Is it true?'

'We didn't find a body, if that's what you mean, and we have no evidence that the tenant of the flat is a Chinese prostitute – that's a bit of creative reporting – but we do have reason to believe that a violent crime was committed there.'

'So of course you know that the flat is above a Chinese takeaway?'

'A hairdressing salon to be precise,' she corrected, 'although there is a takeaway next door. But what's that got to do with anything? It so happens the name of the takeaway came up recently in connection with another case and we checked it out; it doesn't employ any illegal immigrants and the drugs squad have given it the all clear as well. We've no reason to connect it with this case – or to suspect it of fronting any other illegal activity.'

'Wait till you hear this – it might make you change your minds.'

'Well?'

'The last bit of our body to be found – apparently quite a long time after the rest of it – was the right arm. There was a rather strange tattoo on it that looked like something in Chinese. It so happened one of the investigating officers had a daughter who was learning Mandarin Chinese at school. He drew it for her and she asked her teacher what it meant . . . and guess what?'

'You tell me.'

'It's a single character and it means "Death". How about that for a clue?'

'Clue to what?' said Sukey. Mentally her synapses were buzzing, but she managed to keep her voice casual as she added, 'It doesn't seem to have got the police in your case anywhere if they haven't even got an ID. Anyway, what makes you think we'll be interested?'

'Don't you see, the takeaway under Connie's flat – one of the Chinese workers there might have murdered her.'

'Gus, there are any amount of Chinese restaurants and take-aways in Bristol. Just because one of them is in the same building as a flat where a crime was committed doesn't mean anyone who works there is involved. Besides, it was the victim in your case who had the death tattoo. Now, if the police had reason to think it was the *killer* who had it on his arm . . .' She broke off, aware that she'd said too much. Her son's track record in worming information out of her was quite impressive and at this stage she needed time to get her own thoughts in order.

As she expected, he pounced. 'That would make a difference?' he said eagerly.

'Not necessarily,' she said, mentally cursing herself.

'Then why . . . ?'

'Look, Gus, I'm tired so please, no more questions. Just tell me how you think this could be of help in our case.'

'All right. Suppose they both – your murderer and the victim in our case – belong to the same gang and this is their membership badge,' he said eagerly, unwilling to abandon what he evidently considered a promising new line of investigation. 'Maybe our victim broke their code or something, like what happens in the Mafia sometimes, and they made an example of him. Why don't you suggest to DS Rathbone that you check all the employees in your takeaway for a death tattoo?'

'I'll bear it in mind,' she said, having already made a mental resolve to do exactly that. 'Gus, it's been great talking to you but I haven't had anything to eat since a sandwich at lunchtime.'

'Oh sorry, Mum, you must be ravenous. Are you busy at the weekend?'

'Not so far as I know.'

'Could I pop down on Saturday and stay till Sunday?'

'Sure, that'd be great. See you then.'

When they reported for duty the following morning, Sukey and Vicky were greeted by a glum-looking DS Rathbone with the news that the surveillance team, put together at short notice and with some difficulty to observe fourteen Tyndale Gardens, reported that there had been no sign whatsoever of suspicious activity.

'Either the villains have been scared off or somehow they've found out Mayhew's dead,' he said morosely. 'I moved heaven and earth to get that team set up at short notice and they've had a wasted weekend – my name'll be mud in certain quarters.'

In the hope of lightening his mood, Sukey took the opportunity of telling him about her conversation with Fergus, but his reaction was dismissive.

'Sukey, you're like a dog with a bone,' he said. 'Just drop it, will you?'

'But surely it's worth at least a quick check of the Oriental Garden employees,' she pleaded. 'It wouldn't take long. After all, we haven't got that many leads.'

'Don't remind me. All right, I'll mention it to the SIO,' he said grudgingly.

'And what about this stuff about a computer programme to analyse behavioural patterns? Have you heard anything about it?'

He shook his head. 'Can't say I have. It might be interesting – get your son to let you have a copy of the article and I'll show it to the SIO as well.'

'Will do, Sarge.' At least he hadn't brushed that one aside.

'By the way,' he said, 'we've just had an opinion from our tidal expert about the most likely area where the bits of Annie O were dumped. For various reasons he doesn't agree with Ken Lowe's "guesstimate". Basing his calculations on the estimated time the killing took place and the movement of the tides that night, he thinks the most likely scenario is that the killer had access to a motor boat moored somewhere round Portishead – possibly in the marina – although it's difficult to judge how far out he went or in what direction. It's obvious that the bits would have been moved up and downstream by successive tides before they were finally washed ashore – it was pure chance that the head ended up at Clevedon in such a short time.'

'So what's the next move, Sarge?'

'House to house enquiries among the residents near the marina, for a start,' he said resignedly. 'Some of them are only week-enders, so it's going to take time.'

'Do you want us to make a start this morning?'

'No, we'll get uniformed on to that. We're sweeping Mayhew's house today and I want you and Vicky to go along and see what they come up with.'

'OK, Sarge. What time are they starting?'

'In half an hour, so get moving.'

On the way to Tyndale Gardens Sukey told Vicky about the 'death' character found on the arm of another dismembered victim. 'DS Rathbone wouldn't even consider checking with the personnel at the Oriental Garden,' she complained.

Vicky chuckled. 'I'm not surprised – you really have got a bee in your bonnet over the Chinese connection. I'm beginning to wonder if you're planning to write a crime novel featuring a wicked character like Doctor Fu Manchu.'

'Oh, why can't anyone take me seriously,' said Sukey in mock despair. 'I've a good mind to do a bit of private snooping on my own. It'd serve him right if I came back with a red hot lead!'

'So what have you got in mind? Go marching into the take-away and demand that everyone show you their tattoos?' Vicky taunted. 'Just the staff, or would you ask any oriental-looking customers to roll up their sleeves? You'll be thrown out on the spot – or worse, the manager might call the police and complain a member of the public is causing a disturbance. How will you talk yourself out of that one?'

'I'll have to think about it.' Privately, Sukey had already begun considering such a course of action, but she kept her thoughts to herself for the time being. Meanwhile, they had arrived at Tyndale Gardens, where the dog handlers were about to start their sweep at number fourteen.

SEVENTEEN

'There are Toby's parents.' Vicky nodded in the direction of a dark blue car parked inconspicuously in one of the spaces at the far end of Tyndale Gardens. The two DCs went over to greet them.

'Oh, I'm so glad you're here,' said Mrs Mayhew. 'It's going to be an ordeal for us and it's such a relief that someone we know is going to search Toby's house.'

'It doesn't work quite like that,' said Sukey. 'The dog handlers will be going in first; they'll be sweeping the house and grounds for drugs and when they've finished we can go in. We're here initially as observers, like yourselves.'

'Oh dear!' Already Mrs Mayhew was becoming tearful. 'Can't we go in and at least take some of Toby's personal things before they start poking around?'

'I'm afraid not,' Vicky said gently. 'Nothing must be touched until the police give permission.'

'Fair enough,' said Joe Mayhew. He stared at the house with a puzzled frown on his face. 'Where the hell did he get the money to put down on a house?' he muttered.

'Why didn't he tell us?' wailed his wife. 'Why didn't he invite us to visit him? And isn't it our house now anyway? As Toby's next of kin . . .'

'In the circumstances you have the right to be present during the search in place of your son,' said Sukey, 'but as we've already explained, unless he left a will leaving the property to you and your husband, the question of ownership will be decided by the court.'

'She's right, Millie,' her husband said gruffly as she opened her mouth to protest. 'We just have to be patient. He put an arm round her and she hid her face against his shoulder. 'How long will the search take?'

'Probably all morning,' said Vicky. 'What happens will depend on what – if anything – of interest is found, but in any case we suggest you just stand and watch while the officers are working.'

'In other words, shut up and keep out of their way,' said Mayhew.

'That's about it, yes,' Vicky agreed, 'and I should warn you that if you say anything during the search it may be recorded by the officers.'

'Suppose they find something and ask us questions?' said Mrs Mayhew anxiously.

'They won't,' Sukey assured her. 'If as a result of the search we want to interview you, we'll do it later. You don't have to be present if you think it will upset you.'

Mrs Mayhew was still on the verge of tears, but she shook her head. 'I want to stay the whole time,' she said firmly. 'And besides, I want to see where my son's been living since we last saw him.' She dried her eyes and, clinging to her husband's arm, resolutely followed the two detectives.

Sukey explained the situation to the sergeant in charge of the team. He nodded and beckoned to the Mayhews. 'I'm Sergeant Stafford and I'm in charge of this operation,' he informed them. 'We shall sweep every room in the house in turn; if the dog finds anything suspicious in one room my team will record the find while the handler moves on to the next. You are free to observe the entire operation provided you touch nothing and do not interfere in any way with the officers or the dog.'

'We'll do exactly as you say, Sergeant,' Mayhew assured him. Sukey handed over the keys that had been taken from Toby's pocket after the accident; Sergeant Stafford selected one and opened the door. He stood aside to admit three uniformed officers, one leading a black and white dog. 'I must ask you to remain outside until we've finished with the hall,' he said.

Mrs Mayhew put her hands to her face. It was clear that she was finding the whole situation extremely stressful. 'Oh, I don't know,' she began. 'I hadn't realized . . . I mean, I'm not sure I want to watch strangers going through Toby's things.' Her eyes were full of tears as she looked up at her husband. 'What shall we do, Joe?'

'We might as well see it out,' he said.

'All right, if you say so.'

Sergeant Stafford had left the front door ajar and the four of them stood outside watching as the handler released the dog from its leash. It ran the length of the narrow, carpeted hallway and back, sniffing the floor from side to side and briefly paying attention to a heap of mail lying on a mat just inside the door, pushing the items aside with its muzzle but showing no evidence of excitement. The handler opened a cupboard under the stairs and the dog disappeared for several minutes; when it emerged it was plain it had found nothing of interest in there either.

'All clear so far, Sarge,' said the handler. 'Where next?'

'In here.' Stafford opened the door to the front room, at the same time beckoning to the Mayhews. 'As you can see, we've found nothing suspicious up to now. You may come in, but please remain in the hall for the time being.'

A little hesitantly, Toby Mayhew's parents stepped across the threshold. The mother bent down and reached for the pile of mail, but Sukey put a hand on her arm.

'Please leave those where they are,' she said sharply.

Mrs Mayhew straightened up and stepped back in alarm as if the scattered heap had suddenly become red-hot. 'But there may be something there that would help us,' she said timidly.

'Millie, Sergeant Stafford told us not to touch anything,' her husband reminded her. There was an edge to his voice; Sukey sensed that his patience was being considerably tested.

'I'm sorry,' his wife faltered. She turned and took a step towards the open door and peered into the front room. She put a hand to her mouth and whispered brokenly, 'At least he had some nice furniture. It's a relief to know that our poor boy could still live in some comfort, isn't it Joe, but . . . oh, Toby, you didn't have to be alone. Why did you have to shut us out?' This time she broke down and wept uncontrollably; with a word of apology her husband, also visibly moved, led her away.

'Poor things,' said Vicky. 'This must be even worse for them than the PM. Maybe they should wait in their car. Shall I go with them?'

'If you like,' said Sukey, 'I'll stay here.' She watched as the dog and its handler carried out a sweep of the room while Sergeant Stafford and two other uniformed officers stood by to record possible finds. It was the first time she had witnessed the procedure and was fascinated by the way the dog ran hither and thither, exploring every nook and cranny that could possibly conceal a stash of drugs.

'Sooty's a top performer,' one of the officers, a woman constable, informed her with some pride. 'He won an award recently for nosing out the largest quantity of heroin in a month.'

'Let's hope he chalks up a success here,' Sukey commented. 'DS Rathbone and the SIO are getting pretty tetchy about the lack of progress on all fronts at present. It would cheer them up no end to have a good fat lead in at least one case.'

'Well, it doesn't look all that promising so far,' said the officer with a shrug of her shoulders as the team finally emerged from the sitting room.

'Try upstairs next,' said Sergeant Stafford.

Halfway up the staircase the dog at last began to show signs of excitement, but it wasn't until they reached the upper landing and entered the front bedroom that he began, as his handler put it, 'to go bananas'.

'Quite a substantial stash, Sarge,' said Sukey when she and Vicky reported back after the search of Toby Mayhew's house. 'A sizeable quantity of amphetamines and class A drugs according to Sergeant Stafford – subject to weighing and analysis of course – plus the usual paraphernalia for cutting and wrapping.'

'They also turned up cash amounting to several thousand at a rough estimate,' added Vicky. 'Sergeant Stafford reckoned that if he was dealing he was most likely collecting cash so he got the handler to bring in a second dog specially trained to sniff out money.'

'All in all quite a fruitful exercise,' said Rathbone. 'How did Mayhew's parents react when you told them?'

'They already knew their son was a user of drugs but they were very upset at the revelation that he'd been a dealer,' said Sukey. 'After the dog handling team left we invited them back into the house while we did our search, but they couldn't face it and went home.'

'Did you find anything useful?'

'Not really,' said Vicky. 'He had a bank account – we already knew that because he had the card in his wallet – but he hardly

ever used it. We found an unused paying-in book and the last
cheques he wrote were dated around the time he moved into the
house.'

'How much money is there in the account?'

'Just a few hundred. We found receipts for water and elec-
tricity charges so presumably he used cash from his dealings to
pay them, as well as his other shopping. We found food in the
fridge – most of it well past its sell-by date – and a reasonable
stock of groceries suggesting he lived to a reasonable standard.'

'What about booze?'

'No spirits, just a few bottles of wine.'

'What about the stuff pushed through the letterbox?'

'Nothing of any significance – a freebie newspaper and junk
mail.'

'Hmm.' Rathbone thought for a moment before saying, 'So
Mayhew was definitely a dealer and almost certainly a user –
although we have to wait for forensics to confirm that – and the
kids Mrs Scott had noticed talking to him over the garden wall
were probably his runners. Well, it confirms our suspicions but
it doesn't help much in our search for other members of Chesney's
mob. And it doesn't tell us what the thug who was hanging
around outside his house was after, or why he's given up since
Dobbie tackled him.'

'Maybe Toby owed Chesney but saw no need to pay his debts
after Chesney got busted,' Sukey suggested.

'And another member of the mob took a chance on Chesney
being sent down for a long stretch and decided to take over his
territory, but wasn't familiar with Toby's movements,' said Vicky.

'Or was detailed to collect on Chesney's behalf while he's
waiting for his case to come up,' Sukey continued.

'All reasonable possibilities,' Rathbone agreed. 'So tell me
why he didn't just break in and search for the cash himself.'

'If he's working on his own account, it might be because apart
from calling in the debt he reckoned Toby could still be useful
to him in the same way as he was to Chesney?' Vicky suggested.

'That still doesn't explain why he's called off the search.'

'Perhaps he's figured that with Chesney banged up on remand,
Toby reckons he's off the hook for the time being and has gone
off on a jolly somewhere,' Vicky persisted. 'My guess is he's

planning to come back in a few days. I can't imagine anyone in that line of business willingly giving up on an outstanding debt.'

'Unless,' said Sukey with a flash of inspiration, 'he's found out Toby's dead.'

'In that case he would have broken in to collect whatever Toby had in the house in the way of cash and drugs,' said Rathbone.

'Maybe he somehow found out we have the house under surveillance and has decided to write it off as a bad debt,' said Sukey. 'It must happen sometimes.'

Rathbone frowned. 'It's possible, I suppose, although the press have respected our request not to release Mayhew's name and there was hardly anyone at the inquest except you two and his parents.'

'But supposing,' Sukey went on, 'some member of the press has a link with the gang and passed the message on? There was at least one reporter at the inquest – I recognized him, he's on the staff of the *Evening Echo* and I happen to know him a little because his father's a neighbour of mine. Suppose I ask him how many people in his office know Toby Mayhew was the subject of that inquest. He's sure to have told his editor, of course, as it would be his decision not to publish Toby's name, not Harry's. Suppose one of his colleagues is a user and Toby was his supplier . . . or he might have mentioned it to his supplier who's also one of Chesney's men. It's worth considering, don't you think, Sarge?'

'I agree the fact that Toby's name wasn't published, doesn't necessarily mean it wasn't revealed to someone else who might be interested,' he said. He thought for a moment. 'It wouldn't do any harm, and we seem to be scraping the barrel for leads at the moment, so all right, see what your friend's got to say.' He turned to Vicky. 'You spent some time with Mayhew's parents while the sweep was going on, didn't you? Did they have anything to say that might help us trace his other contacts?'

'Not a great deal,' said Vicky. 'His dad said he'd offered to give him a mobile phone so they could keep in touch, but he said he already had one but wouldn't reveal the number. He said he never used the phone anyway except to order takeaways and it was switched off the rest of the time. Mr Mayhew mentioned that his son was in what he called a funny mood that day and he thought that was when they first began to suspect him of being on drugs.'

'Did they say when this happened?'

'They couldn't remember offhand, but Mrs Mayhew keeps a diary and she's going to check. She promised to let me know.'

'Now that could be helpful.' Rathbone's mood appeared to lighten a fraction. 'All right, you talk to your reporter friend, Sukey. Vicky, you follow up with the Mayhews. Ask Mrs M if you can have a look at her diary – better still, ask her to lend it to us so we can go through it with a toothcomb. With luck it could reveal something even more interesting. At least, I can tell the SIO that we aren't sitting on our hands.'

'Any idea as to how you tackle your friendly news hound?' asked Vicky as she and Sukey were clearing their desks to go home.

'I'll have to think about it,' Sukey replied.

But as it happened, the solution to the problem presented itself very shortly.

EIGHTEEN

During the drive home, Sukey turned over in her mind various ways of broaching the subject of Toby Mayhew's death with Harry Matthews, the son of her neighbour Major Matthews. She had met him only once, at a drinks party a few weeks ago; the majority of the guests were in the upper rather than the lower age bracket and he had held her in conversation for some time before his father bore down on him and carried him away to meet a former comrade in arms. She recalled the look he had given her over his shoulder, half whimsical, half apologetic, as if he regretted the interruption.

He had, she recalled, shown a considerable interest in her work in the CID. 'I might have gone for that as a career instead of journalism,' he told her. 'You and I have a lot in common.'

'We have?'

'We both like asking questions, don't we?'

'You could say that, I suppose, but there's more to detective work than interviewing.'

'You're still asking questions, even when you're not talking to witnesses or grilling suspects,' he pointed out, 'and I'll bet,' he went on after taking a swig from his wine glass, 'you often lie in bed asking yourself what line to take in the latest case of murder and mayhem to hit the headlines.'

She remembered informing him that most of her cases were run-of-the-mill rather than murder and mayhem and that in any event it was her superior officers who decided what line to take in an investigation. As at the time there was no spectacular case to occupy the attention of the local press, the conversation passed on to other topics and they had spent some time chatting about their respective careers to date. After leaving university, where he graduated in English, he had worked for several years in administrative jobs before taking a crash course in journalism and joining the staff of the *Evening Echo* after a spell as a stringer.

'When people asked me what I did for a living I used to say, "Just call me 'Autolycus'!"' he proclaimed, with a dramatic flourish of his by now empty glass before holding it out to be refilled by a passing waiter.

'A "snapper up of unconsidered trifles"?' she responded with a smile. 'Is that what stringers do?'

He raised the recharged glass in acknowledgement. 'More or less – they pick up stories and try and flog 'em to some rag they think will be interested.' He swallowed a mouthful of wine before saying, 'Do I gather you did English Lit too?'

'No, media studies and photography. After uni I joined the police in the uniformed branch, but life got in the way for a few years and I had to resign. I rejoined later as a Scenes of Crime Officer and eventually managed to get fast-tracked into the CID.'

It was at that moment that his father put an end to the conversation. She had a feeling at the time that had they not been interrupted he would have asked how and when 'life had got in the way' and on the whole she was glad he hadn't had the opportunity. The next time she saw him was in the coroner's court. She recalled noticing that he was the only reporter who had attended the inquest on Toby Mayhew.

What you don't want to do, she told herself as she parked her car outside her flat in Clifton, is give him the idea that we want him to do a bit of what he'd no doubt think of as 'investigative journalism'. Jason Dobbie's lucky to be alive after his unplanned intervention; if the thugs who attacked him thought a journalist was on their track they'd make sure he didn't survive to tell the tale. It was going to be tricky.

She went into the kitchen and assembled the ingredients for her evening meal, then went into the sitting room and settled down with a glass of wine to think over the problem. Barely five minutes passed before someone pressed the buzzer to her recently installed entry phone. With a sigh of exasperation she put down her glass and lifted the receiver.

'Hullo,' she said, trying not to sound impatient.

'Matthews here, Matthews senior that is. Sorry to disturb you, Mrs Reynolds; I wonder if you could spare a moment.'

'Good evening, Major,' she said more cordially, 'Yes, of course, do come up.' She pressed the lever to release the lock on the front door and went to greet him as he came puffing up the two flights of stairs.

'Good system that,' he said when he had recovered his breath. 'Saves you running up and downstairs every time someone calls.'

'I bought this flat because of the view from the roof terrace,' she said, 'but there are times when I wish I didn't have to climb two flights of stairs to reach my living quarters.'

'Especially when you've got something heavy to carry,' he agreed.

'Do sit down.' She indicated a chair and he waited while she returned to her own before sitting down. She held up her glass. 'Would you like a snifter?'

He looked startled – 'almost shocked' as she later confided to Fergus, 'as if he didn't think it was quite the proper thing to do.' After a moment's hesitation he accepted the glass of Merlot she handed him and took a couple of mouthfuls before putting it down carefully on the small table she placed at his elbow.

'Not sure if I ought to be doing this,' he began. 'I mean, it's usually the police doing the interviewing, isn't it, not the other way around?'

'That depends on what you want to talk about,' she replied, 'but it's only fair to tell you that I can't give you any information that hasn't been officially released.'

He nodded. 'Quite so.' There was a short silence; then he said, 'It's about young Harry.'

Her first thought was that his son had fallen foul of the law and he was seeking her advice or even asking her to put in a good word for him. That would be out of the question, of course – after all she had met Harry only once – and she was mentally rehearsing the most diplomatic way of responding when he spoke again. 'Part of his job is attending the courts and writing reports for the *Echo*,' he began. 'Last Friday he attended two inquests; one on that dreadful case of a woman's dismembered body being washed up on the coast and the other of a man killed in a car crash. You probably know the cases I'm talking about.' Sukey nodded. 'Harry doesn't often talk about his work for the *Echo*,' he went on, 'he says if I'm interested I can read it in the paper, but for some reason he seemed particularly keen to talk about these two cases. You know the details of course – Harry said he saw you in court so it's obvious you're on them. And I know,' he hurried on as if anticipating a negative response from her, 'there's a news blackout on both cases so I'm not trying to pump you.'

'It isn't exactly a news blackout,' said Sukey. 'In the case of the dismembered woman, she hasn't yet been identified and as you know we're still making extensive enquiries. In fact, an artist's impression of her was released to the press yesterday – you may have seen it.' The major nodded. 'As far as the other case is concerned,' Sukey went on, 'the coroner asked them not to release the name of the victim because our enquiries are not yet complete there either.'

'Yes, we understand that, and as far as I'm aware the request has been respected – certainly as far as the *Echo* is concerned,' said the major. 'In any event there doesn't seem to have been much interest in that one – Harry said he and a woman from the *Gloucester Gazette* were the only two reporters who bothered to attend the inquest on young Mayhew. The dismembered woman story had much more of what they're pleased to call "public interest",' he added with a contemptuous sniff.

Sukey fiddled with the stem of her wine glass for a few moments before saying, 'Major Matthews, you've told me nothing so far that I don't know already, and you've assured me you aren't after further details of these cases, so what exactly is on your mind? It's pretty obvious that something's bothering you, so please tell me what it is.' *Otherwise finish your drink and go home so that I can finish mine in peace and have my supper* was the unspoken rider to her remarks.

'Yes, yes, I apologize for beating about the bush,' he said hastily, 'the fact is, young Harry's got some bee in his bonnet about Mayhew's death. He thinks there's something suspicious about it.'

'Whatever gave him that idea?' Sukey asked.

'He was in the khazi at the office, that is, er, sitting in one of the compartments, don't y'know.' The major looked at his feet as if he found this part of his story somewhat embarrassing. 'He heard someone come in, thought nothing of it until he heard this person – he assumes it was one of his colleagues but he isn't sure which one – talking on his mobile. He heard this chap say, "Delta? We've got a problem" and then, "Hermes is dead. Thought you should know right away". And then after a few seconds he said, "Will do. Cheers". And then Harry thinks the chap had a . . . well, anyway, he heard him washing his hands after a few moments before he went out again.'

'So what did Harry do?' Sukey asked.

'He stayed where he was for a moment or two longer and then went to the coffee machine before going back to his desk.'

'Because he didn't want this chap to twig someone had overheard his conversation?' Sukey suggested.

'Right. The thing is –' the Major leaned forward and lowered his voice as if he was suddenly afraid that they too were likely to be overheard – 'Harry's got a hunch that when this chap mentioned someone he called "Hermes" he was actually referring to Tobias Mayhew.'

'Why would he think that?'

'He says this conversation took place a short time after he got back from the inquest on Mayhew. He went and spoke to the editor and told him of the police request not to include his name in his report. The editor agreed, of course – you've probably noticed there was no mention in the *Echo* – but there were other people in the office at the time and some of them must have heard Harry talking to him.'

'You're saying Harry believes the person who made that phone call was passing on to someone else information the police didn't want made public?' said Sukey. The major nodded. 'Does Harry have any reason, other than this phone call that might or might not have been referring to Mayhew, to suspect him of being involved in something criminal?'

'Not really. He says it's just a hunch. He often has those and they've got him into scrapes more than once.'

As someone prone to hunches herself, Sukey was beginning to feel some sympathy with Harry Matthews. However, she was careful to sound matter of fact as she asked, 'I take it Harry didn't recognize the voice of the person who made the phone call?' The major shook his head. 'So what is he proposing to do about it?'

'He says he's been doing a bit of "ferreting around" as he calls it. I've told him that's a job for the police and he shouldn't meddle with it, but he says investigative journalism is perfectly legitimate as long as you don't tamper with evidence or withhold information from the police. And that's not all. He suspects a connection between Mayhew and the case of the dismembered woman.'

Up to this point Sukey, although interested in what the major had to say, had been inclined to take Harry's interpretation of the phone call with some reservations. Now, she sat up with a jerk, almost spilling her wine. 'What in the world . . . ?' she began and the major waved his free hand in a gesture that was almost apologetic.

'For a start, he says it's too much of a coincidence that the two inquests should be held on the same day. Mrs Reynolds –' he leaned forward and looked at her with an earnest expression – 'he's been in one or two scrapes in the past for poking his nose into what he's called "dodgy deals", and to put it frankly, I'm concerned for his safety.'

'That means you believe he's on the track of something big?' she said slowly.

'Yes, and I want him to drop the idea. When I asked him if he'd learned anything useful from his "ferreting around" all he would say was, "watch this space". All right, I admit I'm a bit of an old woman where Harry's concerned. He's all I've got since his mother died. I've never tried to cosset him or be overprotective – rather the contrary – but I've got a bad feeling about this.'

Sukey gave a sympathetic nod. 'You've got a hunch as well?'

'You could call it that, and that's why I'm here. Will you have a word with him, try and talk him out of it? Don't say I've spoken to you, of course,' he hurried on. 'I was wondering if you could say something on the lines of . . . the police think someone in the office might have revealed Mayhew's name to some unauthorized person and, well, ask if he's got any idea who it might be, something like that, and impress on him that if he has any information it's his duty to tell the police.'

'I could certainly do that,' said Sukey. She resisted the impulse to tell him she already intended, with her sergeant's approval, to do exactly what the major asked.

'Splendid! Well, I mustn't keep you, thank you for listening.' The final words came out in a rush and the major drained his glass, put it down and leapt to his feet as if he had a train to catch. At the door he said, 'Harry's at home this evening, if you'd care to give him a call.'

'I'll think about it,' she said.

NINETEEN

'Nice try, but I don't think so,' Sukey said aloud as she closed the door behind Major Matthews. From their short acquaintance she had already judged the son to be considerably more sharp-witted than the father and she had a shrewd idea that if she were to call Harry a matter of an hour or so after his father returned home – doubtless without revealing where he had been – it would appear more than a coincidence. So she finished her supper and ate it on a tray in front of the television while watching her favourite quiz programme before picking up her notebook and jotting down a few ideas for an approach to Harry Matthews.

The next morning she reported her conversation with Major Matthews to DS Rathbone, who seized on it like a drowning man clutching at a lifebelt. 'This may be the breakthrough we need to help us track down the rest of Warren Chesney's mob!' he said. 'I'll tell the SIO.' He grabbed the telephone, spoke a few words, listened intently for a couple of minutes before saying, 'Yes, sir, I'll make sure she understands that.' He put the phone down and turned back to Sukey. 'Get young Matthews on his own away from the office to make sure there's absolutely no chance of being overheard. Get what you can out of him and remind him of the consequences of withholding information – and at the same time discourage him from doing any more "ferreting around", as he calls it. Tell him that apart from putting himself in danger he could interfere with our own ongoing enquiries. No need to let on that they seem to have run into the sand,' he added wryly.

'Right, Sarge.' Sukey went back to her desk, called the office of the *Evening Echo* and asked to speak to Harry Matthews. 'Mr Matthews,' she began, 'I believe you attended the two inquests held in St Andrew's church hall last Friday?'

'That's right,' he said. 'Who's speaking?'

'Before I go any further I want to ask you to treat this call as completely confidential and not reveal who is making it to anyone,' Sukey continued. As she spoke, she pictured him at the other end; intrigued, a little wary perhaps but, sensing an exclusive story or possibly a fresh piece of information from someone he had spoken to in the course of his 'ferreting around', he would probably give a sharp glance around the office to see if anyone was within earshot or paying any particular attention to him.

'Understood,' he said after a brief pause. 'Go ahead.'

'This is DC Reynolds of the Avon and Somerset CID. Do you know Stacey's Café in Corn Street?'

'Yes.'

'Can you meet me there in about half an hour?'

She pictured him glancing at his watch before saying, 'Sure.'

'Good. See you then.' He's a real pro, she thought as she put down the phone. He had asked no questions and no one would have guessed from his neutral tone that he attached any importance to the call.

The café was half full when she arrived; most of the customers were women and from the bulging shopping bags on the floor by their feet she guessed that they had been shopping in the nearby Nicholas Market. It was an ideal environment for a private conversation since it was unlikely that anything she and Harry said would be heard above their chatter. He was already there, sitting at a corner table holding a large mug of coffee in both hands while apparently engrossed in the early edition of the *Echo,* which was spread out in front of him. As she approached he stood up to greet her with a smile of welcome.

'Sukey! I had a feeling I was talking to you; the voice was familiar although I couldn't be sure I'd remembered your surname. We met at the Gaddens's drinks party, didn't we? Do sit down and I'll get you a coffee.'

'Thanks.'

He went to the counter, bought the coffee and returned to the table. 'So,' he said. 'You want to talk about one of the inquests I attended recently? Would that be,' at this point he lowered his voice, 'the one on Tobias Mayhew, aka "he who must not be named", by any chance?'

'Got it in one,' she said with a nod of approval, 'and as you know, the circumstances surrounding his death are still under investigation, which is why the press were asked to withhold his name from their reports.'

Harry nodded. 'I can assure you the *Echo* has complied with the request,' he said. 'If there's anything we can do to help your enquiries, I'm sure everyone here will be more than willing to help. But why the cloak and dagger stuff?' Sukey was conscious of a searching glance from a pair of keen greyish blue eyes. 'Why not suggest we have this conversation over the phone, or in our office?'

'There are two reasons why we asked the press to withhold the name of the RTA victim,' Sukey replied. 'One is that we have evidence connecting the victim with a known drugs supplier and we are still looking for other members of his mob.'

'I guessed that was the case,' said Harry, his eyes twinkling at Sukey over the rim of his coffee mug, 'but that doesn't account for your wanting to talk to me sub rosa.'

'You're right, it doesn't,' she agreed.

'So what's the second reason?'

'We suspect that at least one member of the gang who, not knowing of Mayhew's death, has been trying to contact him in connection with some criminal activity, possibly connected with drugs. However, the fact is that despite the press co-operation we have reason to believe that the person who has been trying to contact him has found out that he's dead. And we're very keen to lay hands on that person.' Harry made no comment but she could almost hear his synapses clicking away. 'That's why I'm asking for your help. Is it possible that someone in the *Echo* office has passed on the information?'

'In other words,' said Harry as she sipped her coffee while waiting for his reply, 'you think one of our staff has connections with the underworld?' When she did not reply for a moment he added mischievously, 'How do you know I'm not the guilty party?'

'Let's just say I know your background and I believe you have inherited your father's integrity,' she replied.

'You haven't been talking to my dad by any chance?' he said.

The unexpectedness of the question caught Sukey off guard. A mouthful of coffee went the wrong way and it took her a minute or two, with the aid of a glass of water that Harry hastily

obtained from the woman behind the bar, to recover her breath.
'Sorry about that,' she said when she was able to speak, 'what
were you saying?'

'I asked if you'd been speaking to my dad,' he said simply,
'and before you start prevaricating, he came home yesterday
evening after "just popping out for half an hour" as he put it,
and when I asked him where he'd been he said something vague
about "having a chat with a neighbour" and "nothing of any
significance". So,' he continued as she remained silent, 'was it
you, and did he tell you stuff about my interest in the death of
the man we're talking about?'

There seemed little point in denial; he was obviously far too
shrewd to be deceived. 'As it happens he did come and see me,'
she admitted. 'He's concerned for your safety in the light of
certain things you've told him and he asked me to talk to you.
In fact, he hinted I could catch you at home that evening.'

'Why didn't you?'

'I didn't think I could justify working overtime,' she said flippantly.

'Is that the only reason?'

'No,' she admitted. 'I figured that if I knocked on your door
just after your dad had come home you might smell a rat.'

'Good thinking – but as you see, I've smelt one anyway.'
Harry drained his coffee and put down the empty mug before
adding, 'So that's the reason for this meeting – to warn me off
in case I tread on police toes or beat you to it in hunting down
the master crook?'

'On the contrary, the reason I asked you to meet me is that
after a discussion with my sergeant yesterday he agreed that I
ask you about the possibility of a leak from the *Echo* office. It
was pure coincidence that your father came to see me shortly
after I got home.'

'So you aren't here because of what he told you?'

'No, but he told me enough to make us want to know exactly
what you're up to. He said you've been ferreting around, and
I'm sure you don't need reminding that if you've uncovered
anything significant it's your duty to tell us – and an offence if
you fail to do so.'

To Sukey's discomfiture he burst out laughing. 'If you could only see yourself with your official face on!' he chuckled. 'Don't worry, I know the score and if I'd come up with one significant new piece of evidence I'd have passed it on straight away. You know, of course, about the phone conversation I overheard?'

'Yes, your father told me. He said you have no idea who was making it.'

'None whatever.'

'Then what makes you think the reference to "Hermes" had anything to do with Mayhew's death?'

'Have you ever heard of anyone whose real name is Hermes?'

Sukey shook her heard. 'I can't say I have.'

'I'm sure you know enough about classical mythology to know that Hermes was the Greek messenger of the gods. Supposing –' although there was no one within earshot, Harry leaned forward and lowered his voice – 'Tobias Mayhew, alias Hermes, was so-called because he was a kind of go-between, carrying messages of some kind on behalf of Delta, whoever he might be. And another thing; I believe there's a connection between his death and the disappearance of a prostitute living above a hairdressing salon in Bradley Stoke – a disappearance that seems to have aroused an unusual amount of police interest. All right, I know it sounds far-fetched, wildly improbable even,' he went on, evidently noticing the change in her expression and mistaking it for a mixture of astonishment and scepticism, 'but stranger things do happen, especially in the underworld.'

'I'm sure they do,' she murmured. Her thoughts were racing, but the last thing she intended at this stage was to let him know how close he had come to her own hunch that, despite having been brushed aside by both DS Rathbone and DCI Leach, had been fretting away in the back of her mind. 'Do you have any evidence to support this theory?'

'Not so far,' he admitted, 'not evidence, just a string of co-incidences – bits and pieces I picked up from neighbours. Nothing they haven't already mentioned to the police.'

'How can you be sure of that?' Sukey said sharply.

'They all said so,' he said simply.

'Isn't that a bit naive? They may think they have, but it's possible something slipped out that we don't know about. I take it you've been making notes of everything you've been told?'

'Of course.' He pulled a notebook from his pocket and put it on the table. 'You're welcome to read them – if you know shorthand.'

'I do, as is happens,' she said, a little smugly. She scanned the neatly written pages and realized that the information they contained added nothing of any substance to what the police already knew. 'You'd have made a good detective,' she said as she handed the notebook back to him and he acknowledged the compliment with a sly wink. 'All right, I believe you, but there isn't enough here to suggest a connection between Mayhew's death and Connie Gilbert's disappearance.'

'Let's just say that we of the fourth estate have very sensitive antennae and they often lead us in unexpected directions.' His grin was deliberately provocative and she couldn't help smiling back at him.

'In other words, you've got a hunch – no more than that.'

'If you want to put it that way.'

'All right.' Not for the world was she going to admit that her own antennae, as he put it, had been leading her in the same direction. While she was reading his notes a question had popped into her head. 'I presume you have your colleagues' mobile numbers?'

'Sure. Why?'

'Would you let us have a note of them – or at least, the ones who were in the office the day you heard that call being made?'

Harry hesitated. 'I'll have to think about it,' he said after some moments' thought.

'All right.' She took out one of her cards and gave it to him. 'Call me on this number and let me know what you decide.' He nodded, took the card without comment and put it in his pocket. 'Just be careful, that's all – and if you do find anything significant, please call us right away and leave it to us to follow up. If you're right about Tobias Mayhew being "Hermes", it could mean he was involved with some very dangerous and ruthless people.'

TWENTY

B ack at headquarters, Sukey settled down to write her report. She had just finished when Vicky returned from her visit to Toby Mayhew's parents.

'I thought I was never going to get away!' she exclaimed as she sat down at her desk next to Sukey's. 'They seemed to think of me as some kind of FLO – it's done wonders for my counselling skills.'

'I guess they were really glad to have the chance to get some of their grieving out into the open,' Sukey said. 'It must be a strain to have to bottle it up.'

'It's not only the grieving,' said Vicky. 'What troubles them even more is that they feel a strong sense of guilt; they blame themselves for not having done more to help Toby although from what they told me they were up against a typical case of addiction. I tried to explain how it could cause personality change and the destructive effect it could have on relationships and I think that gave them some degree of comfort, although they're still hurting badly. And all the time they were talking,' she went on reflectively, 'I kept thinking of what he told Colonel Driver about the hard time his parents – particularly his father – had given him. If they knew the way he'd bad-mouthed them when they'd been so caring and supportive it would just about break their hearts.'

'Thank the Lord they don't,' Sukey said fervently. 'So I gather they weren't able to add much to what we already know?'

'That's not quite true. He stayed with them for a while after coming out of prison because before the bust-up he and his wife had been living in service accommodation and of course he'd been booted out of that so he had nowhere else to go. He found it difficult to get a job, so they suggested he might do some voluntary work dishing out what his father called "soup and sympathy" to dropouts. They hoped it would help him regain some of his self-respect, which had taken a bit of a hammering, but instead they have an idea it was at the centre that he came into contact with junkies and started experimenting with drugs.'

'That's what some philosopher called "the irony of Fate",' Sukey commented sadly. 'I suppose the fact that it was their idea made them feel even more guilty?'

'Exactly. At first all seemed to go well, but after a while they noticed a change in Toby's behaviour; he became subject to mood swings and it was then his father suspected he was on drugs. He tackled him about it and there was a hell of a row, after which he became more and more withdrawn. Then one day he didn't come home and from then on he simply dropped out of their lives. They tried everything they could to find him, even contacted his ex-wife, but she couldn't help so they were left in limbo. The diary entries suggest this was shortly before the time when he moved into the house in Tyndale Gardens.'

'Any other clues?'

'There's a reference to some new clothes he'd bought – quite expensive ones. They assumed he'd at last got a job, but when they questioned him about it he flew into a rage, said it was none of their business and stormed out of the house. There might well have been more useful references in the diary but Mrs M was getting agitated by then so it seemed a good time to leave.'

'No chance of borrowing it for further study?'

'That's what I really needed, but when I suggested it she clung to it like a child clutching a comforter. It's as if she feels it's her only link to her son.'

'Poor soul,' said Sukey. As a mother herself, she had some inkling of what the woman was suffering.

'How did you get on with your journo friend?' asked Vicky.

'I'm just about to print off my report. Want to have a read?' Sukey moved aside so that her colleague could read her computer screen.

Vicky scrolled back to the beginning and scanned the text without speaking for several minutes. When she came to the end she said, 'Two things in that have hit me.'

'And they are?'

'This reference to Delta – Mrs Mayhew wrote in her diary that Toby mentioned someone he called "Delta" not long before he disappeared. They can't recall the context but they thought it was about something he had to do or someone he had to see. She said he seemed uneasy about it – frightened almost – but he refused to answer any questions.'

'And the person Harry heard making that phone call was speaking to someone he addressed as Delta,' said Sukey. 'It looks as if Harry could be right in thinking "Hermes" was a code name for Toby Mayhew. Do you suppose the envelope he handed over to that chap in the car park contained a message either to or from Delta?'

Vicky frowned. 'It was hardly a message – just a few odds and ends with no particular relation to each other.'

'Maybe some sort of code?' Sukey suggested.

'Could be, I suppose,' said Vicky. 'Or maybe Delta has a senti- mental streak and was sending some family mementoes to his old nanny?' she added flippantly. 'Still, it doesn't alter the fact that between us we've come across a possible link between Toby's shady contacts and someone on the staff of the *Echo*.'

'By the way,' said Sukey, 'you said two things struck you. What's the second?'

'Only that you and Harry seem to have got on particularly well,' said Vicky with an impish grin, 'even down to sharing a hunch.'

'I thought you'd have something to say about that,' Sukey retorted. 'You'll laugh on the other side of your face if we're proved right.'

'Time will tell.' Vicky hung up her jacket, sat down at her desk and switched on her computer. 'I'll bash out my report and then we'd better grab some lunch.'

After a canteen lunch they joined DS Rathbone in DCI Leach's office.

'I've been reading through this summary you've prepared for me, Greg,' Leach began. 'Apart from having established that the dismembered woman is the prostitute known as Connie Gilbert and that Tobias Mayhew was an associate of Warren Chesney, the only concrete pieces of evidence we have are the blood- stained underclothes and the bits of Connie's body, beginning with the head and eventually the torso and limbs. There's a vague possibility that the person who attacked Jason Dobbie outside

Mayhew's house is the man seen entering Connie's flat shortly before her head was washed up on Clevedon beach, with vague being the operative word.'

'That's about the size of it, sir,' Rathbone replied.

'And I note that the DNA on the cigarette butts found at the end of Mayhew's garden is a match for his, but the one picked up under the front room window is different, so it's possible that was dropped by Dobbie's attacker.'

'That's right, sir, and I've just learned there's no match with any sample on our records.'

'I suppose that was too much to hope for.' With an air of resignation, Leach put Rathbone's report aside. 'Now, Sukey and Vicky, according to your reports there's a possible link between young Mayhew and an unknown member of the staff of the *Echo*. Any further thoughts on that, either of you?'

'We don't know when Toby's association with Delta began, sir,' said Vicky, 'but it definitely dates from before he moved to Tyndale Gardens, just over two years ago.'

Leach made a note. 'We need to know more precisely when his parents first noted the change in his behaviour, get the name and address of the soup kitchen and find out if any of the regulars or their hangers-on around the time he was there are known to the drugs squad. Now, let's hear from you, Sukey.'

'Well, sir, if we accept the theory that "Hermes" is a code name for Toby Mayhew, then the obvious conclusion is that he and the mystery caller both had links with Delta.'

'It's a big "if",' Leach said doubtfully, 'but in those circumstances, yes that would seem to follow. It's a pity Harry didn't recognize the voice. Any other suggestions?'

'Suppose the mystery caller isn't on the staff of the *Echo*?' said Sukey. 'Isn't it possible it was someone who happened to be in the office on some business or other when Harry came back from the post-mortem on Toby and heard him tell the editor of the police request not to publish his name?'

Leach raised an eyebrow. 'There's nothing about this in your report.'

'No, sir, it's only just occurred to me that it might be the reason why Harry didn't recognize the voice.'

'It doesn't explain why it was necessary to pass on the

information immediately, or why he had to make the call from the john instead of out in the street.'

'Unless, sir, time was of the essence?' suggested Rathbone.

'Well, we can't exclude any possibility,' said Leach doubtfully. He thought for a moment and then nodded. 'Have another word with your friend at the *Echo*, Sukey. I see he wasn't all that keen to hand over his colleagues' mobile numbers so, Greg, give some thought about another way of checking them without letting Delta's messenger know of our interest in him.'

'Will do, sir. Is there anything else?'

Leach turned back to an earlier page in the file. 'I recall Sukey suggested a possible link between Mayhew's antics in the car park before the RTA and the attack on Jason Dobbie. She was, as I recall, hinting on the existence of some sinister oriental influence, due also to the fact that one of the numbers on Mayhew's mobile is a Chinese takeaway. Right, Sukey?'

'Yes, sir.'

'You and I discounted it at the time, Greg, although it was noticed that the dismembered corpse of Connie Gilbert, when reassembled, had a slightly oriental appearance. Incidentally, I note the only responses we've had to the artist's impression have been from local people who've seen her around, but nothing from further afield. Someone out there must know her, but either they haven't seen the picture or they've got their own reasons for keeping quiet. I'm beginning to wonder whether what's been happening on our patch is part of a wider picture.' He returned to the latest reports. 'We now have information on another dismembered corpse – not on our patch and not recently – where the victim had a Chinese character tattooed on his wrist. It may be nothing more than a bizarre series of coincidences, but just the same it wouldn't hurt to run a check on the people at the Oriental Garden.'

'If you say so, sir.' Rathbone's tone was far from enthusiastic. 'Will there be anything else?'

'Not for the time being.' Leach closed the file as a sign of dismissal and the three returned to the CID office. 'OK, Sukey,' said Rathbone, 'get back to Harry Matthews and ask him to think back carefully about who was in the office at the time he returned from the inquest on Mayhew.'

'Will do, Sarge.'

'Vicky, you and I will check out the soup kitchen, as the SIO calls it. There can be some dodgy characters hanging around these places so I'm not sending you on your own.'

'What about the Oriental Garden, Sarge?' said Vicky.

'First things first,' Rathbone grunted. He checked the time. 'Get a car and pick me up downstairs in ten minutes.'

'Right, Sarge,' said Vicky. 'What's with all this gallantry, I wonder?' she whispered slyly to Sukey as he marched out of the room.

'You tell me,' Sukey replied with a grin. She was about to call Harry on his mobile when her own began to ring.

'Sukey? Harry Matthews here.'

'Harry! I was about to ring you.'

'What about?'

'You go first.'

'All right; I've got a bit of info for you.'

'What is it?'

'Why don't we meet? Same place as before?'

'I assume you'd rather not talk on the phone.'

'Correct.'

'OK. When?'

'Say in twenty minutes.'

'I'll be there.'

When Sukey entered Stacey's Café she found Harry sitting at the same corner table as before. He jumped to his feet and said, 'Hi! Sit down and have a coffee!'

'Thanks.'

'I've been doing more ferreting around,' he said as he put her coffee in front of her and sat down again.

'Yes?'

'I thought it might be an idea to find out how long Mayhew had been living at fourteen Tyndale Gardens,' he began.

'I could have told you that.'

'But could you have told me who owns the property?'

'We assume it was Toby's. At least, we've no reason to think otherwise.'

'But have you carried out a search?'

'Not so far as I know,' Sukey admitted. 'We do know his parents are wondering where he got the money for a deposit on a house, but some time before he disappeared they noticed he suddenly seemed rather flush and assumed he'd found a job. Harry, what exactly are you getting at?'

'Let's just say that according to the Public Records Office it certainly didn't belong to him although the last time it changed hands was shortly before he moved in. And who do you think owns it now?' Harry put down his cup, took a piece of paper from his pocket, pushed it across the table and sat back to await her reaction.

She gaped in astonishment at the name written on it. 'You're saying Toby was living in a house belonging to a relation of Warren Chesney?'

'Not a relation. When Chesney appeared in court after his arrest he was charged under his real name of William Arthur Robert Chesney. It looks as if he invented Warren from the initials of his three given names.'

'You're joking!'

'It's true.'

'Are you suggesting Chesney could be the mysterious Delta?'

'I'm not going so far as that at the moment, but it's worth considering.'

Sukey shook her head doubtfully. 'He was nicked for running a local network of pushers and suppliers, but it looks as if he's an even bigger fish than we suspected and he's been stashing his ill-gotten gains in property. I wonder how many others he's got tucked away?'

'It's worth looking into, don't you think?' said Harry, evidently well pleased at the effect of his bombshell.

'I'm sure it is; I'll pass it on and many thanks for the tip. Anything else?'

'Isn't it time you told me why you were going to call me?'

'Fair enough; apropos of that phone call you overheard, my superiors would like to know if you're anywhere nearer finding out who was making it.'

'I expected you to say that,' he replied with a grin. 'If you remember, you asked me to let you have my colleagues' mobile numbers.'

'Yes, and you weren't too happy about it.'

'No I wasn't, so I tried to think of some other way I could help you.'

'Any joy?'

'Maybe. I'm pretty good at recognizing voices – accents and so on – but at the time I must have been more interested in what the chap was saying than who was actually speaking. By the time I twigged what he was talking about he'd ended the call.'

'And you've had further thoughts?'

'Just after our last meeting my editor sent me to cover a protest about a proposed site for travellers that was getting a bit lively; while I was on my way I thought back to that call and tried to play it over in my mind, as it were, and the more I thought about it, the more I became convinced that the voice I heard was unfamiliar.'

'And?'

'After I got back I checked who was in the office at the time and I soon felt certain that no member of staff had made that call. By the way, have you read Chesterton's Father Brown stories?'

'Yes, but a long time ago. Why?'

'Do you remember one called "The Invisible Man"?'

Sukey thought for a moment. 'It rings a bell . . . yes, I do remember that one!' she exclaimed excitedly. 'There was a series of murders but people swore no one had entered or left the house where the killings took place . . . and then it turned out they'd all seen the same man going in and coming out at the crucial time, but discounted him because he was . . .'

'The postman!' said Harry triumphantly.

'Just a minute before we get too carried away,' said Sukey. 'Is this chap your regular postie and have you spoken to him?'

He assumed an aggrieved expression. 'What do you take me for? I made a point of passing the time of day with him when he came in with today's delivery and there's no doubt in my mind whatsoever. He's the man who made that call.'

TWENTY-ONE

When Sukey, bursting with excitement, returned to the office she found DS Rathbone hunched over his desk with his eyes fixed on his computer screen. He glanced up as she approached, his expression wooden.

'You're looking mighty pleased with yourself,' he remarked. 'Got something interesting?'

'Yes, Sarge. You'll never guess who . . .'

'Save it till Vicky gets back.'

'Is she still at the soup kitchen?'

'It's called The Cleft Stick and it's closed on Friday afternoons. The only person around was a cleaner who barely understood English so we gave up and went to the Oriental Garden. And guess what – that doesn't open until five o'clock. It was gone four by then so I told Vicky to hang around until the staff turned up while I came back here to catch up with some paperwork.'

'Sounds like you've had a pretty frustrating time,' said Sukey. 'Here comes Vicky now,' she added, glancing across the office.

'Learn anything?' asked Rathbone as Vicky slipped off her jacket and perched on the edge of her desk.

'Yes and no,' she said. 'Two cooks turned up at about half past four and I showed them my ID and asked for a few words. They looked very worried . . . maybe they thought I was going to tell them their work permits had run out or something. Their English was a bit rudimentary but a short time later the owner arrived. His English was OK and I explained we were investigating a case of GBH and there was a chance the assailant had some Chinese characters tattooed on his arm and had he or any of his staff noticed anything like that among their customers. And before you ask, Sarge, both cooks were working in sleeveless vests and Mr Chang, the boss, was wearing a short-sleeved shirt and there was no sign of any tattoos.'

'And had any of them noticed anything significant?'

'The cooks don't have much contact with the customers; they

just prepare the food from orders given to the counter staff or on the phone, pack it up and pass it across a shelf behind the counter, so there wasn't much joy from them. Chang sits at the till and takes the money so he probably gets a closer look at them, but he didn't see anyone with that kind of tattoo.'

'Did any of the staff show any sign of uneasiness?'

'No, Sarge, just mild curiosity.'

'You said "yes and no"; so I suppose you've got some gem up your sleeve?' There was more than a hint of scepticism in Rathbone's tone.

'Not exactly a gem, Sarge, but I remembered what Sukey's son told her about a tattoo of a Chinese character that some kid said meant "death" on the arm of another dismembered body. I thought that was worth checking so I asked Mr Chang if there was such a character and if so could he kindly draw it for me. I'm not sure whether or not he thought I was joking, but anyway he obliged, and here it is.' Vicky put a page torn from her notebook on Rathbone's desk. 'A woman who works on the counter had turned up by then as the place was opening any minute. I kept an eye on her as well as the two cooks while Chang was doing his art work, by the way, and they looked first puzzled and then faintly amused, but I saw no sign of any suspicious reaction.'

Almost grudgingly, it seemed to Sukey, Rathbone picked up the paper and studied it for several seconds. 'I suppose we can eliminate them, for the time being at any rate,' he said. 'What do you suggest we do with this thing?'

'I thought we might show it to Jason Dobbie and Don Wyatt and ask them if it's anything like the marks they saw – or in Wyatt's case, what he thinks he might have seen – on the wrists of the two suspects.'

Rathbone shrugged. 'It's a long shot,' he said, 'but I suppose it might jog their memories. We'll try, anyway. Now, Sukey –' he spun round in his chair – 'tell us what you've found out.'

Sukey quickly outlined the information Harry Matthews had given her. As she spoke, Rathbone's morose expression visibly lightened. 'Is this guy their regular postman?' he asked.

'So Harry says. He doesn't know his name, but he wears an official ID so it shouldn't be difficult to track him down. I made

Harry promise not to go tackling him by himself, by the way,' Sukey added.

'Good.' Rathbone made a few notes and then sat back and thought for a few moments. 'We still can't be sure Harry's postman was talking about young Mayhew when he made that call, but if he was then he's our first serious link with this mysterious Delta character who seems to have been an associate of young Mayhew and is more than likely part of the drug supply chain. We need to talk to that postie and see how he reacts, but if we are on the right track and we put the frighteners on him he'll simply refuse to answer questions and we'll get nowhere. I'll have a word with DCI Leach and ask him for his thoughts on how best to tackle it.'

'What would you like us to do in the meantime, Sarge?' asked Sukey.

'Make photocopies of that Chinese character, one for the file and one each for you and Vicky. On your way home, drop in on Dobbie and Wyatt and ask them if there's a cat in hell's chance that that's what they saw.' Sukey guessed from his tone that he had very little hope of a positive result, an impression that was confirmed by his next words. 'Since one of them was on the point of passing out and the other one was pissed to the eyeballs, I doubt if either will recognize it, but I suppose it's worth a try. If there's a miracle and one or both gives a positive reaction, let me know.'

'There has to be a breakthrough some time, Sarge.' said Vicky. She received a non-committal grunt by way of a reaction. 'By the way, is Dobbie still having round-the-clock protection?'

Rathbone shook his head. 'DCI Leach referred that to the Super who said the risk isn't high enough to justify the expense, especially as we've swept Mayhew's house and taken away his stash of drugs. I guess the villains will have to write that lot off.'

'What about The Cleft Stick? Shall we try them again next week?'

'I was coming to that. They're open on weekday mornings from nine until one, so you and Sukey take yourselves down there first thing on Monday and see what you can find out. Take a mug shot of Chesney and see if any of the people there recognize him. And while you're at it, show the death symbol around as well.' He glanced at the clock, shut down his computer and stood up. 'I'm off home. Have a nice weekend everyone.'

'What happened to the "perfect gentle knight"?' said Vicky mischievously as she and Sukey returned to the yard to collect their cars.

'He knows I work out at a gym so he obviously thinks I'm tough enough to protect you,' Sukey grinned. 'Now, who shall we call on first, Jason or Don? It might be an idea to check they're both available before we go any further, don't you think?'

There was no reply from Wyatt's mobile. They had better luck with Jason Dobbie, who had a night off and was taking his girl-friend out to supper followed by the show at the Hippodrome. After a brief discussion it was agreed they would meet at the Watershed at six o'clock. When they arrived they found Jason sitting at a table by a window overlooking the Floating Harbour with a slim blonde girl whom he introduced as Lotus. A waiter was filling two glasses from a bottle of white wine, which Jason politely offered to share with them. They declined – equally politely – and Vicky went to the bar to order coffee.

'We don't want to take up too much of your time,' said Sukey. She turned to Lotus. 'You have an unusual name,' she remarked. 'It's very pretty, though, and it really suits you.' The girl gave a shy smile at the compliment. 'While we're waiting for Vicky to come back,' Sukey continued, 'has Jason told you of his adventure the other night?'

'Yes, and it sounded really scary,' said Lotus. 'I was on holiday with my parents when it happened so I didn't learn about it till we got home at the weekend.' She took his hand and gave it a squeeze. 'He's lost his personal protection, by the way. Are you sure it's safe?'

'It's now considered highly unlikely that he poses a risk to whoever was trying to get into Toby Mayhew's house,' Sukey assured her.

At that moment Vicky returned and sat down. 'Coffee on the way,' she announced. 'What was that about risk?'

'Lotus is worried that one of the villains might take a further swipe at me,' Jason explained.

'And I've been reassuring her,' added Sukey.

'But you must think he still knows something that could lead you to them or you wouldn't have asked to meet him,' the girl persisted.

'You're right, although it's a bit of a shot in the dark. Jason, when you came round after that attack on you, you remembered seeing a mark – possibly a tattoo – on the attacker's arm, a mark that might have been a Chinese character.'

Jason swallowed a mouthful of wine before replying. 'I've thought a lot about that,' he said. 'I've tried seeing it in my mind's eye, even writing down bits that might have been part of it, but all I can recall is a few black lines that mean nothing to me. If this is why you want to see me I'm sorry, but . . .'

'Just stop there a moment,' said Sukey. She tore a page from her notebook and put it and a pen on the table in front of him. 'Could you just draw the bits you can recall? Thanks,' she added over her shoulder as a waiter put two large cups of coffee on the table.

Jason hesitated for a moment before picking up the pen. 'There was a horizontal line,' he drew on the paper as he spoke, 'with a curved bit under it.' He drew some more and then closed his eyes and sat back. After a moment he opened them and put the pen down. 'Sorry, that's really all I can think of, and I can't be sure I've even got that right.'

'Did it by any chance look anything like this?' Sukey gave a glance round to make sure there was no one close enough to see Mr Chang's drawing before she unfolded it and spread it out in front of him.

Jason stared at it for several seconds, but eventually he shook his head. 'It could be, I suppose, but I've really no idea,' he said helplessly.

'Well, it was worth a try, and thanks for your time,' said Sukey. She picked up the papers and was about to put them away when Lotus, whose attention had been distracted by a street entertainer on the opposite side of the water, reached out a hand.

'May I see?' Sukey handed over Mr Chang's drawing and the girl gave a little gasp of surprise. 'I've seen this before – or something very like it, but smaller than this – tattooed on someone's arm, or rather on his wrist.' She put a hand to her mouth and her eyes grew round. 'It looks spooky. What does it mean?'

'Never mind that for the time being,' said Sukey. 'The important thing is you've seen it before. Can you remember when this
was?'

'I noticed it the first time he came to our office – I can't
remember exactly when that was but it was some weeks ago.'

'Have you seen him since?' Lotus nodded. 'Do you happen
to know who this person is, or where we can find him?'

Lotus hesitated. 'I don't understand,' she said. 'He's just an
ordinary guy; I can't believe he'd be capable of attacking anyone.
I wouldn't want to make trouble for him.'

'The most unlikely people are sometimes capable of doing
the most unexpected things,' said Vicky, 'so please leave it to us
to decide whether he's likely to attack anyone. Just tell us who
he is and where we can find him.'

For several seconds Lotus still appeared reluctant to answer,
but at last she said, 'He's a postman. He delivers the mail to the
office where I work.'

'Will you tell the DS or shall I?' asked Sukey as she and Vicky
headed for home.

'Will you do it?' said Vicky. 'Chris and I have got some people
coming in for drinks later on.'

'Sure. No problem. See you Monday.'

As soon as she arrived home Sukey called Rathbone with the
news of their discovery. 'At last, something's going our way!'
he exclaimed. 'Good work, Sukey. I don't suppose you got a
name, by any chance? No? Never mind, see if young Harry can
tell you where the local sorting office is and we'll pick him up
on Monday.'

'What about The Cleft Stick, Sarge? You told us to go first
thing Monday.'

'It depends what time this guy delivers the mail to the *Echo*
office. Check that with Harry as well and we'll sort out timings
then. Cheers!'

TWENTY-TWO

On her way home Sukey called at a supermarket to stock up on food for the weekend. Back at the flat she packed everything away, set her own pre-prepared evening meal in the oven and sat down to relax with a glass of wine while it was cooking. Five minutes later her phone rang. Harry Matthews was on the line.

'Remember me?' he said breezily.

'It is rather a long time since we last met, but I do have a vague recollection,' said Sukey dryly, 'and before we go any further, if this is an attempt to pick my brains while I'm off duty, forget it.'

Harry gave an exaggerated sigh. 'Why do people always attribute the basest motives to me?' he said plaintively.

'It goes with the job, doesn't it?'

'I suppose so. Anyway, this is a strictly social call. The fact is, my dad has invited his lady friend for a meal tomorrow evening and he thought it would be nice to have another lady in the party so he – we, that is – wondered if you'd care to join us?'

'Harry, that's really kind of you both, but my son is coming for the weekend, so—'

'Your son?' He sounded taken aback. 'I didn't know . . . I mean, is he at boarding school or something?'

Sukey chuckled. 'No, he's in his second year at uni.'

'Oh!' The monosyllable expressed a mixture of surprise and relief. 'I had no idea . . . I mean, I wouldn't have thought you were—'

'The maternal sort?' Sukey suggested teasingly as he seemed to be floundering.

'No, that isn't what I meant, it's just you don't . . . anyway, why don't you bring him as well – that is, if you don't think he'd be bored. What's he reading by the way?'

'Psychology and law. His ambition is to be a forensic psychologist and he takes a great delight in passing on bits of expertise gleaned from his tutors that he thinks will help me solve tricky cases.'

'He sounds a lad after my own heart. I'm sure he and I would get on famously.'

Sukey chuckled. 'I think you're probably right; in fact, I've a feeling the two of you will gang up on me if I'm not careful.'

'So you'll bring him along?'

'If you're sure it'll be all right with your dad. What time shall we turn up?'

'About seven o'clock?'

'Fine. See you then.'

'A crime reporter? Great! Harry sounds just the sort of guy I'd like to meet!' was her son's enthusiastic response on hearing of the invitation. 'You haven't mentioned him before, Mum,' he added with a sudden change of tone. 'Is there something you think I should know?'

She gave him a gentle cuff on the arm. 'Don't be a chump,' she said, knowing what lay behind the question. Ever since her relationship with Jim Castle ended the previous year he had shown extra concern for her. 'He lives next door with his dad,' she explained, 'but apart from the odd "hello" and wave as we go in or out I've met him socially just once – at a drinks party a little while after I moved to Bristol. It so happens our paths crossed again a couple of days ago when he was reporting on one of our cases.'

'The one about the chopped up Chinese lady?'

'Er, no, another one.'

'Which one's that?' Seeing her defensive expression he raised both hands in a gesture of surrender. 'All right, no leading questions. Anyway, it should be a fascinating evening – and who knows, maybe I'll get something useful out of Harry,' he added with a provocative wink. 'What shall we do this afternoon?'

'I don't know about you, but I need some fresh air and exercise.'

'Me too. The sun's shining and spring is busting out all over, so how about a brisk walk over the Downs?'

'Why not?'

*   *   *

The house where the Matthews lived was called The Stables. It was, like a number of dwellings in Sherman Lane including Sukey's own flat, a conversion of a building that had once formed part of a country estate on the northern edge of the city. The knocker on the front door was, unsurprisingly, made from a horseshoe, and promptly at seven o'clock Sukey and Fergus arrived and did a discreet rat-a-tat.

A voice from within shouted, 'Coming!' and the next moment the door was flung open by a beaming Major Matthews. His face was slightly flushed and he held a glass of wine in one hand. 'Good evening, welcome, welcome!' he said expansively. 'Come along in! This way!' He preceded them along a carpeted passage, opened a door at the end and ushered them into a cosily furnished sitting room where Harry and a simply but elegantly dressed lady with short, neatly styled grey hair were seated on either side of an imitation log fire.

'Now, introductions!' continued the Major. 'Freddie, may I present our charming neighbour Mrs Reynolds and her son – Fergus, I think you said his name is – a student from the University of Gloucester. Mrs Reynolds, this is my dear friend Lady Frederica Sinclair.'

The lady shook an admonishing finger at the Major. 'Oh, George, there's no need to be so formal,' she said. 'I'm delighted to meet you, Mrs Reynolds, and you, Fergus – and do please call me Freddie.' Her smile as she held out a hand had a warm and friendly quality to which Sukey instinctively responded.

'Thank you, Freddie,' she said. 'I'm Sukey.'

Major Matthews cleared his throat and said self-consciously, 'Well, Sukey, I suppose you and I will have to, er, "go with the flow" as the young people say, so you must call me George.'

He eyed Fergus a little uncertainly as if wondering how he would feel at being so familiarly addressed by someone many years his junior but, with a spontaneous tact for which he later received his mother's congratulations, that young man solved his dilemma immediately by saying, 'Everyone calls me Gus, and thank you for including me in the invitation, sir.'

'Glad to have you with us, Gus. Now, what about some drinks? There's white or red wine, or maybe you'd prefer a beer, Gus? Harry, will you—?'

'Leave it to me.'

When they were settled with drinks, Freddie said, 'I understand you're in the CID, Sukey? That must be very interesting.
I used to be a lawyer, but I dealt with mostly civil and domestic
cases – nothing very exciting, I'm afraid.'

'My job certainly has its moments, but it's not all wild chases
and dramatic showdowns with arch criminals,' said Sukey.

'Freddie's retired,' explained George. 'She tells me she's busier
than ever and I tell her if she didn't take on so many good works
she'd have more time for me.'

'What kind of good works do you do?' said Sukey.

'Before I retired I used to help out every so often at a drop-
in centre called The Cleft Stick, mostly giving advice to people
with matrimonial difficulties. Since I retired I've become one of
their regular volunteers and I have to admit it seems to take up
more and more of my time.'

'That's a coincidence,' said Sukey. 'It so happens my colleague
and I have to call at The Cleft Stick on Monday in connection
with one of our cases. We're looking for information about
someone who used to help there a couple of years or so ago.'

'Really? Maybe I can help you. What's this person's name?'

Sukey hesitated, aware that Harry's eyes were on her. 'It's
someone whose name we've asked the press not to release at
the moment,' she said.

'Well, you can certainly count on my discretion, but I'm not
sure I can answer for our news hound here,' said Freddie with
a smile.

'If it's Toby Mayhew, we know about him already. In fact,'
Harry went on, a little smugly, 'I'm involved in the case myself
– helping with enquiries and all that.'

'Mum, who's Toby Mayhew?' Gus wanted to know. 'You
haven't mentioned him before. Has he been topped as well?'

Reminding herself that she was a guest in the house, Sukey
tried to hide her exasperation. 'No, he died in a road traffic accident a couple of weeks ago,' she said.

Her son pounced. 'Is that the one you told me about . . . the
man you and Vicky saw acting suspiciously in the motorway
services and told the local police, and then found it was all
perfectly innocent?' he went on eagerly. 'You said you passed

an accident a bit later and his car was involved . . . does that mean there was something suspicious about the stuff in that package after all?'

Sukey was beginning to wish both of them a hundred miles away. 'No, it doesn't; this is something completely different so drop it, Gus, please.'

Fergus, aware that he was being gently reprimanded, took refuge in his glass of beer and it was left to Harry to stir the pot. 'What's all this about a mysterious package?' he wanted to know. 'Is it connected with the Toby Mayhew case?'

'Not really – or rather, we thought it might be the start of a case, but it turned out to be a red herring.'

'Then you can tell the others, can't you, Mum?' said Gus persuasively.

Sukey put up a hand in mock surrender. 'All right, if you must know, Vicky and I – she's my colleague – rather made fools of ourselves. We saw a man in the motorway services car park who seemed to be acting suspiciously. He handed what looked like a padded envelope to another man; we thought it might be drugs and alerted a couple of uniformed officers we'd seen in the coffee shop. So the second man was followed, intercepted and questioned, but there were no drugs or anything else suspicious in the envelope, only a few odds and ends that he said were of sentimental value.'

'What were they?' asked Freddie, who had been listening attentively to the conversation.'

Sukey thought for a moment. 'There was a locket with a cutting of hair in it, like the Victorians used to wear,' she said slowly. 'I remember that because my grandmother had one with a curl from one of her babies who died. And a pendant with some kind of carved ornament . . . and what was the other one? Ah yes, a bit of fabric – a woman's handkerchief I think it was.'

'You don't suppose there were drugs hidden in the locket?' said Gus.

'Theoretically I suppose there could have been, but only a small quantity. And can you think of a reason why anyone would choose such an elaborate way of passing them on when the pros have much slicker arrangements for delivering supplies.'

Gus shrugged. 'No, I guess not.'

'The chap was pretty miffed about being "harassed" as he put it,' Sukey added. 'I think he even threatened to complain to his MP or the Chief Constable or someone.'

'So did you get a ticking off for wasting police time, Mum?'

Sukey shook her head. 'Actually, DCI Leach was very nice about it – said he'd probably have done the same in our place.'

'Would I be right in thinking the first man was Toby Mayhew?' asked Harry.

'Yes, but it doesn't have anything to do with the current enquiry. And I'm not answering any more questions,' she added firmly.

At that moment there was a knock at the front door. George leapt to his feet. 'That'll be my lovely catering ladies,' he said. 'You've probably been wondering if you were going to get anything to eat, ho! ho!' he guffawed as he headed for the front door. 'Harry, top up the glasses, please. Dinner in fifteen minutes.'

By general consent, no further controversial topics were allowed to ruffle the relaxed atmosphere of the remainder of the evening. Sukey had been hoping for an opportunity to check with Harry the approximate time when the *Echo* received the daily postal delivery without inviting further questions. None arose, but when they were leaving and Harry helped her on with her jacket, he whispered in her ear, 'There's a note in your pocket.' The note, which Sukey delayed reading until Fergus was out of the way, simply read, 'Normal time for delivery nine thirty to ten a.m., but later than that on the day in question.'

'Mind if I turn on the telly for the football scores?' said Fergus when they got home.

'Sure, go ahead.'

He switched on and settled down to watch while Sukey went into the kitchen to get a glass of water. When she joined him in the sitting room he was watching the end of the late news bulletin. 'Anything special?' she said as she joined him on the couch.

'Not really.' He picked up the remote control and switched off. 'That was a good evening, wasn't it? I like your friend Harry, by the way.'

'Gus, he's not exactly a friend. It just happens that we're both interested in the same case.'

Her son gave a knowing grin, but all he said was, 'If you say so. I think I'll turn in,' he added with a yawn. He stood up and gave her a peck on the cheek. 'Goodnight, Mum.'

While Sukey and Fergus were preparing for bed after a quiet evening in the company of neighbours, in the Stompers Club a couple of miles away things were beginning to warm up. The punters were packing in, drinks, laughter and conversation were flowing while multicoloured strobe lights flashed and dancers gyrated to the throbbing rhythm. Jason Dobbie was presiding over the sound system with his usual panache and enthusiasm under the admiring gaze of Lotus as on the dance floor she and her friend Tricia whirled and kicked and wriggled their hips in time to the music.

During a break between numbers the two girls sashayed back to the bar and ordered more drinks. As Lotus picked up her glass and turned round to look for a seat, a man's voice said, 'Hullo! Haven't I seen you somewhere before?'

She flicked him a sideways glance. 'I don't think so, but nice try!' she said with a cheeky grin that faded as she caught sight of the tattoo on his wrist. Her eyes travelled back to his face. 'Wait a moment, don't you deliver our mail?'

'Well done!' He gave a little smile of triumph. 'You work in Wilson and Taylor's office in Corn Street, right?' She nodded. 'Your name's Lotus, innit? How do I know that? I've heard one of your mates speak to you, that's how,' he went on. 'Pretty name, suits you. I'm Ron, by the way.'

'Hi, Ron.' Instinctively, Lotus cast a wary glance in Jason's direction, but he was miming to the trumpet soloist on the current number and oblivious to everything but the music.

Thankful that at least Ron hadn't appeared to notice her momentary interest in his tattoo, she took a long draught from her glass of lager. Recalling the encounter with the two detectives the previous evening, she had a sudden urge to put space between him and herself, but to her dismay, Tricia – who had already had two drinks to her one and was casting an approving eye on him – said with a tipsy simper, 'Her bloke's the DJ, but I'm available.' As Ron gave a polite nod and raised his glance in mock salute, she caught sight of the tattoo. 'Ooh, Lotus,' she hiccuped, making a stabbing gesture with a scarlet fingernail, 'is that the one you were telling me about – like the one that Jason saw when that chap knocked him out . . . ow!' She gave a squeal as Lotus gave her a sharp kick on the ankle. 'Mind where you put your feet, Lottie!'

'You've seen one of these before?' said Ron and this time he was looking directly at Lotus.

'No, only yours, and that was ages ago,' she said, trying to sound casual but conscious that her voice was unsteady.

'But her boyfriend over there has,' Tricia said with a nod in Jason's direction and oblivious to the mute rage in her friend's eyes. 'She told me all about it, she saw a picture.'

'Trish, you've got it all wrong so just drop it will you,' Lotus pleaded, but Tricia paid no heed.

'What's it mean anyhow?' she wanted to know.

Ron shrugged. 'Search me. It's just a design I spotted in a tattoo artist's place and liked the look of.' With a sudden change of attitude, he grabbed Tricia's empty glass and said, 'Same again, my lover?'

'Ooh, ta!'

The minute he left them to go to the bar, Lotus grabbed her friend's arm and hissed, 'For God's sake, Tricia, don't say any more about what I told you.'

'Wha's that?' Tricia shook off the restraining hand and did a sexy gyration as the next number started. 'He's quite a smooth talker, innee? Ooh ta!' she said again as Ron returned and put a replenished glass into her hand.

'Come on, Trish, you can drink that later and this is one of your favourite numbers, so let's dance,' pleaded Lotus.

'Dance? G'd idea.' Tricia put down her glass on an adjacent table and grabbed Ron's free arm. 'C'm on Ron, let's you and I boogie.'

'Sure, why not?' He put down his own glass and the next moment the two of them were lost in the gyrating throng. Lotus could only look on in despair as she frantically tried to decide what to do, to think how to warn Jason of the possible danger he was in, and above all how to prevent Tricia from blurting out even more damaging information. For the moment at least she appeared to be more interested in the dance, but if Ron had a mind to get more information out of her there seemed no way of preventing it.

The music ended and Ron led a breathless Tricia back to where Lotus was waiting. 'Ooh, that were great, Ron,' she panted. 'We must have another when I've had a drink.'

Ron drained his glass, put it down and said, 'It'll have to be another time, Trish, I've gotta go now.'

'Oh no!' Tricia looked devastated. 'You can't go now, the music goes on for hours yet!' she whined.

He shook his head. 'Sorry, I've got things to do. See you around.' With a brief wave he was gone.

Tricia rounded on Lotus. ''s all your fault, being such a misery,' she grumbled, picking up the drink she had left on the table.

'Give that to me, you've had enough.' Lotus took away Tricia's glass and held it out of her reach. 'What else did you tell Ron about Jason?'

Tricia scowled. 'Why would I want to talk about Jason?'

'Did he ask you any questions while you were dancing?'

'Can't remember. I want a drink!' Tricia made a grab at the glass, missed and knocked it from Lotus's hand. 'Now look what you've done. Get me another.'

'You've had more than enough already. I'm going to get a taxi and take you home.'

TWENTY-THREE

Within a few minutes of switching off her light, Sukey fell asleep. At some stage during her slumber she began to dream. In her dream, she and Vicky were peering through the windows of a drop-in centre whose walls were decorated with huge posters bearing the Chinese symbol for death. The place was dimly lit and apparently deserted, but suddenly a telephone began to ring. Convinced that the call was for her and that it was vital that she should take it, Sukey – on her own now as Vicky had disappeared – struggled frantically to open the door, which was securely locked.

It seemed an eternity before she escaped from the dream into wakefulness and the realization that the ringing was coming from the mobile phone on her bedside table. She rolled over, picked it up and mumbled sleepily, 'Sukey Reynolds here.'

A woman's voice gasped, 'Oh Sukey, thank God you've answered! I'm so frightened . . . please help us!'

Sukey sat up in bed, wide awake in an instant. 'Who is this? What's wrong?'

'It's Lotus . . . Jason's girlfriend . . . we need help . . . protection.' The girl was beside herself; the words tumbled out in a breathless stream.

Sukey was already on her feet, the phone clamped between ear and shoulder as she reached for some clothes. 'Lotus, please calm down and tell me where you are and what's happened.'

'I'm at the Stompers Club . . . where Jason works . . . Sukey, he was here; he's going to kill Jason . . . please come quickly.'

'Who was there? Who are you talking about?'

'The postman . . . the one with the tattoo . . . his name's Ron . . . he was here and now he's gone. My friend Tricia was here with me and she had too much to drink and she went on about the tattoo and how Jason had seen it . . . I tried to shut her up but she kept mouthing on. Then she almost passed out so I took her home and came rushing back here to warn Jason . . .

he thinks I'm being paranoid but I'm sure Ron means to kill him before he can tell the police . . . oh *please* help us.'

Sukey, struggling into jeans and sweatshirt, was thinking on her feet. 'OK, calm down and listen,' she said. 'What time does Jason finish at the club?'

'It shuts at two but he has to pack up his gear so he leaves a bit later.'

Sukey glanced at her bedside clock. 'That give us a little under two hours. Are you sure Ron has left?'

'I think so. He said he had things to do and he disappeared, but I didn't actually see him leave the club. He may be some-where outside, lying in wait for Jason. Sukey, what are we to do?'

'I doubt if he'll do anything with other people around,' said Sukey, trying to sound more confident than she felt. 'Just the same, we can't take any chances. Stay where you are and I'll contact my sergeant for instructions. Keep your mobile switched on and I'll get back to you as soon as I can.'

'Oh thank you . . . but please . . . hurry!' The words ended in a sob.

Sukey keyed in DC Rathbone's number. 'What the hell?' he growled, becoming immediately alert as Sukey passed on the message. 'Right,' he said, 'we need armed back-up at the club and at Dobbie's home, but it's got to be covert; we want to nick the bugger in the act, not just scare him off. Does the tattooed postman know you by sight, by the way?'

'No, Sarge, he wasn't at the *Echo* office the day I called and so far as I know we've never set eyes on each other anywhere else. Even if we have, there's no reason why he should know I'm a police officer.'

'Good. You get down to the club and make sure Dobbie and the girl stay there until I give you the word it's OK to leave. I'll let you know when everything's set up so keep in touch for further instructions.'

'Right, Sarge.' Sukey ended the call and got back to Lotus. 'I don't hear any music or noise,' she said anxiously when the girl answered. 'You aren't outside, are you?'

'No, I'm in the loo. I've been here waiting for you to call . . . there's so much racket in there, you can't hear yourself think. What's happening?'

'I've spoken to my sergeant and he's told me exactly what to do. I have to come to the club and stay with you, but I'm not a member so . . .'

'That's no problem; as long as you're decently dressed and can still stand up you just pay and they let you in.'

'Have you got any other friends there?'

'Not friends exactly . . . but I do know a few of the people here tonight.'

'That's good. I'll be leaving here in a few minutes.'

'Will you be on your own?'

'Yes, but there'll be other officers around. You won't know who or where they are but I promise they'll be there.'

'Sukey, I'm scared. Are you sure this'll work?'

'It will if you do exactly as I tell you. As soon as we end this call you're to go back and hook up with your mates – and try to look as if you're enjoying yourself,' she added, sensing from the girl's hesitant manner that she was far from reassured. 'When I get to the club I'll make my way to the bar and get a drink and act as if I'm there to meet someone. That's you, of course. When you spot me, come over and say something like, "so glad you made it",' she continued. 'You can do that, can't you?'

'I s'ppose so.'

'Good girl! And whatever you do, don't say anything about all this or tell people who I am, just greet me like an old friend and make sure Jason does the same, all right?'

'All right.'

Sukey ended the call, hurried to the spare room where Fergus was sleeping and shook him by the shoulder. 'What's up?' he mumbled sleepily. 'It can't be time to get up yet.'

'It's only half twelve, but I have to go out and I'm not sure when I'll be back,' she said.

'Go out where?' He was awake in an instant. 'Is it police business?'

'Yes. We're on the trail of a villain who attacked someone recently and we think he's going to have another go tonight. The potential victim works in a nightclub in the city and I have to keep an eye on him and his girlfriend until back-up gets there.'

Fergus was out of bed like a shot. 'Hang on for a tick, I'm coming with you.'

'No, Gus, that's not on. It might be dangerous and anyway my sergeant will go ballistic if I involve you.'

'So you're planning to go clubbing by yourself . . . and in that outfit?' he said, eyeing the jeans and sweatshirt. 'Or were you just planning to flash your ID and tell the bouncers there's a covert police operation in progress?'

'Gosh, I hadn't thought that far,' she admitted.

'Good job you've got me to put you straight. The jeans are OK,' he went on, 'but trainers are out. Put on some proper shoes – no stilettos though – and a funky top. That number you wore this evening will do. And a bit of make-up would help. Don't argue,' he added as she still wavered. 'I'm your date for the evening so go and get into some suitable gear while I do the same.'

Recognizing that it was pointless to argue, Sukey did as he told her. Ten minutes later they were heading for the city centre; on the way she filled him in with a few details about the background to the enterprise. 'Just bear in mind you're only here to give me street cred – and whatever you do don't call me Mum,' she added with mock severity.

'You can trust me, Mum,' he assured her cheerfully. 'There's no prob, it's cool nowadays to have a girlfriend twice your age. I'll bet you can still wiggle your bum with the best of 'em,' he added cheekily.

'I'll do my best,' she grinned and then became serious. 'This isn't a party, Gus; like I said we're after a killer and my job is to let the police know – unobtrusively of course – which people they're protecting. So if anything unexpected happens we behave like part of the crowd, OK? Stompers is just up there on the right,' she added as she pulled into a vacant space by the kerb. As she switched off the ignition her mobile rang. DS Rathbone was calling.

'Where are you?' he said.

'Parked near Stompers, on the opposite side of the road. We're meeting Lotus inside.'

'We?

'My son's with me. I need him for cover and I promise he won't do anything daft,' she hurried on before he had a chance to object. 'We're going in as a couple having a night out.'

'That makes sense, I suppose,' he admitted. 'Do Dobbie and the girl know you're there?'

'Not yet. The plan is to go in, make contact as if we've arranged to meet up there, have a drink and mingle with the mob. I've impressed on Lotus that they must both continue to act as normally as possible. He seems pretty laid back, but she's as jumpy as a cat on hot bricks.'

'Let's hope she can hold it together. Now listen. I'm in my own car a bit farther up the street and there's an unmarked police car close by with a couple of armed officers. There are also two DCs – Tim Pringle and Penny Osborne – inside the club. They'll be looking out for you, but won't necessarily make contact right away. We're in sight of the club entrance; there are still people going in and out so you won't have a problem. Stay in there until Dobbie and Lotus leave.'

'He has to pack up his gear so that'll be a little after chuck-out time.'

'OK.' There was a brief silence. 'Right. In that case you, your son and Lotus, together with Penny, will come out with the mob and stand in a group chatting. You'll be under observation from then on. It's just possible the target may be hanging around – maybe having a smoke or something as an excuse to keep an eye out for Lotus and Dobbie with the intention of tracking them. If he is, tell her to say goodnight – very casually, just a smile and a wave'll be enough for us to identify him. After a couple of minutes of chat your son will take her to your car and drive her home. Call me the minute they're on their way. Got that?'

'Yes, Sarge, but it could be tricky prising her away from Jason.'

'You tell her if she doesn't do as she's told we call the operation off and they're on their own.' Sukey could tell from his tone that he was running out of patience. 'Not that we would, of course, but we're having to play this by ear at very short notice so no more ifs or buts.'

'OK, Sarge. Let's hope she keeps her head.'

'It's up to you to make sure she does. Once she's gone you're to hang around chatting with Penny until Tim and Dobbie come out. The armed officers will take over at this point and shadow Dobbie back to his house, where the other half of the team is already in position and waiting to hear that he's on his way home.

You, Tim and Penny will get in this car with me and we'll head there as well. Got all that?'

'Yes, Sarge.'

'Right, on your way and fingers crossed.'

'I think a prayer might be more to the point,' Sukey said to herself as he ended the call. 'Right, Gus, here's how we play it.' She relayed Rathbone's instructions and got him to repeat them. 'OK, we go in now. You'd better have some cash, by the way.' She fished out her wallet and handed over some notes. 'I just hope DCI Leach will sign my expenses chit, that's all.'

It was some years since Sukey had been in a nightclub, although she had often seen them featured in films or in news items on the TV. Just the same, she was momentarily stunned by the blast of sound that battered her eardrums as she and Fergus passed through the swing doors and threaded their way through the forest of tapping feet and waving arms towards the bar. On the opposite side of the floor she saw Jason Dobbie, flanked by his audio equipment, microphone in hand and a dreamy smile on his face, hips swaying to the rhythm of the music. Overhead, strobe lights spun and flashed in a dizzying succession of colours. Sukey perched on a stool and began searching the crowd for Lotus.

'What can I get you, Suko?' asked Fergus.

Sukey blinked, recovered, and said, 'I'll have a lager please, Fergo.'

Fergus beckoned the barman. 'Two lagers.'

'Coming up.' The barman put two small cans and two glasses on the bar and held out his hand. 'That'll be four quid.'

Fergus pretended to be shocked. 'I only want a couple of cans, not buy the brewery,' he said, handing over a fiver.

The barman, who looked like a student himself, gave a sympathetic grin as he handed over the change. 'Cheap drinks ended at half-twelve,' he explained. 'Too many people leaving here rat-arsed lately; the boss is worried about his licence.'

'My heart bleeds for him.'

While Fergus opened the cans and filled the glasses, Sukey was scanning the crowd. 'Seen any of your mates yet?' he asked.

'Not yet . . . oh yes, there's Lotus,' she replied as the girl suddenly detached herself from the heaving, gyrating throng and hurried towards them, followed by a tall, white-faced girl with two black pigtails hanging forward over her thin shoulders.

'Hi, Sukey,' said Lotus breathlessly. 'Glad you could make it,' she added hastily. She spoke like an actress who had almost forgotten her lines. 'Jo, this is Sukey.'

The two nodded at each other and Sukey said, 'Fergo, meet my friend Lotus and her friend Jo.'

Everyone smiled and nodded. Jo eyed Sukey and then turned to Fergus. 'Big sister?' she asked.

'Well done, you spotted the likeness!' he said blandly. 'You girls want a drink?'

'Orange juice, please,' said Lotus.

'No drink for me, I'd rather dance,' simpered Jo, who had obviously taken an instant shine to Fergus. He bought Lotus her juice and allowed Jo to drag him on to the floor.

'She'll have him off you if you don't watch it, she's a real maneater,' said Lotus, who had obviously missed the exchange while her mind was elsewhere.

'I can live with it,' Sukey replied with a shrug.

Lotus picked up her drink. Over the rim of her glass her eyes were wide with apprehension. 'Is everything OK?' she whispered.

Sukey, glass in hand, was gently rocking to and fro in time to the music. 'Fine, just fine!' she said gaily. 'Did you give Jason his orders?' she added in the same casual manner without looking at Lotus. Her eyes searched the crowd, trying to spot Tim and Penny.

'Yes, of course, and this time I really think he's taking it seriously,' said Lotus. 'Look, he's spotted you. He'll be over to say "hi" in a minute, when he's put on the next number. Oh, Sukey, I'm so scared.'

'It'll be all right as long as you do as I say . . . and for goodness' sake, try and act normal.'

It was Jo, not Lotus, who almost led to the operation being aborted. As closing time approached, Tim and Penny linked up with Sukey, Fergus and Lotus. Jo was still clinging to Fergus, whom she had inveigled into buying her an alcopop, and from its effect on her it was evidently not her first drink of the evening. To complicate matters still further, when Fergus declined to buy her any more, she decided to transfer her favours to Tim, with the same lack of success. Penny acted her part with gusto, telling Jo in no uncertain terms to keep her hands off him. By now it was closing time and as the revellers flowed out into the street, Jo began screaming abuse at Penny and instead of dispersing a number of people lingered, scenting the possibility of a cat-fight. Sukey was becoming desperate when Lotus – who, surprisingly in the circumstances, had remembered her instructions and whispered 'No sign of Ron' in her ear – came to the rescue.

'Pack it in, Jo, or Penny'll tear your hair out,' she said, grasping her friend firmly by the arm. 'Fergo's giving me a lift home and he'll drop you off at your place on the way. You will, won't you, Fergo . . . *please*?'

'No probs,' he said manfully, catching his mother's eye.

'Ooh, you are a love!' Jo was by now rocking unsteadily on her feet; she lurched towards Fergus and grabbed his arm. Sukey held her breath as with Lotus supporting her on one side and Fergus on the other, they led her to the car and the loiterers drifted away.

'I hope she doesn't throw up in my car,' Sukey muttered as she watched them go.

Fortunately it was a mild night and Penny and Sukey were not the only people to linger chatting with friends before heading homewards. The next stage of the operation went according to plan and it was with a sense of relief that the three detectives climbed into DS Rathbone's car.

'Let's hope we get a result,' Rathbone observed as they headed towards Tyndale Gardens.

There was certainly a result, although not the one they had all expected.

TWENTY-FOUR

On the way to Tyndale Gardens, Rathbone questioned Sukey about the layout of the area.

'It's a cul-de-sac with about eighteen houses on either side and a few spaces for visitor parking at the far end,' she explained. 'The houses are numbered consecutively; Jason lives at number twenty-five, immediately opposite the Scotts at number twelve.'

'Isn't Mrs Scott the neighbourhood watch supremo?' he asked.

'That's the one. If it hadn't been for the note she sent round, Jason Dobbie wouldn't have bothered to say anything about the movement he saw – or thought he saw – outside Toby Mayhew's house. He might not even have spotted the chap who was actually there – the one who attacked him.'

Rathbone grunted. 'She's been something of a mixed blessing, in fact.'

'From Jason's point of view, I suppose, but it wasn't her fault that he went and challenged the intruder the second time instead of calling us. All I hope –' she went on as a sudden thought occurred to her – 'is that she hasn't spotted our heavy mob taking up their position and called 999. The last thing we want is a patrol car turning up at the crucial moment.'

'If you mean the armed response unit, they won't have been announcing their arrival,' he assured her. 'Come to think of it, this is the first time you've been involved in this kind of operation, isn't it?'

'If by that you mean my previous encounters with guns has been unexpected rather than pre-planned, you're right,' she admitted. 'I'm finding this pretty nail-biting,' she added. 'How are we going to play it?'

'*We* aren't doing anything except stick around and wait for the action to start. This is their show. This might be a good moment to say one of your prayers, Sukey.'

'I already have,' she replied quietly.

'Let's hope God's listening. Now, you mentioned a lay-by just before Tyndale Gardens . . . yes, there it is. I'll pull in and wait for the fun to start.' He parked, cut the engine, switched off the lights and turned up the volume on his two-way radio. The only sound was a faint crackling. 'Any moment now,' he muttered.

The silence that followed seemed interminable. Sukey found herself imagining a nightmare scenario when the entire operation turned into farce and the anticipated attack failed to materialize because Ron the postman was fast asleep at home and the wild fears that had prompted Lotus to make her panic-stricken call were nothing but an overreaction to seeing him at the Stompers Club. She found herself mistrusting her and Harry's hunch that there was a connection between Toby Mayhew's attacker and Connie Gilbert's killer – the hunch that had enabled her somehow to convince DS Rathbone and DCI Leach that it was worth further investigation. She visualized the mortifying scene in Leach's office after it turned out that they'd been on a wild goose chase and . . .

She was jerked back to reality by Rathbone's radio. Over the airwaves came a shout of 'Armed Police, drop the weapon!' followed by sounds of a struggle accompanied by a stream of obscenities that continued for a considerable time until an authoritative, but slightly breathless voice said, 'You're nicked.' Rathbone rubbed his hands together.

'Looks like they got the bugger,' he said and switched on the ignition. 'Let's get a look at him.'

When they arrived in Tyndale Gardens the lights were on in most of the houses, dogs were barking and people were leaning out of their front windows to see what was going on. There was even a light in an upstairs window in Colonel Driver's house, but it came as no surprise to Sukey that every light in the Scotts' house appeared to be on and the front door was open. As they got out of the car and approached Jason Dobbie's house Mrs Scott, in dressing gown and slippers and with her hair hanging loose around her shoulders, darted out and came running across the road towards them, only to be gently but firmly turned back by one of the armed officers. Two others were propelling their prisoner towards a car; he suddenly ceased to struggle and hung limply between them with his feet trailing on the ground so that they had to drag him the last few yards and lift him bodily into the back seat. Catching a glimpse in the headlights of a sullen expression, a narrow, shaven skull and a lean but muscular frame, Sukey was reminded of a bad-tempered whippet. 'Not sure I'd want him delivering my mail,' she remarked to Rathbone.

'He won't be delivering anyone's mail for quite a while,' he replied gleefully.

On Monday afternoon DCI Leach summoned the team to his office.

'So you made an arrest,' he said, indicating the report that lay on his desk. 'Congratulations to everyone concerned; that was really good work all round.' He turned to DS Rathbone. 'So what do you reckon, Greg? Have we nicked the mysterious Delta?'

'It would be nice to think so, sir, but we really don't know at the moment I'm afraid,' said Rathbone. 'Our prisoner has been uncooperative, to say the least. He's given what we're pretty sure is a false name and address, he denies intending to attack anyone and claims the knife he was carrying was for self-defence because he lives in a dodgy part of the city where everyone carries them in case they're attacked.'

'We've heard that one before, haven't we?' Leach remarked. 'I presume he wasn't carrying any ID?'

'No, sir.'

'Nor a mobile?'

'No, sir. Apart from his underwear he wore nothing but joggers and a sweat shirt and the only thing in his pocket was a bunch of keys.'

'I suppose that's a start. What reason did he give for lying in wait outside Dobbie's house and trying to attack him?'

'He claims he needed money for drugs and was looking for a likely house to burgle when he found himself surrounded by heavies and pulled the knife to protect himself.'

'Which I take it doesn't exactly tally with the police version?'

'No, sir,' said Rathbone without a hint of a smile in response to the sardonic lift at the corners of Leach's mouth. 'All four of the armed officers are quite clear that Ron – that's the name he gave the girls in the nightclub although the one he gave us is Wally Price – was lying in wait behind Dobbie's front gate and approached him from behind with the knife raised as he was putting his key in the front door. He was challenged, dropped the knife and tried to make a dash for it but was quickly grabbed and brought under control.'

'Is he a junkie, do you reckon?'

'He hasn't shown any serious withdrawal symptoms so far.'

'What about the tattoo on his arm?'

'He says he has no idea what it means and chose it at random from a book of designs offered by some tattoo artist.' Rathbone turned to Sukey. 'That ties in with what he told Lotus, doesn't it?'

Sukey nodded. 'That's right, Sarge. If I might make a point, sir?' she went on, turning to DCI Leach, 'I had the impression during the interview that there's something or someone that he's more scared of than he is of us. It was the way he avoided eye contact,' she went on in response to Leach's raised eyebrows, 'and he kept his hands hidden in his lap so we couldn't see whether he was clenching his fists like some nervous witnesses do, but there seemed to be a tenseness in his facial muscles that suggested he might be under some stress. It could be because he needed a fix, I suppose.'

'In the circumstances, you'd think he'd have had his fix beforehand,' Leach commented. 'What about the phone call he's supposed to have made to this Delta character – the one your journo friend says he overheard? What did he have to say about that?'

'He said he had no idea what we were talking about and denied ever being inside the *Echo* offices. To every subsequent question he simply answered, "No comment".'

Leach referred to an earlier entry in the file. 'I take it you also questioned him about the earlier attack on Dobbie? I see from here that no weapon was found, but from the nature of the wound we suspect it was inflicted with a jemmy or something similar that he intended to use to break into Mayhew's house?'

'That's correct, sir, and yes we questioned him about that as well, but he flatly denied ever paying a previous visit to Tyndale Gardens. Made some wisecrack about "spreading himself around".'

'Has he asked for a brief?'

'No, sir. We offered to get him one but he refused on the grounds that he had nothing to add to his story. As – fortunately – he was arrested before he could carry out what we believe was an intended murder we can't charge him with assault, but we have charged him with carrying an offensive weapon without lawful authority.'

'And what did he say to that?'

'He just shrugged. He's been remanded in custody of course until his case comes up and we'll naturally oppose any application for bail. Meanwhile we'll continue with our enquiries.'

'Any progress on checking his identity?'

'The address he gave us exists and uniformed went to the house but it was empty at the time – or if there was anyone in they weren't answering. In any case, none of the keys we took off him fitted the front door. They questioned a few of the neighbours but none of them had heard of a Wally Price. Not that that means a lot, sir; most of the houses in that street are in multiple occupation and the turnover by all accounts is pretty high. We presume he'd have needed a car to get from there to Tyndale Gardens, but we've no idea where he left it. I'm having a check made on all the vehicles that are still parked in the area round Tyndale Gardens this morning. Some of them will belong to the residents, of course, but we can easily eliminate them.'

'Good.' DCI Leach referred again to the report. 'I see you've taken a DNA sample from the prisoner,' he remarked.

'Yes, sir, and we're hoping to find a match with the one we found on the cigarette stub left outside Mayhew's house after the first attack on Dobbie.'

Leach made a note. 'That can take forever if we wait in the queue. We got it fast-tracked last time so let's hope they'll do it again. A match would prove he's been lying, which would be a big step forward.' He slipped the report into a folder and put it away. 'That's it for now; report back to me as soon as there are any developments.'

When the team returned to the CID office DS Rathbone said, a little wearily, 'I've a feeling we've got a lot of leg work in front of us.' He referred to his notepad. 'There's The Cleft Stick to check up on. Vicky, you and Sukey go there tomorrow morning; you might as well take a mug shot of "Wally Price" as well as the one of Warren Chesney and see if he's been seen in there. They might even know his real name, although that'd be too much to hope for. And take a shot of the death tattoo as well in case anyone there has seen anything like it. We know there are at least two in existence – if we count the one on the earlier dismembered body, that is – and if as Sukey suggested it represents membership of some kind of murderous brotherhood there may be others knocking around. Tim and Penny, you follow up the check on the cars and let me know as soon as anything turns up. One of the keys on the bunch has to be a car key, so that should help.' He sat back, flexed his arms, yawned, muttered, 'I need a coffee,' and headed for the machine.

As the others got up to follow, Sukey's mobile rang. Lotus was on the line, and her words came out in a near-hysterical rush.

'Oh, Sukey, I'm so glad you're . . . he was here . . . you said you'd caught him so he must have escaped . . . I rang Jason to try and warn him but he's not answering his mobile. Please . . . you must do something before it's too late . . .'

'Hold on a minute, Lotus,' said Sukey. 'I don't understand what you're talking about. Who was where?'

'Ron . . . the postman . . . he came to the office as usual this morning and . . .'

'This morning?' Sukey exclaimed in bewilderment. 'But he can't have done . . . he was arrested yesterday morning outside Jason's house.'

'That's what Jason told me . . . but he must have escaped because he was here this morning as if nothing had happened.'

'There must be some mistake,' said Sukey, whose thoughts were spinning round in her head with the speed of a Catherine wheel. 'Anyway, if you saw him this morning why didn't you call us right away?'

'I didn't see him myself . . . I had the morning off . . . it wasn't until this afternoon that I had a chance to tell the girls in the office about all the excitement we had on Saturday night and when I broke it to them that our own postman had been arrested for trying to attack Jason they thought I was mad . . . they said it couldn't have been him because he delivered the post as usual this morning. Sukey, are you still there?' she went on urgently as Sukey, stunned by the revelation, was momentarily unable to speak. 'Can you hear me?'

'Yes, I'm still here,' said Sukey. 'Look, Lotus, a man was arrested in the small hours of yesterday morning as he was about to attack Jason and that man is still locked up in a cell so you and Jason have nothing to fear.' She was on the point of adding, 'for the moment', but managed to keep the words back. 'It's obvious that there's been some confusion over identity,' she went on, 'but I promise you the man we arrested hasn't escaped, so tell Jason everything's OK and we'll let you know once we've got it sorted.'

'You're sure?' Lotus asked shakily.

'Quite sure,' said Sukey. She ended the call and went to break the news to the rest of the team.

TWENTY-FIVE

'So now we've got two suspects with identical tattoos,' said
Leach as the team reassembled in his office. 'One caught
in the act of trying to stick a knife in Jason Dobbie's back
and the other a postman called Ron who, according to information received from a member of the staff of the *Echo*, made
a telephone call to someone he addressed as Delta informing
him of the death of a person he referred to as Hermes. The
circumstances under which he made that call suggest that it was
essential to pass on the information without delay. There's also
reason to suspect that Hermes might be a code name for Tobias
Mayhew, a known crackhead and associate of Warren Chesney,
currently awaiting trial for dealing. Mayhew was last seen alive
handing over an envelope to a man in a motorway services car
park; shortly afterwards he was killed in an RTA. There was a
suspicion at the time – subsequently discounted – that the envelope contained drugs. However, information received from his
parents give us reason to believe that he had dealings with Delta.
Anything to add to that, Greg?'

'That's a pretty fair summing up of the facts so far, sir,' said
Rathbone, 'but we should also bear in mind that the dismembered male body found off the coast near the mouth of the Mersey
also had a tattoo on the right arm. According to unconfirmed
reports, that tattoo is also in the form of a Chinese character
meaning "death".'

'It so happens I've been in touch with the Merseyside police
and I've just received this faxed copy of the tattoo on that victim's
arm.' Leach handed a sheet of paper to Rathbone, who glanced
at it, nodded and passed it back. 'It appears identical,' Leach
went on, 'but it may be a coincidence. It could be there are fash-
ions in tattoo design and by chance this one happens to have
caught on. In any case the Merseyside one was on a victim, not
a suspect. Just the same, Greg, it might be an idea to check with
local tattoo artists to see if they can shed any light.'

Rathbone made a note. 'Will do, sir.'

'The fact that Ron the postman was not, as we all expected, Jason Dobbie's attacker doesn't mean he isn't still in the frame and he's to be pulled in for questioning. That will be your priority for tomorrow, Greg.'

'Right, sir. So far as the events of Saturday night are concerned, all we know for certain is that he left the nightclub shortly after learning from a drunken mate of Dobbie's girlfriend Lotus that Dobbie was the victim of the first attack outside Mayhew's house. Was Wally Price the attacker on that occasion? And did Ron leave unexpectedly early because Price had to be warned that Dobbie not only survived the attack but had given important information to the police and had to be silenced? Or is it just a coincidence that a second attack took place on that particular night? Ron will almost certainly deny making the telephone call from the *Echo* office and disclaim all knowledge of anyone called Wally Price, Hermes or Delta, but he can hardly deny the tattoo. When we put it to him that we know of two other people with a tattoo identical to his, one of whom is in custody charged with a serious offence and the other a dismembered corpse, it may be enough to rattle him.'

When the team reported for duty the following morning, Rathbone had already agreed with DCI Leach the programme of enquiries for the day.

'Tim and Penny, I want you to make a start on the local tattoo studios. Take a copy of the death tattoo with you and see if any of them recognize it. If it's a standard design, ask if they can remember doing any and if so show them a mug shot of Wally Price and see if they recognize him. And at the same time, ask if anyone else has had it done and if they can give a description. As you'll see, there are quite a few of these jokers in here, so divide them up between you.' He tossed a copy of the Yellow Pages at them.

'You did tell us to keep a check on the cars, Sarge,' Tim pointed out. 'Are we to . . . ?

'Uniformed have got Price's keys and are scouring the neighbourhood,' said Rathbone. 'This'll keep you occupied until they find his car and depending on what that tells us we decide on our next step. Vicky and Sukey, you're to check out The Cleft Stick as arranged. I've had a word with Harry Matthews at the *Echo* and made an appointment to see him in half an hour – with luck a bit earlier if the traffic isn't too bad. The idea is to be there when Ron turns up with the post. Harry will identify him, I'll invite him to help us with our enquiries and we'll take it from there. All right everyone?'

'I'd love to be a fly on the wall when our Sarge "invites Ron to help with our enquiries",' Sukey remarked as she and Vicky set off on their assignment. 'Suppose he refuses? He hasn't committed any offence that we know of.'

'He's probably smart enough to know that a refusal would look suspicious,' said Vicky.

'Probably,' Sukey agreed. 'Anyway, let's get on with the job and make sure we get back in time to be present at the interview.'

It was still a few minutes before nine o'clock when they arrived outside The Cleft Stick. It was not yet open, but already a small knot of people had gathered outside. They were mostly young men, unshaven and bleary-eyed; all were huddled into shabby clothing with grubby scarves round their necks and woollen caps pulled down over their ears. Some carried plastic carrier bags; one had what looked like a bundle of old blankets roughly tied up with string and they all shivered in the chilly breeze that chased discarded food wrappers and drinks cans along the pavement. It was a depressing sight.

'They look half frozen,' said Vicky. 'I'll bet they've been sleeping rough.'

'At least they'll get some hot food when it opens up,' replied Sukey. One of the lads reminded her of Fergus and she gave silent thanks that he had not come to this.

They wandered a few yards along the street and waited. Promptly at nine o'clock three neatly dressed women, encumbered by a considerable number of bulging shopping bags, approached from the opposite direction. They smiled and said a cheerful 'Good morning' to the waiting group, unlocked the door and went inside. The effect of their appearance was almost electric; backs were straightened, heads raised and bundles lifted from the ground as the first customers of the day trooped in behind them.

'I've heard a lot about places like this, but it's the first time I've been inside one,' said Vicky in a low voice as she and Sukey stepped through the door and closed it behind them. 'I remember peering through the window the day DS Rathbone and I came last week when it was closed and thinking how nice and cheerful and welcoming it looked, with the chairs and tables and those jolly posters on the walls. It must be a godsend for those poor folk.'

In the far corner, an open door gave a view of what looked like a small kitchen. The three women took off their coats, hung them up behind the door and put on aprons. One filled a kettle, set it on a stove and lit the gas before the three of them set to work unloading their shopping bags and setting the contents out on a table. They were so absorbed in what they were doing that it was several minutes before they realized they had some unfamiliar visitors.

The youngest of the three, who nevertheless appeared to be in charge, left what she was doing and came over to them. 'Can I help you?' she said pleasantly. They held up their IDs and her face changed. 'Is one of our clients in trouble?' she asked uneasily.

'Not that we know of,' Sukey assured her, 'but we are seeking information about someone who used to serve here as a volunteer and we're wondering if you or one of your colleagues can help us. Is there somewhere we can talk privately?'

'We have a small office upstairs,' the woman replied. 'I suppose we could . . .'

'Hey, Zoe, what's happened to the tea?' called one of the 'clients', a thin young man with a shaven head.

'Just waiting for the kettle to boil, Scotty,' she called back. She turned to the two detectives. 'Would you mind waiting while I give them their tea or coffee?' she said. 'It'll be their first hot drink for goodness knows how long.'

'No problem,' they assured her. They watched with interest as the women bustled about in the kitchen; within a very short time everyone had received a hot drink and been invited to help themselves from boxes of muffins taken from one of the carrier bags.

'These'll keep you going till we get the hot breakfasts ready,' said Zoe as the muffins were eagerly snapped up. 'The local

supermarkets are so good to us,' she said when she rejoined
Sukey and Vicky a few moments later. 'Anything that's reached
its sell-by date they distribute to local charities – we simply
couldn't manage without them. Now, you wanted a private word
about one of our former volunteers. Come this way.' She led
them to a staircase adjacent to the kitchen, from which came the
appetizing smell and sizzle of frying sausages, and led them up
to a small office on the first floor. 'What name was it?'

'His full name was Tobias Mayhew, but you may have known
him simply as Toby.' said Vicky.

'Toby?' Zoe thought for a moment. 'It doesn't ring a bell.
How long ago was this?'

'We don't know exactly how long he helped here, but we
believe he gave up two years or so ago.'

'In that case I'm afraid I can't help you. I've only been doing
this job for eighteen months. Peggy's been here for quite a long
time; I'll ask her.' Zoe disappeared for a moment, returning shortly
with a tall, grey-haired woman with a slightly harassed expression. 'This is Peggy,' she said. 'She thinks she may be able to
help you. I must go and help with the breakfasts.'

'I do remember a man called Toby,' said Peggy. 'Yes, that's
him,' she added as they showed her the photograph the Mayhews
had lent them. 'He told us he was looking for a job but hadn't
found one that suited him and he offered to help here until something turned up. He never spoke much about his private life but
he used to chat to the clients, in particular one who came in
regularly about that time. The two of them seemed to strike up
some sort of relationship.'

'Can you remember this person's name?' asked Vicky.

Peggy frowned and bit her lip. 'It began with a W . . . not
William . . . something a little unusual . . . maybe Wilfred . . . no,
that wasn't it . . .' She shook her head. 'Sorry, I can't remember.'

'Could it have been Warren?'

'Yes, that's right, it was Warren!' she said eagerly. 'That's
what he called himself. I don't think I've heard the name before.'

'Called himself? You mean you don't think that was his real
name?' asked Sukey.

Peggy shrugged. 'It may have been, I suppose, but there was
something about this person . . . he always looked scruffy and

wore shabby clothes, but to be honest I thought he looked too
fit to be a genuine down-and-out and I had the feeling he was
a bit of a freeloader. The others thought I was being a bit, well,
unchristian, but to be honest I wasn't sorry when he stopped
coming.'

'Is this the man you're talking about?' Sukey held up the shot
of Warren Chesney taken at the time of his arrest.

This time there was no hesitation. 'Yes, that's definitely him.'
Peggy gave Sukey a sharp look. 'That's a police photo, isn't it?
Has he been arrested?'

'He's awaiting trial on charges of drug-related offences.'

'I suppose that means I was absolutely right to be suspicious
of him,' said Peggy soberly. 'I wonder if he had anything to do
with the change in Toby's behaviour?' she added, half to herself.

'Tell us about it,' said Vicky.

Sukey and Vicky arrived back at headquarters to find a message
from DS Rathbone to say that he had spoken to the postman at
the *Echo* office. He had given his name as Ronald Painter and
shown considerable surprise at being asked to 'help with their
enquiries into a serious crime', but agreed provided he was
allowed to finish his round first. While they were waiting, the
two DCs prepared their report on the visit to The Cleft Stick.

'This could be useful stuff during the interview with Ron,'
Vicky remarked when they had finished.

'It certainly looks as if Chesney went out of his way to influence Toby,' Sukey agreed. 'It's all circumstantial, of course, but . . .'

They were interrupted by a further call from Rathbone.
'Uniformed think they might have found the car used by Wally
Price,' he said. 'It was in a side road about a quarter of a mile
from Dobbie's house.'

'Why "used by"?' asked Vicky.

'The key on Price's key ring didn't fit so they discounted it
at first, but it so happens that the car belongs to someone in
Easton who reported it stolen after he discovered it was missing
from his front drive when he went out to fetch his Sunday paper.'

'Well, if Price did use a car – which seems probable – it might
have made sense to nick one that couldn't be traced to him
instead of using his own.'

'That's what I'm thinking,' Rathbone agreed. 'Anyway, the owner's being very co-operative and allowing us to examine his car before returning it to him, in the hope that forensics can pick up something to link it to Price. How did you and Sukey get on at The Cleft Stick?'

'We got some pretty interesting stuff about Warren Chesney. We've done our report but if you've got a moment now . . .'

'Save it till I come in. Painter's just put in an appearance,' said Rathbone and ended the call.

'Price obviously went to a lot of trouble to cover his tracks,' Sukey remarked after Vicky put the phone down. She was about to repeat her earlier premonition – one of her famous hunches, Vicky had teased – that the Chinese tattoo identified those who wore it as members of a secret and potentially murderous society, but changed her mind. She had to admit, even to herself, that there was absolutely no evidence to support the notion. But she resolved not to lose sight of it, just the same.

TWENTY-SIX

'He's in an interview room with a cup of tea and some sandwiches he bought for his lunch,' said Rathbone as he joined Sukey and Vicky in the CID office. 'He seems quite relaxed; I said we'd be with him in a few minutes and all he said was, "No problem". Either he's a tough, experienced operator or he's genuinely got nothing to hide. Right, let's have your report on The Cleft Stick.'

'It's in your in-tray, Sarge,' said Vicky.

He made an impatient gesture. 'I'll read it later; just give me a quick summary.'

'We spoke to quite a few people,' Vicky began, 'but the only one who was able to give us any really useful information about Toby Mayhew was a lady called Peggy who's worked there for a number of years. She remembers him quite clearly; as his parents told us, he went there as a volunteer. He never spoke to the others about his private life except that he'd recently left the army and was living with his parents while looking for a job. He apparently got on well with the other volunteers and the clients, as they call them. He used to chat with them about things in general while serving them or clearing the tables, but after a while Peggy noticed that one of the regulars used to make a point of seeking him out . . . asking him to sit down with him when things got quiet towards closing time and so on. To use Peggy's own words, "they seemed to strike up a relationship" and she noticed this guy would often hang around on the other side of the street, waiting for Toby to leave, and they'd go off together.'

'She made a point of saying she didn't take to the man because she didn't believe he was a genuine down-and-out,' said Sukey. 'We showed her the mug shot of Warren Chesney and she identified him immediately.'

'How long did this go on?'

'She can't recall when it started, but she remembers they all noticed the same sort of change in Toby's behaviour as his parents described – mood swings and so on – and some weeks later both he and the other man stopped coming to the centre and they never saw either of them again.'

'It looks as if Chesney went out of his way to cultivate Mayhew and get him hooked on drugs,' said Rathbone. 'Did Peggy ever overhear anything that passed between them?'

'No, Sarge.'

'How long ago would it be that Mayhew disappeared?'

'She thinks about two years.'

Rathbone nodded. 'Around the time he left home. Interesting. I wonder why Chesney made a point of targeting him? Peggy didn't notice him on particularly intimate terms with any of the other clients?'

'We asked her about that and she said no,' said Vicky. 'It seems pretty obvious, in the light of what we know now, that he had his reasons for thinking Mayhew would serve his purpose. We think he was probably looking for someone to fill a gap in his organization and thought Mayhew a suitable candidate. Maybe Mayhew confided in him and so appeared vulnerable, but at the same time smart enough to play a useful part in his distribution network. It may be he was already using pot and it was easy to introduce him to the hard stuff. Whatever the motive, it seems pretty clear that having got him dependent on drugs, Chesney recruited him and even offered him a home.'

'Has Wally Price ever been seen at The Cleft Stick?

'We showed the mug shot around, but no one there recognized him, Sarge.'

'What about the death tattoo?'

'We showed that around as well, but again no one recognized it. Peggy's there most days; she drew a copy and promised to show it to the people who come in on other days. And by the way, she'd never heard anyone mention "Delta" either.'

'At least we now have a clearer picture of the chain of events that took Mayhew to the house in Tyndale Gardens,' Rathbone observed, 'although it doesn't add up to much more than confirmation of what we already suspected. Right, let's go and see what Painter has to say for himself.'

Ronald Painter was a well-set-up man whom Sukey judged

to be in his early to mid-forties, with neatly brushed fair hair and brown eyes beneath strong, straight eyebrows. He had a clear skin and the healthy appearance of a man who spent much of his time in the fresh air. When Rathbone entered the room, accompanied by Sukey and Vicky, he finished his mug of tea and began folding the wrapper of the sandwiches that he had apparently just finished eating.

'I apologize for keeping you waiting, Mr Painter,' said Rathbone.

Sukey thought she detected a hint of reluctance on Painter's part to meet Rathbone's eye before he replied, 'That's all right, Sergeant, and thanks for the tea.' He finished folding the wrapper and put it in the pocket of his denim jacket. 'So what do you want from me?'

'First of all, I have to make it clear that you are here voluntarily and you are free to leave at any time. This interview is not being recorded on tape, but these officers –' he indicated the two DCs sitting beside him – 'may make a few notes. Do you understand?'

Painter nodded. 'Yes, Sergeant.'

'Good. You are, I believe, a postman and your regular round includes the offices of the *Echo*. Is that correct?' Painter nodded again. 'How long would you say this has been the case?'

'Just over a year.'

'Long enough to become familiar with the layout of the building?'

'I only go into the general office.'

'What about the toilets?'

Painter hesitated for a moment before replying, 'I've used them once or twice. I asked permission,' he added. 'Has someone complained?'

Rathbone ignored the question. 'Have you ever, while in the *Echo* toilets, made a call on your mobile phone?'

'Why would I do that?'

'Maybe it was quiet in there, or maybe it was raining outside,' Rathbone suggested. 'Or perhaps it was about something particularly urgent.' Painter sucked his lower lip and shook his head. Rathbone leaned forward, looked the man straight in the eye and said, 'Does the name "Hermes" mean anything to you?'

Painter showed no reaction other than mild surprise at the detective's sudden change of direction. 'Hermes? Can't say I have.'

'It's the name of a Greek god. In classical times he was known as the messenger of the gods.'

Painter raised his eyebrows. 'Very interesting,' he said. 'I didn't know that.'

'Have you ever heard of someone whose associates refer to or address as Delta?' Painter shook his head. 'You're sure?'

'Quite sure.'

'So if I were to tell you that a witness overheard a man making a telephone call in the toilets at the *Echo* office to someone he addressed as Delta and informed that person that Hermes was dead, it would mean nothing to you?'

Sukey was certain she detected a tightening of the muscles round Painter's mouth, but his voice was steady and he met Rathbone's eyes without flinching as he replied, 'Nothing at all.'

'And if I were to tell you that our witness has identified you as the person making that call?'

For the first time Painter appeared rattled. 'But he couldn't have . . .' he began.

Rathbone pounced. 'You mean, the toilets were apparently empty at the time so there was no one to overhear you make the call?'

'I didn't say that.'

'Do you deny making the call?'

'Of course I deny it. Your witness made a mistake, that's all.'

'I see.' Rathbone sat back in his chair. 'Mr Painter, I believe you have a tattoo on your right wrist. Would you mind showing it to us?'

Again, an unmistakable hint of unease flickered across Painter's features, but he quickly recovered and said, 'Sure.' He pulled back the sleeve of his jacket. 'There it is. Chinese, so the tattoo artist told me.'

'Did he tell you what it means?'

'I asked him, but he said he didn't know. He said it came in a sort of catalogue of patterns that he showed people who wanted a tattoo but didn't have anything particular in mind.'

'And you chose that one?' Painter shrugged. 'Why?'

''Cos it looked different, I suppose. What's so important about it?'

'You were in the Stompers Night Club on Saturday, we believe.'

'That's right. What of it?'

'You spent some time chatting to two girls, one called Lotus who works in an office where you deliver mail and the other a friend of hers called Tricia.'

'What of it? I enjoy chatting to girls.'

'I'm told Tricia showed a great interest in your tattoo.'

Painter gave a half grin and said, 'It always seems to fascinate women. The mystic East and all that.'

'We understand Tricia had a particular reason for her interest. Can you recall what that was?'

'Can't say I do. She was half-cut . . . I didn't take much notice.'

'Was it because someone her friend Lotus knew had been attacked by a man with a tattoo like yours on his wrist?'

'The two of them were rabbiting on together but I don't remember what about. It was girl talk . . . I couldn't be bothered to listen.'

'In fact you left the club soon after?'

'Might have done. I wasn't keeping track of the time. Look, Sergeant, you asked me to help with enquiries into a serious crime, but all you've talked about so far is some geezer making mysterious phone calls, two females who were half-cut and a perfectly harmless tattoo. As I said, I'm always willing to help the police, but I don't see . . .'

'All right, I just wanted to clear up a few minor matters first.' Rathbone's tone was almost affable and he sat back in his chair. 'Now, you may have read the reports in the press of an incident that took place in Tyndale Gardens in the small hours of Sunday morning?'

Painter shook his head. 'Can't say I have. I don't read the papers, except the sports pages.'

'In that case, you will not be aware that a man was arrested and later charged with being in unauthorized possession of an offensive weapon?' Painter shook his head. 'You will certainly not be aware – because what I am about to tell you did not appear in the press reports – that the suspect has a tattoo on his wrist identical to your own?'

'So he went to the same place as I did. There's probably any amount of them knocking around.'

'It so happens we already know of one more. It was on the arm of a dismembered corpse washed up a few weeks ago on the coast near the mouth of the Mersey. In fact,' Rathbone went on, still in the same deceptively conversational tone, 'we're beginning to think it's the symbol of some kind of cult.'

'If it is, I don't know nothing about it.'

'That's what Wally Price said. You don't know him, by any chance?'

'Never heard of him,' said Painter confidently. 'Is he the bloke you nicked yesterday?'

'That's the name he gave us, but we're pretty certain it isn't his real one. In fact,' Rathbone continued, 'he seems to have gone to considerable trouble to conceal his identity.'

Sukey was beginning to wonder where this line of questioning was leading, but at this point there was a tap on the door and DS Tim Pringle's face appeared at the window. Rathbone got up and went outside; when he returned he said, without any preamble, 'I have just received a very interesting report from one of our officers. He and a colleague have been checking the tattoo parlours in the city to try and find one who remembers a client who chose the design that you, Mr Painter, and our suspect are both wearing. And guess what –' this time there was no affability in Rathbone's manner – 'their search was successful. They found a tattoo artist who had been asked to carry out that same design on two men who came to his parlour. Interesting, don't you think?'

Plainly uncomfortable, but evidently feeling compelled to make some response, Painter muttered, 'More of a coincidence, I'd say.'

'Not only that,' Rathbone continued, 'their informant stated that he is quite sure he has never carried out this design before or since, nor – and he has been in the business for a considerable time – has he ever seen it in any pattern book. Both these clients brought a drawing of the design they wanted.' Rathbone paused for a moment and then, in a movement that reminded Sukey of a conjuror pulling a card out of the air, he produced from his pocket a copy of the mug shot of Wally Price and pushed it across the table. 'Ever seen him before?'

Painter took a sharp breath and stared fixedly at the photograph for several seconds before saying in an almost inaudible voice, 'No, never.'

'Supposing I tell you that this man was identified by the tattoo artist as one of the men who asked for that design?' the detective continued, his gaze fixed intently on Painter's face. The man shrugged, but kept his own eyes on his hands, which were tightly clasped together. 'Or that he gave a description of the other man – a description that could very well apply to you?'

For a moment it seemed Painter was about to break, but with an effort he raised his head, pushed back his chair and stood up. 'This has gone far enough,' he said harshly. 'You said I was free to go at any time, and that's what I'm doing. I'm saying nothing more.'

'Just one moment,' said Rathbone. Painter, already on his way to the door, stopped in his tracks, but did not turn round. 'You told us that you chose that design from a book of patterns, I believe?' Rathbone went on.

'That's right.'

'Our suspect – the man who has the same tattoo – told us that same story, which we now know to be untrue.'

Reluctantly, Painter turned round and with what appeared to Sukey to be a supreme effort he looked Rathbone straight in the eye. 'Then all I can say is that we must have gone to different tattoo parlours,' he said.

'Just another coincidence, in fact?'

'It must have been.'

'Then perhaps you would allow us to take your photograph so that we can eliminate you from our enquiries? Before you give an answer, I should make it clear that those enquiries are part of a serious case involving at least one murder.'

'I told you, I've got nothing more to say,' Painter declared, and this time he wrenched open the door and marched out of the room.

TWENTY-SEVEN

'The connection with Chesney needs looking into,' said DCI Leach. 'Any thoughts on that, Greg?'

'I've been having a look over his file, sir,' said Rathbone. 'One thing struck me in particular; he's described as being "heavily tattooed". I can't find a reference to any particular design so I'm thinking it would be worth checking whether he's got one of these Chinese characters on him somewhere, particularly on his right wrist.'

'Good idea; get on with it,' said Leach. 'Now, we have to get a mug shot of Painter but we must do it by the book, so give him another chance to co-operate and at the same time make it clear that if he declines there are other possibilities open to us. He'll almost certainly refuse, of course, so in the circumstances I'll authorize the techies to start setting up a covert operation.' He made a note. 'The CSIs have been working on the car and they've found some fibres on the driver's seat and grit in the foot well that might with a bit of luck match with samples taken from Price's clothing. Not that charging him with one case of twocking will help our case much further forward,' he added with a wry smile, 'although once we establish his real identity we might come across something more useful. Any other ideas?' His eyes swept briefly round the room.

Sukey opened her mouth and then closed it, but Leach gave her a keen glance. 'You were going to say something, Sukey?'

'I keep finding myself thinking back to that episode in the car park, sir,' she said hesitantly. 'I know there's absolutely no connection – not that we know of, at any rate – between the man who received the envelope from Mayhew and anything we've uncovered since, but there might be a connection between Mayhew and the people wearing the Chinese tattoo because it looks as if it was Wally Price who was lurking outside Mayhew's house and attacked Jason Dobbie when he went to investigate.'

'So you still think we should be taking an interest in this individual?'

'Well, sir, when Vicky and I were observing him we made a note of his car registration number. Suppose we were to check the details of the owner on the PNC? It's just possible we might find a link.'

Leach compressed his lips and Sukey found herself wishing devoutly that she had kept her mouth shut. Eventually he said, 'And what sort of link do you expect to find?'

'We've heard several references to someone who calls himself Delta. That's the fourth letter of the Greek alphabet, and Hermes is a Greek god. Suppose the owner of that car is Greek? If he is, wouldn't it be worth finding out a bit more about him? Suppose he wears a tattoo like the others? Wouldn't that put him in the frame?'

By the time she had finished, Sukey was aware that her heart was thumping and her cheeks uncomfortably warm. Leach sat in silence for a few moments and then turned to Rathbone. 'Greg? I can tell by your expression that you don't rate this idea very highly.'

Rathbone shrugged. 'First it's an obsession with Chinamen and now it's Greeks,' he said in exasperation. 'Oh well, it can't do any harm and it wouldn't take long, so I suppose she might as well go ahead. It'll probably come to nothing, but at least it'll stop her nagging.'

Leach nodded. 'All right, Sukey, you have permission to check the owner of that car. And if it isn't someone with a Greek or a Chinese name I don't want to hear any more about it. Understood?'

'Yes sir . . . and thank you,' Sukey said meekly.

'And, Greg,' Leach went on, turning back to Rathbone, 'when you interview Painter about the mug shot, ask him to hand over his mobile so you can check the numbers in his browser. If he really is part of the Delta mob, that should put the frighteners on him.'

'Will do, sir.'

'So get on with it.' Leach gathered up his notes and the team, taking the action as a sign of dismissal, got up and left.

Back in the CID office, Rathbone issued instructions. 'Vicky, Chesney's in the remand wing in Bristol prison. Get in touch with the governor and arrange for me to see Chesney tomorrow. Sukey, I take it you have a note of Painter's address?'

'Yes, Sarge.'

'What about a phone number?'

'No, Sarge.'

'Never mind. It would be better anyway to take him by surprise so you and I will pay him a call before we go home.'

'Suppose he's out?' said Sukey hopefully, with a covert glance at the clock. She had been looking forward to that evening's episode of her favourite soap and it began to look as if she was going to miss it.

Rathbone grinned. 'I doubt it. He's more likely to be getting ready to flash his oriental tattoo at a few more impressionable females at Stompers, so let's not hang about.'

Painter lived in a basement flat in a quiet street in Cotham. When he opened the door and saw the two detectives he appeared startled for a moment, but quickly recovered himself. 'What the hell do you want now?' he demanded.

· 'Just a couple more questions,' said Rathbone smoothly. 'May we come in, or do you want the lady whose curtains are twitching above our heads to hear what we've come for?'

'Nosy old biddy!' Painter muttered as he stood aside to admit them. 'So, what is it?' he asked as they stepped into a brightly lit hallway. 'You'll forgive me if I don't invite you in for a drink,' he added as he closed the door.

'No problem, we can talk here,' said Rathbone. 'Now, you declined earlier to allow us to take a photograph of you for elimination purposes – as of course you had every right to do since you were not under arrest.'

'So?'

'You left in rather a hurry, which meant you didn't give us time to point out – as we are legally obliged to do – that if you persist in refusing, and if we consider such a photograph necessary as part of our investigations, we are legally entitled to obtain it by other means.'

'What other means?'

'Oh, there are various possibilities open to us,' said Rathbone smoothly.

'Then go ahead – see if I care.' Despite Painter's defiant manner, Sukey detected a wary expression in his eyes. 'So what's the next question?'

'You assured us that you have never heard of a person called Delta, or spoken to him on your mobile.' Painter nodded. 'So would you mind letting us check it so that we can be sure you are speaking the truth?'

'I'm not parting with it,' Painter declared. 'I need it to keep in touch with people – people at work as well as mates.'

'That's no problem – just give it to DC Reynolds and she'll do it here and now. It won't take more than a few minutes.'

Painter shrugged and disappeared into a room at the far end of the hall, returning a few moments later with a very smart, state-of-the-art mobile phone. Without a word he handed it to Sukey, who sat down in a chair standing conveniently beside the front door, took out her notebook and began scrolling through the various options for the information she needed. When she had finished she returned it to its owner, who put it in his pocket. 'Anything else you need?' he said with a hint of a sneer. 'Birth certificate? Driving licence?'

'Thank you sir, that will be all – for the time being,' said Rathbone politely. 'Cocky bugger,' he exploded as he and Sukey returned to their car. 'He reckons he's fireproof. We'll show him. I'll give the techies a jog first thing tomorrow and tell them to get a mug shot ASAP. If the tattoo artist can identify him he'll sing a different tune.'

It was seven o'clock by the time Sukey got home. Having prepared the ingredients for her evening meal, she checked her answering service. There was just one message; it was from Harry Matthews, who merely said he would call again later. Her first thought was that he wanted to pick her brains and she decided that he could wait, but she had barely sat down to relax with a glass of wine than he called again.

'Ah, you're home!' he said. 'Dad's a bit under the weather so I've just been doing a spot of shopping at the supermarket for him and I saw your car. Have you been working overtime?'

'A bit,' she acknowledged.

'I notice our postie is still doing his daily round, so it wasn't him your lot nicked on Saturday night?'

'Correct.'

'And you think the reason for this call is to try and get some info out of you, I suppose?'

'It had occurred to me.'

'Well, it so happens this is not a fishing expedition.'

'No?'

'Definitely not. It's to ask if you'll have dinner with me tomorrow.'

Apart from the recent invitation from Harry's father, it was the first time a man had invited her out since the separation from Jim and it came as an unexpected pleasure. 'That's really nice of you, I'd love to – provided of course that I don't have to work more overtime,' she added, almost mechanically, reflecting that such uncertainties went with the job.

'In that case, we'll simply postpone it,' said Harry. They agreed a time when he would pick her up; Sukey finished her wine, put her meal on a tray and watched *EastEnders* with even more enjoyment than usual.

Next morning, Vicky reported that she had arranged the interview with Warren Chesney that Rathbone had requested. 'I understand he's not too happy about it,' she said.

'Too bad,' said Rathbone. 'Mike, you'll come with me; Sukey, while I'm away you and Vicky are to check on all the numbers you found in Painter's mobile browser and at the same time find out if he's been calling any others. Calls received as well. I'd like to think one of the ones you jotted down would lead us to Delta, but I'm not exactly brimming with confidence.'

'We might find a connection with the owner of that white Peugeot,' Sukey suggested, and was rewarded by a cynical curl of the lip from DS Rathbone.

It did not take long to establish that the owner of the white Peugeot was one Daniel Lionel Tanner with an address in Portishead. 'Neither a Greek nor a Chinese,' sighed Sukey as she returned to the office to find Vicky at work on the list of numbers Sukey had given her.

'At least his first name begins with a D,' said Vicky.

'In common with several thousand other people,' said Sukey. 'He's probably a respectable businessman, a pillar of the church and chairman of the Rotary Club. Might as well check his landline while we're at it.' She riffled through the pages of the phone directory, pounced on a name and called out the number. 'Any joy?'

Vicky shook her head. 'There aren't any landlines on here, only mobile numbers. 'Let's call them in turn and ask to speak to Mr Tanner.' They shared them out; it took only a short time to carry out the check and once again they drew a blank.

Vicky sat for a few minutes in silence, turning Painter's phone in her hand. 'This is a very new model,' she said thoughtfully. 'I wonder how long he's had it . . . and whether it's the only one he's got. There's nothing to stop anyone having more than one, is there? I mean, supposing he anticipated being asked to hand this over for examination . . .'

'. . . and bought this one, put in a few of his mates and the odd takeaway and kept it in readiness . . .'

Vicky was busy scrolling through the menu. 'There's no record of any incoming calls,' she commented. I know what!' She took out her own mobile and began jabbing keys. 'I'm on the same system as this phone and I've got a contact . . . hullo? Maisie? Vicky Armstrong here. Listen, can you check on this number?' The conversation continued for a couple of minutes before Vicky, looking extremely pleased with herself, ended the call and said, 'As I thought. The number on that phone was registered to Ronald Painter just two days ago. And he doesn't have another account with Maisie's company.'

'So it couldn't have been the one he used to call Delta,' said Sukey. 'Remember what I said about Wally Price going to a lot of trouble to cover his tracks? It begins to look more than ever as if Painter's doing the same and my guess is the two of them are part of the same mob, but we can't prove it without some cast-iron evidence.'

Their speculations were interrupted by the return of DS Rathbone and DC Mike Haskins. Without saying a word, Rathbone marched over to the coffee machine. His demeanour made it clear that the interview with Chesney had not been fruitful. 'There was no sign of the Chinese tattoo on his wrist or anywhere else,' said Mike. 'He bent over backwards to prove it and he insisted on stripping off to show us his entire art collection – which was quite impressive,' he added with a grin. 'We showed him the design, of course, and he flatly denied ever having seen it or anything like it before.'

'He'd seen it before all right,' said Rathbone, who had just rejoined the group with his mug of coffee. 'It was obvious from his body language that he not only recognized it but knew exactly what it meant. Just like Price and Painter, in fact,' he added moodily. 'It's beginning to look as if there's something or someone really big behind this, and ten to one the key factor is drugs. I must talk to the SIO – my guess is he'll hand the case over to the drugs squad.'

About ten minutes before Harry was due to call for her that evening, Sukey received a call from Fergus. 'Hi, Mum!' he said breezily, 'caught any crooks today?'

'Not so far,' she responded in the same light tone, 'but if you have any useful tips make it snappy as I'm going out in a few minutes.'

'Anywhere interesting?'

'Harry Matthews is taking me out to dinner but he hasn't told me where we're going.'

'Great! He may be interested in this as well. Listen, Mum, have you ever read a poem called "The Vampire"?'

Sukey thought for a moment. 'It doesn't ring any bells. What of it anyway?'

'Listen. I'll read you the first verse and see if it suggests anything to you.'

'All right.' She listened, thought for a moment and said, 'Sorry, I don't see . . .' At that moment her front door bell rang. 'Must go, Harry's at the door. I'll bounce it off him and see if he comes up with any bright ideas.'

As it happened, Harry had a bright idea of his own – one that led to unforeseen and near fatal consequences.

TWENTY-EIGHT

I t had taken some time for Sukey to decide what to wear for her date with Harry. She rejected what Fergus had described as the 'funky top' she had worn the evening she spent with Harry's father and Freddie Sinclair, partly because she wanted a change but also because it would from now on be forever associated in her mind with the night at Stompers, the arrest of Wally Price and the subsequent shock on discovering that he and the man Harry was certain had made the call to Delta were two different people. While she was rummaging through her wardrobe she found herself mulling over the case, even though it now appeared unlikely that she would play any further part in it.

She finally settled on a pair of black silk trousers, a cream shirt and a scarlet velvet jacket, and was rewarded by Harry's reaction when she opened the door to him.

'You look stunning!' he said. 'You should wear that shade of red more often; it really suits you.'

It was an encouraging start to the evening. Harry had ordered a taxi – 'I hate driving into the city; parking's always a problem and anyway, what's a night out without a drink?' he said as they set off. 'I suggest we find somewhere we like the look of, have a preprandial snort and decide whether we're going to eat there or go and look for somewhere else.' The taxi dropped them near the main shopping centre and he took her arm. 'Come on, there's plenty here to choose from.'

Sukey was happy to fall in with his suggestion. It was a mild evening and there were plenty of people about, some passing the time window-shopping, others strolling up and down in the same relaxed fashion as themselves. After inspecting a few menus they agreed to start at a Spanish tapas bar. They found a seat by the window; Harry ordered two glasses of Rioja and they sat sipping and watching the passing show.

After a few minutes he said, 'I see postman Ron has been at work as usual so I suppose he's got bail?'

Sukey eyed him above the rim of her glass. 'I thought we agreed there'd be no fishing,' she said.

Harry helped himself from the dish of tapas before saying, 'Not really fishing, just commenting. If we'd had anyone available we'd have covered his court appearance on Monday.' When Sukey made no reply he went on, 'It was him who was arrested early on Sunday morning, wasn't it – or was there another incident we haven't heard about?'

'The answer's no to both questions,' she said.

'You mean you nicked another bloke and our Ron is out of the frame?' he exclaimed. 'But what about the phone call . . . Delta and Hermes and all that stuff?' he persisted when she made no answer. 'He must be involved somewhere. I can always do some ferreting around on my own, of course – but you did warn me it might be dangerous!' he added with a provocative grin.

'It's no laughing matter; dangerous is likely to be the operative word,' Sukey said quietly. 'The fact is, it's beginning to look a lot bigger than we thought and there's talk of handing the case over to the drugs squad. And anything to do with drugs and drug barons is for specially trained officers to handle, not for amateurs to fool around with.'

Harry did not reply directly. He drained his glass, noticed that hers was almost empty and said, 'Let's have another of these before we start thinking about food.'

The warmth of the wine was already filtering pleasantly through her system. 'That'd be nice, thank you,' she said.

They continued to enjoy their drinks in a companionable silence. Then Harry said, 'I'll tell you what, let's make a deal. You tell me why Ron is still in the frame and I'll promise not to play detectives.'

Torn between her duty of discretion as a police officer and a desire for an independent sounding board for her own ideas about the case, Sukey took only a few seconds to plump for the latter. 'We pulled him in for questioning about the phone call, but of course he denied making it and insisted the names Delta and Hermes meant nothing to him. He also denied knowing anyone called Wally Price . . . oh dear, I shouldn't have said that.'

'Who's Wally Price?' Harry demanded.

'It's the name the guy we nicked on Sunday morning gave us. It's phoney, of course, so naturally Ron didn't recognize it.'

'Which shows he told the truth about something,' Harry remarked.

'Except that when we showed him a mug shot he swore he'd never seen the man before but we're pretty sure he was lying. This man Price – or whatever his name is, and anyway it hasn't been released yet so please forget I said it – has an identical tattoo on his right wrist.' She went on to tell Harry about the evidence of the tattoo artist and how Ron had refused to allow the police to take his photograph for elimination purposes.

'I believe you've got your own methods of doing that,' said Harry.

'Yes, but it'll take a few days to set it up.'

'Do you know which tattoo parlour these two jokers used?'

Sukey thought for a moment. 'Something like "Art for your Skin" – no, that's not it.'

'How about "Art-Full Skin" – with a hyphen?' suggested Harry.

Sukey nodded. 'Yes, I think that was it. Do you know the place?'

'I know of it, although I've never patronized it or any other like it – and I'm willing to prove it!' said Harry with a mischievous glint in his eye that caused a slight but noticeable disturbance to Sukey's pulse rate.

'All right, I believe you,' she said hastily. 'By the way, do you remember I told you about an odd incident in the motorway car park?'

'About the man with the envelope with the collection of bits and pieces in it? Yes, what about it?'

'I managed to get permission to check on his car. It didn't get me anywhere, I'm afraid.' Somewhat ruefully, she recounted her fruitless search for a possible Greek connection.

'What about Ron's mobile?'

'We've checked that without success, although we have our doubts there as well.'

Harry glanced at his watch. His expression had grown serious. 'It so happens that tattoo parlour is just around the corner from here. Some of these places stay open till about eight; why don't we stroll round and have a look at it?'

'What for?' she asked.

'Sukey, you said this was a dangerous bunch. If Ron was the second man and the tattooist can identify him, it would prove he's been lying . . . and even if he wasn't the one who attacked Dobbie it would still take some explaining, wouldn't it?'

'Of course – and that's what we're hoping.'

'So, if you were Ron, would you want to be identified?'

'No, of course not.' Suddenly Sukey took a sharp breath and clapped a hand to her mouth. 'Oh good heavens, are you suggesting . . . ?'

'I'm thinking it might be an idea to warn this guy that he might be in danger.'

'You can't expect me to go barging in without any kind of authority,' she objected. 'If it got back to my sergeant or the SIO I'd be back in uniform on the spot.'

'Suit yourself.' While they were speaking, Harry had paid for their wine. He got up from his chair and said, 'If I'm not back within ten minutes you'd better send in the heavy mob. As you don't want to get involved you can stay here and study the menu.'

'Not likely!' She was on her feet in an instant. 'I shouldn't have told you any of this and the least I can do is back you up.'

'You might need to summon back-up for the pair of us,' said Harry over his shoulder. He set off along the street at a brisk pace with Sukey hurrying along a short distance behind him. He crossed the street, stopped at a corner a few yards further on and waited the few seconds it took for her to catch up with him. 'It's the second shop on the right,' he said, pointing. 'Looks like we're just in time; someone's knocking on the door,' he exclaimed. 'Come on!'

As they hurried forward Sukey caught a glimpse of a man clad in denim shorts and jacket entering the Art-Full Skin Tattoo Parlour. To her horror, Harry sprinted the few intervening yards, reached the door just as it was about to close and hurled himself against it. It flew open under his weight and he all but fell as he stumbled through. Without stopping to think, Sukey rushed after him; seconds later she found herself staring down the barrel of a gun.

'Come and join the party,' said Painter. With a smile that struck
Sukey as having an almost satanic quality, he gestured with the
gun towards a shaven-headed, heavily tattooed young man who
cowered trembling behind a desk in what was evidently a small
reception area. 'Go and stand by my artistic friend over there
while I make sure we aren't disturbed.' Still keeping all three
covered, he walked over to the door, locked it and drew down
the blind. 'I'll take that,' he added, pointing to Sukey's mobile.
'We don't want any more uninvited guests, do we? Throw it on
the floor – now!'

'Better do as he says,' said Harry grimly and without a word
she complied. Painter picked it up, made sure it was switched
off and slipped it into his pocket.

The young tattooist raised his hands in a gesture of suppli-
cation. 'Why are you doing this?' he faltered. 'I opened up for
you specially . . . you said you wanted a new design . . . to please
a girlfriend . . . someone you're seeing tonight . . . a surprise . . .'
His voice trailed away in a half-sob.

'And this is the surprise I promised,' said Painter, 'but it's not
for a girlfriend, it's for you, Billy boy.'

'I don't understand,' said Billy piteously. Tears were streaming
down his face. 'I did what you and your friend asked last time
and I swear I haven't done that design for anyone else. For
God's sake, I'll do whatever you want . . . only please, please
don't kill me.'

'It's too late for that, I'm afraid,' said Ron, 'but don't worry,
you won't have to die alone. These nice people here will keep you
company. Let me introduce you – the lady is a police detective
and the gentleman is a journalist. I'm so sorry –' he made a mocking
bow towards Sukey and Harry without for one second relaxing his
guard – 'but I'm afraid there'll be no commendation from the Chief
Constable and no scoop for the *Echo* either.' His eyes flicked from
one to the other.

Sukey had been observing him closely throughout these
terrifying exchanges and was convinced she detected signs of
megalomania. He was plainly enjoying the feeling of power
over them. *Play for time,* she told herself silently, *flatter him,
keep him talking.* Aloud, she said, 'You really have been very
clever, Ron – you had us all fooled. You even wiped the SIM

card on your mobile so we wouldn't be able to locate Delta on your browser.'

Painter gave a gleeful laugh. 'Wipe my SIM card? Do me a favour! I knew you'd want to check my mobile sooner or later so I bought a new one just for your benefit.'

Sukey affected open-mouthed admiration. 'Gosh, that was a master stroke!' she declared.

Painter smirked. 'Yes, wasn't it? You see,' he lowered his voice to a confidential whisper, the gun still held steady, 'we who wear the Death Tattoo are chosen for our many outstanding qualities.'

Harry, who had remained silent so far, suddenly said, 'If you're such a bloody genius, why are you a postman?'

Painter rounded on him. His mood had changed in an instant. 'Shut up or you'll be the first to go!' he snarled. Mentally cursing Harry for his intervention, Sukey held her breath. She longed to check her watch but was afraid to move. *Oh come on! What's keeping you?* she mouthed silently. Painter relaxed and smiled gently at her. 'Saying your prayers, my dear? What a good idea! Will five seconds be enough?'

There was a hammering on the door and a shout of 'Armed police! Open up!'

As if launched from a catapult, Painter leapt on Sukey, grabbed her round the waist and pinioned her against him. With the gun at her throat he shouted, 'I've got three hostages in here! Break down that door and Detective Constable Reynolds dies first!'

The silence that followed last only a few seconds, yet to Sukey it seemed never-ending. Eventually a man's voice said, 'Are you there, Sukey?'

'Answer!' hissed Painter, jabbing her neck with the gun.

'Yes, I'm here,' she called shakily.

'OK. We'll do whatever you say. Do we back off or what?'

'Well, answer him,' said Painter mockingly.

'I . . . I . . .' Sukey's voice died away; she closed her eyes and allowed her head to roll sideways and her knees to buckle, at the same time shifting her right foot a fraction until she encountered Painter's boot.

'Oh shit, don't tell me your going to pass out,' snarled Painter. 'Trust a bloody woman to . . .'

His words died in a yelp of pain as Sukey raised her right

foot and dragged the heel of her shoe down Painter's shin bone. His grip on her arms slackened; she tore herself free, flung her upper body forward from the waist and screamed, 'Go for it!' The door burst open; there was a click as Painter cocked the gun and then let out a fresh howl of agony as a streak of brown fur shot past Sukey's head and Guy the police dog clamped the upraised arm in his powerful jaws.

TWENTY-NINE

Within seconds of being brought down by the dog, Painter was seized, disarmed, handcuffed and bundled into a waiting police van. Sukey and Harry watched in silence, conscious only of a sense of profound and indescribable relief.

Harry was the first to speak. 'My God, that was a plucky thing to do!' he muttered shakily.

Sukey gave an equally unsteady laugh. 'There wasn't much option, was there? When it's a choice between possible and certain death there's no contest. I bought these to match the jacket,' she added, glancing down at her bright red shoes with their high stiletto heels. 'I never dreamed they'd come in that useful. Bit of luck Ron was wearing shorts and not jeans. The spikes wouldn't have had quite the same effect through denim.'

'I guess someone up there was looking after us!' Harry responded soberly.

'I believe so too,' she replied. She was suddenly aware that not only was she trembling, she was leaning against him. His arm was round her shoulders and she was content to let it stay there.

Billy was slumped at the desk, his face in his hands and his shoulders heaving. A middle-aged uniformed officer stood beside him and touched him on the arm. 'We'd like a statement from you, sir,' he said kindly. 'Why don't you come down to the station with me? You'll find it more comfortable and you can have a cup of tea while we have our chat. Don't worry about this place; we'll take care of it.' His manner was almost fatherly; without a word, Billy got to his feet and allowed himself to be led away.

'I suppose they'll want statements from us as well,' said Harry.

'Too right they will,' said Sukey resignedly. She straightened up and hastily detached herself from Harry's embrace at the sight of a stony-faced DS Rathbone approaching, followed by a team of CSIs. 'Here comes my sergeant. You'll probably get away with a lecture about the inadvisability of "having-a-go". I'll have the book thrown at me.'

For the moment Rathbone ignored Sukey. 'Mr Matthews, I believe?' he said. Harry nodded. 'Would you kindly explain what you were doing in the Art-Full Skin Tattoo Parlour, sir? After a story, perhaps?'

Harry assumed an expression of contrition that Sukey suspected was not entirely genuine. 'I know I made an absolute fool of myself,' he said humbly, 'I was just trying to . . .'

'Never mind what you were trying to do,' said Rathbone sternly, 'the fact is that your thoughtless action nearly cost three lives – your own as well as those of one of my officers and the proprietor of this establishment.'

'Yes, officer, I do understand,' said Harry, 'and I hope you will bear in mind that had it not been for the extraordinary courage and resourcefulness of this lady . . .'

'Yes sir, I'm sure she appreciates your commendation.' Rathbone eyed Sukey up and down and she became conscious of her dishevelled appearance. 'It would seem that you were enjoying an evening out before this sudden change of plan?'

'Er, yes, we were going to have dinner,' said Harry.

Rathbone checked his watch. 'Then you must be feeling hungry.'

'Can we go, then?' said Harry.

'For the time being, yes, but we'll need a statement from you later.' Rathbone allowed himself the briefest of smiles, which faded as he turned to Sukey and said curtly, 'In DCI Leach's office first thing tomorrow.'

'Yes, Sarge.'

They returned to the tapas bar; Sukey went to the powder room to freshen up and tidy her hair, leaving Harry to study the menu handed to him by the same, now slightly bemused waiter who had served them with wine on their previous visit. When she rejoined him he said, 'How did you know the heavy mob was coming? Was it part of an operation that I nearly fouled up?'

She shook her head. 'Not that I know of. While I was chasing after you I was informing HQ where you were going and why. The minute you spotted Ron and went dashing after him I added an urgent request for backup. There wasn't time to go into details – all I could do was hope and pray they got there in time.'

'Only just,' said Harry. 'If you hadn't kept Ron talking . . .'

'Well, I did and it worked, so let's stop thinking about it and decide what we're going to eat before the place shuts down,' said Sukey firmly.

They were halfway through their paella when Sukey suddenly remembered Fergus's phone call. 'Do you know a poem "The Vampire"?' she asked.

Harry shook his head. 'Sorry, never heard of it I'm afraid.'

'It means nothing to me either,' said Sukey. 'Gus seemed to think it has a great significance. He read me the first verse but it didn't make much sense to me. I can't even remember how it went now – something about a fool who made a prayer to a woman who did not care.'

'Sounds like it's been written by a man who's been dumped,' Harry commented wryly. 'Did he go on to call her a vampire?'

'Not in the bit that Gus read out – just the title.' She paused with a forkful of paella halfway to her mouth. 'There must be more to it than that or Gus wouldn't have sounded so excited. I'll Google it when I get home.'

Later, when the taxi dropped them off at Sukey's door, Harry put his hands on her shoulders and kissed her gently on both cheeks. His face stayed close to hers for several seconds as he said softly, 'I hope we can do this again before long.'

She made no attempt to move away. 'Only if you promise not to go chasing after any more homicidal postmen,' she replied.

'Scout's honour!' he assured her.

Before going to bed, Sukey wrote a hasty report of her part in the evening's drama. She then searched the Internet and found the poem, but although she read the first verse several times she failed to see what Fergus had been driving at. It did not trouble her unduly, neither was she disturbed by memories of the recent drama – the fear, the struggle and the narrow escape from death. The evening had ended on a much pleasanter note and she slept soundly until awakened by the alarm.

'I was warned when you first joined our team that you were a bit of a loose cannon,' said DCI Leach. He fixed Sukey with a

penetrating glare. 'This isn't the first time that you've lived up
to that description, is it?' She half opened her mouth to make
some response, but it appeared the question was rhetorical, for
Leach continued without a pause. 'I have here DS Rathbone's
account of the chain of events from the time he learned of your
request for armed back-up; is it too much to hope that you have
prepared one of your own?'

'Well, sir, I did make some notes before going to bed last night
and I added a few more before leaving home this morning,' Sukey
began nervously, 'but they could hardly be described as a full
report so I'd prefer to write them up in detail before submitting
them.'

'Show me.' Leach held out a hand; she gave him the single
sheet of paper, which he scanned briefly before handing it back.
'All right, you can get to work on that as soon as I've finished
with you here. What I want now is, firstly, a full explanation
of why you made that emergency call, and secondly a detailed
account of everything that went on inside the tattoo parlour until
Painter was arrested.'

Anticipating such a command, Sukey had used the journey
time from home to recall the conversation at the tapas bar that
had led to Harry's sudden decision to check whether the Art-Full
Skin Tattoo Parlour was open and if so to warn the proprietor of
his potential danger. 'I told him I couldn't agree . . . that it would
be out of order for me to take any such action without authority . . .
but he went ahead anyway and I thought it best to follow him
and try and stop him doing anything . . . well, stupid,' she finished
lamely.

'So instead of waiting for the back-up you had quite properly
requested, you compounded the error by doing something equally
stupid yourself,' said Leach. 'It's not the kind of action we expect
from a police officer who has been trained to a high professional
standard, is it?'

'No, sir,' Sukey agreed meekly.

'All right, so the damage was done,' he resumed. 'Now tell
me what happened between the time Painter pulled the gun on
you and the moment the dog brought him down.'

Sukey took a deep breath. 'Most of the time I was praying
for the armed response unit to arrive . . . I sensed a hint of

megalomania so I kept him talking . . . told him how clever he was . . . he seemed to enjoy that.'

Until now, there had been a steely quality in Leach's eyes, but when she came to the moment when she made her final, desperate move to break free from Painter's clutches she seemed to detect a fleeting hint of admiration. It was not, however, reflected in his voice as he turned to DS Rathbone. 'Anything to add to that?' he asked.

'Yes, sir. I spoke briefly to young Matthews after Painter's arrest and he made a point of paying tribute to –' he referred to his notebook – 'DC Reynolds' courage and resourcefulness. We'll get a full statement from him later today.'

'What about Painter?'

'He's still cooling his heels in the cells. I'll be interviewing him this morning.'

'You'd better take DC Reynolds with you. She seems to have struck up a relationship with him.' Leach turned back to Sukey. 'All right, go and complete your report while I discuss one or two other matters with DS Rathbone.'

It was evident that the news of the drama at the Art-Full Skin had spread throughout the CID office; the moment Sukey appeared her colleagues surrounded her, demanding a full account. 'Sorry, guys, you'll have to wait till I've done my report for the SIO,' she told them.

She had almost finished when DS Rathbone reappeared and went straight to the drinks machine. He stood staring moodily into space while he slowly drank a large mug of coffee; when he had finished he marched over to Sukey's desk.

'Done it?' he said curtly.

'Just printing it off, Sarge.' Sukey took her report from the printer and held it out to him.

He took a minute or two to read through it before handing it back. 'Right, take it up to DCI Leach. When you come back we'll interview Painter. 'You,' he swung round to Vicky, 'go and get a full statement from young Matthews. The rest of you get back to work.' Without a further word to anyone he went to his desk and sat down.

'Yes, Sarge,' said Vicky to his retreating back. Lowering her voice she murmured in Sukey's ear, 'What's eating him, I wonder?'

Sukey shrugged. 'Search me,' she said.

Back in DCI Leach's office, Sukey handed over her report and was about to leave when he called her back with a gesture and pointed to a chair. She sat down and waited, in some trepidation, while he was reading. She had recounted the entire episode in as much detail as she could remember, including the exchanges between herself and Painter when she had been desperately playing for time. It was several minutes before Leach put the report down.

'At least there was no loss of life and I can't deny your irregular actions brought a result,' he said at last. 'Just the same, our friend Painter spoke the truth on one point: you won't be getting a commendation.'

'I wasn't expecting one, sir,' said Sukey quietly.

'Just as well.' His mouth twitched at the corners in a momentary hint of a smile. 'I'll be reporting details of this latest development to Superintendent Baird and no doubt he'll ask some pretty searching questions.' He paused for a moment before continuing; she had a feeling that he was choosing his words very carefully before saying, 'Police officers are only human and from time to time even the most experienced can miss the obvious. Let's hope you and DS Rathbone manage to get some useful information out of Painter that I can include with this.' He gestured with Sukey's report before putting it into a folder on his desk, his customary signal that the interview was over. On her way back downstairs Sukey found herself wondering whether there was a connection between DCI Leach's slightly cryptic remark and DS Rathbone's apparent ill-humour.

THIRTY

'Painter clammed up in the same way as Price, sir,' said
Rathbone. 'We've charged him with everything from
assaulting a police officer to carrying a firearm with intent
to commit murder, but apart from saying "Yes" when asked if he
understood the charges and "No" when asked if he wanted a brief,
his only response to our questions was "No comment". DS Reynolds
and I both believe that, like Price, he is more frightened of a
shadowy something or someone than he is of anything the law can
throw at him and we can only suppose it's the mysterious character known as "Delta". Here's our joint report of the interview.'

'Thank you.' DCI Leach took the printed sheet Rathbone gave
him and turned to Vicky. 'Have you got the statement from Harry
Matthews?'

'Yes, sir, here it is.'

There was a silence while Leach read through the reports. 'I
see there's a reference here to a mobile phone among Painter's
effects.' He turned to DC Haskins. 'You've been checking it,
Mike; did it reveal anything useful?'

'Not so far, sir. I've made a list of the numbers in the "calls
made" box and I'm running a check on names and addresses
with the service provider.'

'Good.' Leach's eyes swept briefly round the room where the
members of 'team Delta' were assembled. 'Now, as from
tomorrow, Superintendent Baird will be in charge of this operation and he intends to liaise with the Drugs Squad. They're
convinced there's a mastermind running the distribution on our
patch and so far they've only managed to get their hands on
some comparatively minor characters. They're following up a
number of leads but so far there's no sign of a major breakthrough. The common feature in this charade, apart from the
death tattoo, seems to be a kind of vow of secrecy the players
have taken. It's obvious that they fear some form of retribution,
presumably from or by order of Delta. You mentioned Chesney

showing the same attitude, Greg, and I understand he's declined the services of a brief as well.'

'That's right, sir, and like the other two he didn't ask for bail.'

'What about Price? Do we know any more about him?'

'Plenty, sir,' said Rathbone. 'His real name is Gerald de Whalley and he's an ex-army butcher who served five years for GBH and now works in an abattoir. We've interviewed the manager, who spoke very highly of him – said he came with first-class references and was astonished to know he's been in trouble with the police.'

'Anything to link him to the attack on Dobbie or the murder of Connie Gilbert?'

'Not so far, sir. We're still waiting for DNA test results.'

'As least we know he has the necessary skills.' Leach made a note. 'Maybe he's responsible for the other dismembered victim as well. Anyone else like to comment?'

Sukey put up a hand and Leach gave her a nod. 'We all noticed, sir, how much trouble Connie Gilbert had taken to cover her tracks, and in the light of what happened to her it's plain that Delta has a very long arm. And when Painter was taunting us in the tattoo parlour, he referred to "we who wear the Death Tattoo" as if it was some kind of badge of honour.'

Leach nodded. 'I remember you mentioned a while back the possibility of a mafia-like organization. I have to admit neither DS Rathbone or I took it seriously at the time, but it looks as if you may well be right. Maybe that's why those three jokers didn't ask a brief. They might have taken some kind of vow of silence, and not wanting bail could mean they feel less vulnerable in the nick than outside. Maybe just the sin of getting caught merits some kind of retribution.' He gnawed his lower lip for a moment, then said wearily, 'In some ways it'll be a relief to hand over the whole bag of tricks to someone else so that he has the job of finding the missing piece of the puzzle, but on the other hand . . . yes, you wanted to say something else, Sukey.'

'I . . . something else just occurred to me, sir.' As she spoke, Sukey felt a wave of excitement rising from her stomach, almost threatening to choke her. A wild notion had come into her head. *Could this be the missing piece Leach had just referred to?*

'Well, out with it!' he said impatiently.

'It was your use of the words "bag of tricks", sir – it made me think of the envelope that Toby Mayhew handed over in the car park. It contained just three things: a handkerchief, an ornament made of ivory or bone, and a locket with a piece of hair in it.'

Leach frowned. 'I thought we'd already been through this. The items were quite obviously of purely sentimental value, as the owner was at pains to point out.'

'That's what he said, and at the time there was no reason to doubt it. But supposing they represented a coded message?'

'Such as?' Leach's tone was becoming increasingly sceptical.

Sukey drew a deep breath, aware that what she was about to say was a piece of total guesswork on the part of Fergus and herself for which she might well receive a stinging rebuke.

'I've been reading a poem,' she began. 'It's called "The Vampire".'

Leach nodded. 'Rudyard Kipling. Inspired by a painting by Philip Burne-Jones, I believe. What about it?'

'Well, sir, it opens with the line, "A fool there was and he made his prayer" and it goes on to say the prayer was to "a rag, a bone and a hank of hair" – which is how he describes "a woman who did not care".'

Leach raised an eyebrow. 'And the point you are making?'

'Could those three items,' Sukey hurried on, 'a handkerchief, a bone ornament and a lock of hair – could they possibly represent "a woman who did not care"? A woman who treated a man so badly that he arranged to have her killed and the three items were a message to say the job had been done?'

'I take it you have a victim in mind?' It might have been her imagination, but she thought there was a slight softening in Leach's tone.

'Well, sir,' she went on, 'Connie Gilbert seems to have gone to great lengths to hide her identity and she met a very gruesome end. There's strong circumstantial evidence linking Gerald de Whalley, alias Wally Price, to both the attack on Jason Dobbie and Connie's murder. Could she have been killed on Delta's orders, and does the rag and the bone and the hank of hair refer to her?'

'Are you saying that the envelope Toby Mayhew handed to the man he met in the car park – what was his name?'

'Daniel Lionel Tanner, sir.'

'You're suggesting that those bits and pieces were to tell Daniel Lionel Tanner that his orders had been carried out?'

'I know it sounds fantastic, sir, but isn't it worth looking into?'

There was a heavy silence. Sukey stared down at her hands, aware that her face was burning and that a number of pairs of eyes were turned on her. Eventually Leach muttered, 'Could it be that this has been staring us in the face all this time?' No one answered and after a few moments he said, almost to himself, 'Why call himself Delta . . . unless . . . Daniel Lionel Tanner . . . Delta Lima Tango . . . leave out Lima and you have Delta Tango . . . DT . . . Death Tattoo?' He thumped the desk with his fist. 'My God, I believe we've hit on it!' He grabbed the telephone and keyed in a number. 'Leach here, sir. It's possible we've found a lead in the Delta case.'

Little by little over the ensuing weeks the intricate layers of Daniel Tanner's murderous organization were peeled away. After making a fortune from lucrative drug dealings he had bought a large property in Portishead, where he had been living for several years, a man of apparently independent means who quickly became a popular figure in local society. In fact, Vicky's light-hearted suggestion that he was probably 'a pillar of the church and chairman of the Rotary Club,' proved surprisingly accurate. His outward respectability, apart from concealing his involvement with an international ring of drug dealers, hid an even more sinister aspect to his character.

'A psychopath with overtones of megalomania' was the consensus among the team of psychiatrists who examined him after his arrest. 'We found a copy of a poem among his effects,' said Doctor Springwell, who submitted the report on behalf of his colleagues, 'it had one of the verses underlined, something about destiny playing with men for pieces.'

Baird nodded. 'The Rubaiyat of Omar Khayyam,' he said. 'Kipling and Fitzgerald – quite the literary genius, isn't he? In other words, he saw himself playing God,' he added soberly.

'Exactly,' said Springwell. 'He assumed the persona of a philanthropist who went to a lot of trouble to help ex-servicemen with the right sort of skills who had been discharged for serious crimes and therefore found it difficult to obtain employment. They were naturally appreciative of his efforts – until they found there was a price to pay. He kept an iron control over them by various means: threats to their families: loss of their livelihoods by revealing their past were just a couple. In return he required them from time to time to perform other services including in extreme cases the disposal of someone who stepped out of line. In effect, he had a small army of hired killers who were allowed to wear the death tattoo.'

'I take it he's shown no remorse?' said Baird.

'On the contrary, he openly boasts of his "successes", among them the killing – or "execution" as he calls it – of his former wife Miriam. She changed her name to Connie Gilbert in a futile effort to escape from him after he found out she had worked as a prostitute before he married her. He used the same word – execution – about the death of the second headless victim, whose crime had been nothing but a failure to carry out his orders.'

'What about the minor characters who didn't wear the tattoo? Chesney and Mayhew, for example?'

'They were his foot soldiers,' Springwell explained. 'Chesney's latest job, apart from being part of the drugs distribution network, was to recruit someone – Mayhew as it happened – to replace the previous occupant of fourteen Tyndale Gardens who had been what Tanner describes as "a disappointment".'

Many weeks of painstaking detective work lay ahead before the case was ready to be submitted to the Crown Court, and in the meantime it was the subject of much discussion in the CID office.

'You know something,' Sukey remarked to Vicky over lunch in the canteen, one day shortly after Tanner's arrest. 'It might sound heartless, but in some ways I think it was a mercy that Toby died in that RTA. The fact that he was so jumpy when he handed over that envelope might have meant he didn't have all the qualities needed to be part of Tanner's organization.'

'You could be right,' Vicky agreed soberly. 'Imagine his parents' grief if he'd fallen victim to one of Delta's hit men.' After a moment her expression lightened and a gleam of mischief shone in her eyes. 'I noticed you never mentioned it was Fergus who put you on to that poem,' she said. 'I hope you'll see he gets the credit for having provided the vital clue?'

Sukey chuckled. 'I haven't decided yet. He's cocky enough as it is – but I'll think about it!'